BOUND BY THE NIGHT

MEGAN HART

First Published in Great Britain 2016
By Mills & Boon, an imprint of HarperCollins*Publishers*
1 London Bridge Street, London, SE1 9GF

© 2016 Harlequin Books S.A.

The publisher acknowledges the copyright holder of the individual works as follows:

Dark Heat
Copyright © 2016 Megan Hart

Dark Dreams
Copyright © 2016 Megan Hart

Dark Fantasy
Copyright © 2016 Megan Hart

ISBN: 978-0-263-92165-6

89-0316

Our policy is to use papers that are natural, renewable and recyclable products and made from wood grown in sustainable forests. The logging and manufacturing processes conform to the legal environmental regulations of the country of origin.

Printed and bound in Spain
by CPI, Barcelona

Megan Hart is an award-winning and *New York Times* bestselling author of more than thirty novels, novellas and short stories. Her work has been published in almost every genre, including contemporary women's fiction, historical romance, romantic suspense and erotica. Megan lives in the deep, dark woods of Pennsylvania with her husband and children.

You can contact Megan through her website at www.MeganHart.com.

These stories are for everyone who knows to keep their toes under the blankets so the Bogeyman can't tickle them.

CONTENTS

DARK HEAT

Prologue

Everything had gone dark.

And oh, there was pain, great slashing waves of it washing over her as though she'd fallen into an ocean of agony and was being swept away to drown. Blindly, Monica raked the air in front of her and found nothing but emptiness. Hot and stinking breath assaulted her. Then the ground came up to slam into the back of her head and the darkness became sprinkled with the sharp white points of painstars behind her eyes.

She rolled onto her hands and knees, already pushing upward. She had to get to her feet or it would open her throat with teeth and claws like razors. And this rancid cave, this pit, was not the place where Monica intended to die.

She'd lost her knife but swept the ground to look for it and found it with her fingertips. The slice of pain was brief but would ache and burn later. If she was lucky enough to survive being mauled, she'd take those scars gratefully. She found the hilt and grabbed it up as she got to her feet. She turned, slashing outward, nothing but blackness in front of her.

She hit something solid, the blade sinking deep, and Monica didn't wait but pulled it out and stabbed again. Sticky heat flooded her hands. She kept going. Something shoved her again, at the same time grabbing with thick, scaly fingers so she couldn't fall. Couldn't get away.

Teeth on her throat.

Her own voice, screaming.

Then, the blood.

Chapter 1

Monica Blackship woke with a gasp, her hands slashing at the air in front of her before she realized she wasn't in the cave but in her own bed. Alone, thank God. Though in the next moment as the sob wrenched out of her throat, she desperately wished she had someone to cling to.

Brad was gone. A whole month, by now. She didn't blame him, not really. He'd stayed longer than she would have if the situation were reversed. But that was the kind of man he was. The good guy, the hero. He'd tried to save her, but she was past saving. It had been too much for him, in the end.

Still, the bed was vast and empty without him, and though she wasn't *afraid* of darkness, it was so much easier to bear with someone else beside her. She gave in to tears. They leaked from the corners of her eyes and slid down to fill her ears, which was annoying as hell and effectively stopped her from totally surrendering to the indulgence of her misery.

She wouldn't be able to sleep again. The dream always meant the end of the night for her, no matter what time it occurred. Monica rolled to look at the clock, relieved to see that at least it would be morning soon. She wouldn't have chosen to be awake at this hour, but at least she could get up without feeling as though the entire night had been wasted. She could maybe even be a little productive—she'd pay for it later in the day when she couldn't keep her eyes open, but there was nothing to be done about it now.

She swung her legs over the edge of the bed, unable to stop herself, as always, from hesitating just that little bit as her feet hit the floor. Monsters were real, though she'd never encountered one that lived under the bed. It never stopped her from imagining the bite of talons severing her Achilles tendon, of writhing tentacles dragging her under the bed. She settled her feet firmly onto the hardwood planks and used her toes to find the soft edges of the braided rag rug her grandmother had given her.

She didn't turn on the lamp. She knew her way to the bathroom without it, and she'd learned long ago that anything that was afraid of the light was small enough to be dealt with in the dark. Monica shucked off her pajamas and turned on the shower, giving it a few minutes to get hot while she brushed her teeth to clear away the final sour taste of her nightmare. Once under the scalding spray, she pressed her hands to the tile wall. Willing away the bad dreams. Willing away the loneliness.

Monica had already learned there was only one sure-fire way to push the thoughts away. A good, hard old-fashioned hair-pulling, ass-slapping fuckfest. Brad had not quite been the man to give it to her—even after nearly four months of steady dating, he'd often been too timid with her. Afraid of hurting her. He'd wanted candlelight dinners, stuff like that. Monica had been honest with him from the start—she wasn't looking for that. At first he'd been happy to fuck her in the middle of the night when she woke up, sweating and gasping, reaching for him, but then things had changed.

"There's more to me than being your cock on command," Brad had complained.

Monica hadn't tried to dissuade him from the notion that was how she thought of him. Yes, Brad made a stellar cup of coffee and remembered to put the toilet-seat lid down, and yes, he knew how to match his belt to his shoes. For a lot of women he'd have been a perfect boyfriend, but she was so far from being any kind of perfect anything it would've been unfair of her to try to convince him to stay. Even if it did mean now she stood in a steaming-hot shower with her own fingers sliding between her thighs so she could find some sort of release. Some way to wipe away the horror that crept so regularly into her dreams.

Her fingertips stroked, moving faster. There was nothing of romance in this. Nothing of love. She knew her body well enough to push it into pleasure fast and hard and sharp, just the way she wanted it. Ecstasy spiraled upward, urging her to cry out. Shuddering, Monica climaxed. The pleasure didn't linger. In another few seconds she was simply shivering under the spatter of water, feeling empty inside.

At least the dream had been pushed away.

Dripping, Monica wrapped her hair in a towel and then grabbed another to use on her body. She caught a flash of her reflection in the mirror. You couldn't miss the scars, several long slashes sweeping over her belly. She could look at them impassively now. She put her

hand over them, aligning her fingers with the marks.
The official report had been a bear attack. The wounds
didn't match anything familiar or animal; she'd spent a
few nights in the psych ward before giving up her insistence that she hadn't been hurt by a bear. A beast had
torn her open, but Monica had done her own work on
her wrists and that sort of thing had a tendency to make
people give you the side eye about everything else.

She touched those marks, too. The one on the right
was precise. The one on the left, ragged. Four inches
long, lengthwise, not across. She'd been serious about
wanting to die.

"But not anymore," she whispered to herself, just to
be sure the face in the mirror was really hers.

She would put on some comfy clothes and make
herself some coffee and eggs and toast, she decided
firmly. She would not text Brad to see if they could
get together—he'd made noises about the two of them
staying "friends," but she knew well enough how that
would work. As in, it wouldn't.

She'd barely started the eggs frying when her phone
rang. At this hour it could only be Vadim, which could
only mean one thing. Monica thumbed the screen of
her phone, not bothering with a hello.

"This is the job," Vadim said without a greeting of
his own, and suddenly Monica wasn't sleepy any longer.

Chapter 2

Jordan Leone had no patience for rich fucks who thought a hefty bank account equaled free rein to buy and sell any other creature's life. Paul DiNero wasn't usually that sort. The guy genuinely cared for his animals, though his hard-on for the exotics meant he had quite a number of pets that weren't the cuddly kind. It was how the guy acquired the animals that lit a slow fire under Jordan's skin.

DiNero wanted what he wanted and he had the money to get it, even when legal channels failed him. Maybe especially when that happened, since that was often the only way he could procure the pets he wanted. He had contacts all over the world, from legitimate and licensed breeders to poachers to other collectors who were looking to sell off their animals or their offspring. Sure, the guy had a bunch of documentation proving his backyard menagerie was a private zoo used for "educational" purposes, but the fact was, DiNero's collection was for his own private pleasure and nothing else, and when he wanted something, that meant he was willing to put up with the sort of arrogant douche bags Jordan hated.

Today it was some guy with a weird accent that sounded French but wasn't. His greasy black mustache glistened from the bison burger he'd scarfed down while sitting on DiNero's terrace. His beady eyes narrowed while his mouth stretched into a grin Jordan wouldn't have trusted on a great white. He waved a languid hand.

"The price," he said, "is nonnegotiable."

"You understand I'll need to have my man here give the animal a full health check," DiNero warned, though he didn't look concerned. He'd dealt with this dick-blister before.

Jordan hadn't eaten a burger, even though the smell of it had flooded his mouth with greedy, ravenous saliva. His stomach clenched, not so much in physical hunger as in simple longing. He'd restricted his meat eating for over fifteen years, and though his vegetarian diet was self-imposed, he'd never quite managed to convince his body he wasn't missing out. He took a long drink of his beer instead, savoring the hoppy flavor.

"Of course, of course. I wouldn't have it any other way. Not for one of my best customers." The guy, whose name was something like Algiers or Algernon or maybe it was Addison, flicked his gaze at Jordan and gave him another smarmy smile.

DiNero nodded at Jordan and bit into his own burger. Juice squirted. Jordan had to look away.

"Go make sure my new girl is healthy, Jordan, while Mr. Efforteson and I chat about some things," DiNero said.

It was a dismissal, but Jordan didn't mind. With

barely a nod at Efforteson, he headed for the stone stairs off the terrace, toward the driveway and the truck parked there. Unmarked, without even ventilation, the inside would be pitch-black and stinking of frightened animals, but Jordan had seen worse conditions. Sometimes when he'd had to travel to pick up a new pet, the sights he'd witnessed were so horrible they'd left him shaking and furious. Violent.

With a nod at the armed bodyguard, Jordan yanked on the truck's rolling door in the back and hopped into the bed. Inside were rows of cages, all empty but for the one at the back. In it, a cowering female silver Russian fox yipped and rolled her eyes as he approached. He soothed her with a low murmur and put out a hand for her to sniff, his fingers against the bars of the cage. The foxes had been bred for generations in Russia as an experiment at domestication, and now the animals were more like dogs than their ancestors had been. They'd gained in popularity as exotic pets, expensive and limited in where they could be legally kept, rare only because of how difficult it could be to acquire one. This pretty girl was a replacement for one DiNero had lost.

"Hey there, pretty girl. Sweet girl," Jordan soothed, settling close to the cage so the fox could get used to him. "I won't let anything happen to you."

Not like the other one, he thought with a hard swallow of anger. He'd fucking warned DiNero about fixing the barriers between the zoo and the bayou, but the man had been more concerned about keeping away nosy neighbors or thieves than anything else. Gators couldn't climb brick walls or smash them, either, but something had scaled the ten-foot wall. The barbed wire on the top had been torn and tossed aside like candy floss. This last time, the intruder had left behind a pen full of dead foxes.

Jordan opened the cage and the fox crept closer with a small yip. She'd clearly been socialized thoroughly, something DiNero wouldn't bother to do once he had her ensconced in the zoo. The fox had been bred as a house pet, but to DiNero she was an ornament.

"C'mere, little girl." Jordan stroked the soft fur, feeling for any obvious lumps or bumps. He gave her some cuddling time before scooping her up to take her outside. The bodyguard looked surprised, but Jordan ignored him to take the fox across the long expanse of soft green grass to the small bungalow he used as an office.

The fox yipped and buried her face against him when they went inside, but Jordan continued to soothe her with murmured words and gentle touches as he examined her. Her paws scrabbled on the steel tabletop, but she quieted when he gave a warning noise under his breath. She still trembled, but she wasn't trying to get away.

She looked good, at least as much as an animal could when it had been kept caged in the dark and improperly fed and watered for the past few days. But she was healthy, without any signs of abuse or genetic flaws as the result of inbreeding. Jordan finished the exam and slipped a treat from his pocket that the fox took eagerly. She butted her head against him, and he took her narrow face in his hands.

"Pretty girl," he said quietly. The fox licked his face.

Once she'd been put away in her own habitat, separated for now from the three surviving foxes for a quarantine period before he introduced them, Jordan made the rounds of the other habitats in this section. He'd spent long hours building most of them, re-creating different terrains or climates to provide the best possible housing for their inhabitants. The animals were under his care, and that meant their living conditions, too.

Veterinarian, handyman, lion tamer. That was his job here at DiNero's, and it was the best one he'd ever had. The man gave him a good salary and free room and board on the property in a tiny but cozy bungalow with full catering privileges from the main-house kitchen. Most important, DiNero usually left Jordan alone.

Until today, apparently. Jordan rounded the corner of a low stone wall meant to keep the prairie dogs from getting out—DiNero loved prairie dogs and would often spend hours feeding them peanuts and watching them pop in and out of their holes. Today, though, he stood with his back to Jordan. Efforteson wasn't with him. DiNero's companion was a woman, her long dark hair the color of black cherries. It fell in soft waves to the middle of her back, and when she turned, eyes like a summer sky opened wide beneath dark arched brows.

"Jordan, come say hello to Ms. Blackship."

Reluctantly, Jordan came closer. DiNero had been married four times, no children unless you counted the third wife, who'd thrown tantrums like a three-year-old. Now the man claimed he would never get married again, which only meant that he brought around his one-night stands to impress them with his menagerie, and Jordan had to make nice and pretend to give a damn.

"Monica," the woman said as she gave him a firm, brief handshake.

"She's the... Whattaya call it, honey?"

If the endearment raised her hackles, Monica Blackship didn't show it. She gave DiNero a flicking glance but then put her focus back on Jordan. "I'm a crypto-zoologist."

For one awful moment, Jordan thought maybe DiNero was trying to replace him. But then he understood, having heard the term somewhere. "A crypto…"

"I research unusual or what some might consider legendary creatures," Monica replied calmly. "Bigfoot. That sort of thing."

"You think Bigfoot jumped our wall and killed our animals?" Jordan didn't even care what DiNero might think of him taking any small part of ownership. "That's ridiculous."

"Of course it is. By all accounts, the Sasquatch is a vegetarian," Monica said without so much as a quirk of her smile.

DiNero chuckled. "Just like you, Jordan."

Jordan scowled, crossing his arms. "Sasquatch also doesn't exist."

"That remains to be disproven, actually." Again, that calm, almost blank look without a hint of any expression. It made him want to do something to see if he could shake her up.

"Hasn't been proven," Jordan added.

DiNero gave him a look. "Something came over our walls, Jordan. And you said yourself it wasn't human."

"I didn't say it was Bigfoot, either!"

"That's what Ms. Blackship is here to help us figure out. She works with an organization that studies this sort of thing." DiNero, who could be a pain-in-the-ass wisecracker most of the time, looked serious. "You know animals, dude. You know this is some kind of animal that keeps doing this."

Jordan involuntarily thought of the first slaughter he'd found three months ago. The scent of blood, the patches of fur. It was more than the loss of the animals, or even the money they'd cost. It was how they must've suffered that made his stomach tense and churn. He wasn't convinced whatever had killed the zoo animals didn't wear boots and kill with knives.

"Something didn't just kill them," DiNero continued, now facing the woman. "It ate them, we're pretty sure."

Jordan shook his head. "You don't know that."

Monica nodded. "I've seen similar cases. I'm thinking it might be something like a chupacabra…"

"The hell…?" Jordan snorted derisive laughter. "What the hell is that?"

"They're usually found in Puerto Rico and Mexico," Monica went on as though he hadn't spoken, and damn, if there was one thing Jordan couldn't stand, it was being dismissed as if he were nothing. "But there have been cases of them moving north, more and more often now. They typically prey on smaller animals, but several of the cases my colleagues have worked on dealt with what looks to be a different breed of chupacabra, maybe…"

"Hold on. There's more than one breed?" Jordan shook his head. "Please."

"Like dogs," Monica said. "Or wolves."

DiNero had watched the interchange with rapidly rising brows, but now he held up a hand. "Jordan, listen. Monica was sent here by a friend I trust. He's dealt with things like this before, and I want to know what's going on. What's breaking in here, what's eating my pets."

"So you can kill it," Monica said softly.

"Hell no," DiNero said. "So I can put it in my collection."

Chapter 3

It was better than a sleeping bag on the ground or a bedbug-ridden hotel room, that was for sure. DiNero had put her up in one of the guest bungalows scattered throughout the private zoo. Kind of a safari experience for his guests, she supposed and curled her lip. Monica had never liked zoos, seeing the animals in cages. Lions pacing and miserable. DiNero's menagerie was housed in better habitats than any she'd ever seen, but they were still kept captive. Not free.

In her lifetime before, when she'd been attending veterinary school, Monica had dreamed of getting a job at a big zoo. Maybe a circus. She wanted to work with exotic animals, not just dogs and cats. She hadn't finished school, because the attack had screwed that up for her, big-time. Yet she'd ended up working with exotic animals just the same, hadn't she? The deadliest ones, too, nothing soft or fluffy, because people never called for help when they came across a mewling, fuzzy bundle of fur with big eyes. Nope, the Crew got the calls only for the things that chewed your head off and spit down your neck.

Damn, she was tired.

She'd been up for most of the night because of the dream. Then she'd been on a plane from her place in Pennsylvania with a layover in North Carolina and this final stop in Louisiana. Then another four hours or so driving through the bayous to get here. Where here was, she didn't exactly know. Vadim had told her that DiNero demanded secrecy so he could avoid getting caught with his illegal collection. Personally, Monica had no interest in fucking with his animals, so long as they were cared for.

Which made her think of Jordan Leone. That long, tall drink of water was in charge here, and he'd made sure to let her know it. Not that it mattered, really. She was here to figure out what had killed a silver fox, four prairie dogs, a couple chimps and, more frighteningly, a tiger. The tiger had been, by Jordan's account, old and blind in one eye. Raised in captivity, it had come from another collection, where it had been treated like a house cat and overfed, allowed to live with its owner in a tiny two-bedroom cottage until it had pissed one too many times on the couch. It hadn't been full of much fight, Jordan had told her. But still. What could attack and kill a tiger and also drag it half a mile and through or over a ten-foot-high brick wall topped with barbed wire?

After pouring herself a glass of what turned out to be very good whiskey, Monica turned out the lights in the small kitchenette and then the equally compact living room. On bare feet, she crossed the bamboo floors with her glass in her hand and made her way out onto the small terrace. She'd brought a book but didn't feel like reading. The mosquitoes were going to eat her alive out here, she thought, but settled into one of the comfortable chairs and put her feet up anyway.

From here she had a good look directly across into Jordan's bungalow. She hadn't been given her choice of places to stay, and if she had, she wouldn't have picked one so close to his. He was a man who cherished privacy, she could tell that right off. He wasn't going to be popping over asking to borrow some sugar, that was for sure. And there were other guesthouses—she'd seen them when DiNero gave her the tour of the estate. So why this one, then?

It had something to do with Jordan protecting her, she thought with a low chuckle and a shake of her head. DiNero hadn't said as much, but he might as well have patted her on the head when he called her *honey*. She'd figured it out. He didn't seem to have a problem believing in her credentials or ability to find out what was stalking and killing his pets, but he didn't think she could defend herself. Monica gave an internal shrug. She hoped she wouldn't have to, but if she did, she doubted she'd need Jordan Leone's help.

Never mind those long, strong arms and legs. Those big hands. Never mind the muscles cording in his back and shoulders, clearly visible even through his shirt when he bent or lifted anything. Never mind that mouth…

Monica stopped herself. She wasn't here for that. Sure, he pushed just about every one of her buttons, aside from the fact he didn't seem to have a sense of humor. Oh, and that he obviously didn't like her at all, was suspicious of her being here and had no faith in anything she'd already proven to herself as truth. She could get over him not believing in Sasquatch, but Jordan had been blunt and up-front about his utter lack of even an inkling of belief in anything other than what he could read about in a textbook. A man like that wasn't for her. No way.

Still, it couldn't hurt to admire the shape of him through the sliding glass doors at the front of his bungalow as he moved around inside. Cooking dinner, judging by the good smells of onions and garlic in olive oil. She'd eaten at the main house with DiNero, slabs of steak as thick as her fist and wine she bet cost more than her rent. He'd have someone stock her fridge for her tomorrow, he'd promised. Until then, if she wanted a late-night snack, she was out of luck.

At least if she wanted food, Monica thought, watching Jordan's silhouette, and then she reined in her hormones and went inside.

Jordan woke early, as he always did, though this morning he'd actually needed his alarm to rouse him. He'd been dreaming, jumbled images that made no sense. Nothing he could remember, really, but for the first time in forever, he couldn't seem to shake away the sleep.

Breakfast didn't satisfy him, either. Granola and soy milk. Healthy, yes. Satisfying? Not when he really wanted a platter of fried eggs, a rasher of bacon, a fistful of sausages… Shit. His stomach rumbled angrily as he made himself some sourdough toast spread thickly with strawberry jam. Strong coffee eased the cravings a little bit, but not entirely.

It definitely didn't help that when he headed up to the main house to see if that woman DiNero had hired was ready to join him on the daily rounds, Jordan discovered Magnus had laid out a spread. DiNero's personal chef believed in hearty, down-home cooking. Gumbo, jambalaya, but also breakfasts that could feed an army. Jordan nodded at Karen and Bill, two of his assistants, who were helping themselves to the buffet on the sideboard, but he didn't dare get any closer to the food. He'd fall on it like…well…like a starving man.

He spotted Monica and DiNero on the terrace overlooking the yard. She looked fresh faced and ready to take on anything, her dark red hair pulled into a neat ponytail at the base of her skull. He gave her a grudging nod, noting her work pants and boots. At least she'd dressed appropriately.

"Morning, Leone. How the hell are you? I was just telling Ms. Blackship here about the elephant." DiNero gave Jordan a gator grin.

"We don't have an elephant," Jordan said.

DiNero waggled his brows. "Not yet."

Jordan sighed. He'd told his boss an elephant was too much to handle. The sheer size of it would mean a habitat that would require far too much upkeep, unless the man wanted the poor thing to be hemmed in. Not to mention that elephants were smart and could be vengeful if mistreated—not that Jordan would ever mistreat an animal, but you never knew how they'd been treated before. Elephants did not belong in a private zoo. Then again, he thought with a bland smile as DiNero kept blabbing away, no animals really did, even if it meant Jordan would be out of a job.

"Grab a plate," DiNero said.

"Already ate. Thanks." To Monica, Jordan said, "You want to come on my rounds with me today?"

She tucked a final bite of toast into her mouth and

nodded, wiping her hands on a napkin. She swigged some coffee and stood. The way DiNero ogled her ass when she turned made Jordan want to punch the other man in the face.

"He's kind of a douche bag, huh?" she murmured as they left the dining room.

Jordan gave her a glance. "He's my boss."

"He's totally looking at my butt, isn't he? I can tell." She slanted Jordan a sideways smirk.

Jordan didn't answer her, but Monica laughed softly anyway. They'd just started heading for the golf carts when Jordan's third assistant, a white-faced and shaking Peter, ran toward them. Jordan knew before the other guy had even said a word what had happened.

"Where?" he asked.

Peter shook his head and pointed toward the mountain-lion habitat. Jordan took off running, Monica on his heels. In minutes they made it to the habitat, where Jordan skidded to a halt. The entire interior of the habitat had become an abattoir. There was no sign of either of the mountain lions.

"It took both of them." Peter sounded as if he was going to be sick.

Jordan knew how he felt. He ran his hands through his hair, stalking, pacing. He became aware of Monica next to him.

"Can you let me inside?" she asked.

Jordan nodded. "Yeah. We need to check everything out."

They spent the next hour doing that. Monica took notes on the drag patterns in the dirt and blood spatter while Jordan had Peter, Karen and Bill ready for the cleanup. All of them were silent as they worked.

"No signs of damage to the habitat walls. The lock on the gate looks picked," Jordan said.

"Scratched." Monica looked at him. "All around it."

Jordan shook his head. "An animal didn't do this. You can't tell me that something came and picked the fucking lock."

She tucked her notebook into her pocket and then pushed her hair behind her ears. "There have been instances of tool use in some—"

"I need to check the outer wall. See where it got in." Jordan wasn't interested in her lame theories about tool-using monsters.

Monica followed him. "Jordan, wait."

He stopped but didn't turn. He could tell that Karen, Bill and Peter were watching, though none of them said a word. Jordan waited for her to continue, but she didn't. After another minute, he stalked off.

There was nothing. No breaks in the wall. No holes. No bent barbed wire this time. The lock on the gate nearest the mountain-lion habitat had similar markings to the one on the habitat gate. Scratches.

"It's something smart," Monica said from behind him.

Jordan frowned and shook his head. "Smart enough to pick a lock? I'm telling you, poachers are doing this. Someone with a grudge against DiNero, maybe…"

"Poachers would take the animals. They wouldn't kill them. Would they?"

He looked at her. "About seven years ago, DiNero got into a fight with some Japanese billionaire over a rare breed of panda they both wanted. Neither of them had the right habitats for it, but they were going head-to-head over it anyway. DiNero won the auction. The billionaire had someone come in and kill the panda before DiNero could take delivery. Some people don't want anyone else to have what they want."

She gave him a long, steady look, then reached to touch his shoulder. Just briefly. Just once. "Jordan, I know this is killing you. Believe me, I want to find out what's going on."

He put a hand on the wall and leaned, shoulders hunched. "This is fucked up, Monica. I know DiNero brought you in here because he thinks you can help figure out what's happening. But I just can't…"

"You don't have to believe me," she said. "Honestly, if it's a chupacabra or a poacher, does it matter, so long as we find out and stop it?"

Grudgingly, he looked at her. "No. I guess it doesn't."

"We're going to find out what…or who…is doing this." She looked grim.

Though he hadn't known her long at all, Jordan had no doubts that woman meant what she said.

Chapter 4

Vadim's face was a little blurry for a moment on the computer screen before the picture cleared. He was sitting, as he almost always was when they video-chatted, behind his oversize mahogany desk. Behind him, bookshelves overflowed with textbooks and papers. He adjusted his glasses and leaned forward to look at her.

"Strong enough to drag a tiger over a wall but now picking a lock instead?" he asked.

Monica sipped some more of DiNero's excellent whiskey and nodded. "Yes. Maybe whatever it was got tired of the heavy lifting. It looks like it figured out how to get through one of the gates along the perimeter wall, then let itself into the mountain-lion cage. Both were missing. Some blood, some hair, but nothing else. No bones, even. If it's actually eating the animals, it's consuming them entirely."

"DiNero's man thinks it's human, eh? An inside job?

Does he have a grudge against his boss?" Vadim sat back in his chair.

Monica shrugged. "It's possible. DiNero is kind of a dick. But Jordan seems to really care about the animals. If he was somehow working with an outside source to steal the animals away from DiNero, he couldn't hurt them."

"He could be making it look as though they're hurt," Vadim pointed out.

"He could, I guess. Seems pretty elaborate to me. And he seems genuinely upset by what's going on. He runs a clean house here. The habitats are expensive and well maintained, not just cages. There's a wide variety of animals, but they're all really taken care of." She paused, sipping. "He's a little odd. The zookeeper."

Vadim grinned. "Handsome?"

"Ugh, stop." She made a face. Vadim was always trying to set her up with some Crew member or other. Then she laughed a little. "Very."

"I have Ted ready to head down to you once you think you might know what's going on. I'd send someone sooner, but…"

"I know. Too many investigations, not enough Crew. I got it. I'll be careful," she put in before Vadim could lecture her.

Crew rules stated that no investigator try to hunt something alone. They worked at the minimum in pairs. Her role here was to assess the situation and try to get a handle on what they were looking for. No use coming loaded for bear, as Vadim said, if they were really hunting rabbit.

Something told Monica this was no bunny.

"Have they added any security measures?" Vadim asked. "I warned DiNero that your safety was my priority. Not that of his collection. You're not to go off on your own, do you understand?"

He was nowhere near old enough to be her father, though he tried to act as much as a patriarch to the Crew as a leader. Sometimes Vadim's protective nature warmed her. Other times, like now, it left her with the urge to roll her eyes and stamp her feet like a teenager reminded over and over again to "drive carefully." Monica kept her expression bland.

"Don't give me that look," he said.

She raised both brows, innocence personified. Vadim sighed. Monica raised her whiskey glass. After a moment, he shook his head.

"Something that can haul away a tiger could certainly do a lot of damage to you, Monica."

She had, for a period after losing Carl, done many reckless things. But time had passed and her life had gone on, whether she liked it or not, because that was what life did. "I know. And believe me, I'm not… I'm not trying to get myself killed. I'm here to study and assess, and then the team will come in and we'll catch this thing."

"If we're lucky," Vadim said.

They both knew how infrequently the Crew got lucky. There was a reason why people kept repeating that monsters weren't real, after all, and it mostly had to do with how hard it was to find proof. Monica raised her glass again, draining it, and this time, Vadim signed off.

Chapter 5

Ten guesthouses, and DiNero put the woman in the one closest to his. Jordan fumed, though it was pointless. DiNero would do whatever he wanted. And, Jordan grudgingly admitted, it made sense to have Monica closer to him, if only because she'd be walking the zoo with him for the next few days.

He'd seen her out on the terrace earlier. Sipping a glass of whiskey he could smell across the lawn and through his open windows. He could smell her, too. The soap she'd used, the laundry detergent seeping from her clothes. Those were good, clean scents. So was the lingering scent of wine she'd had with dinner. She'd be mortified to know he could smell the meat she'd eaten still on her breath, though she'd covered it with toothpaste.

She made him *hungry*.

Damn it.

Dinner for him had been some pasta with olive oil and some fresh-baked bread. A salad. The food filled him up but didn't sate him. That was why, he told himself, he was up at nearly two in the morning to rustle around in his fridge for some scrambled tofu and cheese when he really wanted to gorge himself to bursting on a thick slab of beef still dripping with blood... Jordan shook himself. He shoveled the food in his mouth, barely tasting it, trying to fill the emptiness. When he'd finished, he rinsed his plate and looked out the kitchen window to the guest bungalow where Monica was staying.

Her lights were off, which made sense at this time of night. The bedroom window was open, though, like his own. He could hear her inside. The slide of limbs on the bedsheets, the whisper of her hair on the pillow. She murmured something sleepy.

He needed to stop being a freaking creep about it. Jordan shook himself and put the plate in the drainer, then froze, head going up, ears straining at the change in her voice. He couldn't make out the words, but the tone had changed.

Carefully, slowly, he put the knife and fork he'd been using in the drainer, too. Still listening. He closed his eyes, opening his senses.

Her scent had changed, becoming bitter. The low mutter of her voice rose, edging toward hysteria. Not quite screaming, but definitely in distress.

Jordan didn't think twice. He was out the back door and heading for the guest bungalow in seconds. He leaped the low brick wall of his back patio and landed hard on the other side, bare feet slapping at the grass DiNero paid so much to keep looking nice. He hit the guesthouse's back patio in three strides after that. She'd locked the door. One hit with his shoulder and the door frame splintered.

She was in the bedroom, and Jordan barreled through the door ready to battle whatever was attacking her. He'd been unable to save the animals, but there was no way he was going to let something hurt anyone or anything else. He skidded on the hard floor, moving too fast to stop himself when he saw the woman was alone.

She sat up in bed at the sound of him coming into the room. Her hands punched at the air. Her low cry changed as her eyes opened and she focused on him.

He'd been moving so fast that he'd ended up next to the bed. Breathing hard, he stared down at her. He looked everywhere, trying to make sure nothing was there ready to pounce on them both.

"Am I still dreaming?" she asked in a totally clear, absolutely calm voice that sounded nothing like the terrified cries he'd been hearing earlier. "Because if I am, goddamn, please get over here and fuck me."

She wasn't still dreaming. Monica hadn't ever been able to control what happened while she was—she had friends who could lucid-dream, and there was a whole squad of people in the Crew who dealt with the monsters that lurked in the realm of the subconscious. The words had tumbled out of her before she was fully awake, though, and she wasn't going to take them back.

The man in front of her had grumbled his way through their earlier introductions. He wasn't someone she'd ever have considered in a romantic way. She was here on a job, not to get laid. Yet of course right now, after the nightmare, which had been even more intense than ever, all she could think about was getting fucked right through the mattress. It didn't matter much who did it.

"Shit," Jordan said.

Shirtless, jeans hanging low on lean hips, bare feet. If she'd ordered him from a catalog, he couldn't have arrived in more perfect condition or with better timing. And, she realized as she took in the heave of his chest and the way his fists were clenched, he'd burst in here to…save her?

She was naked. The covers had come down. He could see her completely, and was he looking? Oh, yeah. He definitely was.

The dream was fading but her hands were still shaking. Now not just from terror. Her nipples had gone hard, and without thinking, Monica cupped her breasts. Not necessarily to hide herself from his gaze. More to draw his attention.

"Jordan," she whispered. "Come here."

He did, two hesitant steps until his knees brushed the edge of the blankets. He licked his lower lip, looking her over. His breathing had slowed, but only a little.

"Did you come here to save me?" Monica asked in a low, rough voice.

He nodded. "I thought whatever killed the animals was in here with you."

"Do you still want to save me?" She shuddered, closing her eyes for a moment to push away the memories. Without opening them, she added, "I need you."

The bed dipped beneath his weight. When his rough hands skimmed up her bare sides, Monica let out a small gasp and allowed herself to arch back onto the pillows. His breath gusted over her cheek and she turned her face, lips parting, waiting for him to kiss her. She thought he wouldn't.

But he did, oh, he did. Hard and fierce and sharp, the way she liked it. The way she needed it. His tongue stabbed into her mouth as his hand slipped to cradle the back of her head. Then his mouth was moving down her throat to nip and nibble and then, yes, oh God, yes, to scrape along her flesh in that beautiful burst of pleasure-pain she craved.

When his lips closed over one nipple, Monica threaded her hands through his thick dark hair, fingers tangling. "There. Yes."

She still hadn't opened her eyes again. She wanted to be lost in this, all the sensations sweeping over her. She gave up to him.

When Jordan's mouth moved lower, though, she tensed. His lips tickled the scars on her ribs and belly. She waited for the questions, but all he did was kiss her softly and then move lower to nip at her hip bone. When he parted her thighs, again she tensed, though this time not out of trepidation.

At his first slow, long lick, she cried out. She lifted herself to his mouth, but Jordan had moved to slide his hands under her ass and his grip stilled her. When she tried to move again, his fingers tightened on her skin hard enough to bruise. She didn't quiet at the sting. She writhed.

His tongue flickered along her clit, then switched to flat, smooth strokes that had her bucking beneath him in a few minutes. Desire was already building, surging. She always woke from the dreams desperate for sex, but this, oh, shit, this was amazing. Brad had been a competent, considerate lover. Jordan, on the other hand, was eating her pussy as if he meant to destroy her with his mouth.

Monica's orgasm tore through her, leaving her gasping. Her fingers tightened in Jordan's hair again, involuntarily yanking. He made a noise, something like a low...growl?

Startled, Monica opened her eyes at last. With her climax still washing over her, all she could do was ride it as, seemingly without effort, Jordan pulled away just enough to flip her over. Hard. Reckless. Not at all gentle—in fact, her head butted the headboard for a second before she managed to look over her shoulder.

He was on his knees behind her, already tearing open his jeans. His cock, thick and gorgeous, sprang free into his fist. His other hand slapped her ass as he gave himself a few strokes. He looked at her, eyes gleaming.

A flash of red.

In the next moment, he was inside her, thrusting so hard she again moved forward and only her hands pressed to the headboard kept her from hitting it. He fucked so deep inside her that she cried out, expecting pain but feeling only the hot, slick engulfing of his cock by her still-clenching pussy. Again Jordan thrust inside her. Again.

When his nails raked down her back, she screamed, breathless and gasping. His body covered hers in the next moment as he leaned to find her clit with his fingers. No soft strokes now. He pinched, jacking it as he fucked into her, and it was too much, too much—she was going over again. Spiraling. Exploding.

Jordan's growl this time sounded like her name, which sent one last wave of ecstasy pulsing through her. He shuddered against her and...oh, fuck, he bit down on her shoulder as his fingers gave her one last pinching stroke and he came inside her. Monica couldn't come again, not after that, but it was close.

Spent, she collapsed onto her face in the pillows. His weight pressed her for a few seconds before he moved off her to flop onto the bed beside her. Boneless, sated, exhausted, Monica couldn't move.

She ought to say something, she thought blearily but couldn't make her mouth form any words. The dream had always made her crave sex exactly how she'd just had it, but this was the first time she'd ever had it exactly how she needed it. She tried to roll over onto her back to at least see if she could get up and go to the bathroom, but her body refused to do anything but sink back into dark and dreamless sleep.

When she woke up to golden streams of late-afternoon sunlight streaming through the window, Jordan was gone.

Chapter 6

As much as Jordan might have loved to take care of everything all by himself simply so he didn't have to deal with other people, there was no way he could possibly manage to feed and clean the habitats of every animal in DiNero's menagerie. Not even if he worked twenty-four hours a day. That was why he had a small rotating staff of three workers who took care of the daily care under his charge, while he spent his days visiting each habitat to be sure the animals were safe, healthy and as happy as they could be in captivity.

The woman was supposed to be with him again today on his rounds. He didn't need her advice on how to keep his animals safe, he thought sourly, just some thoughts on what the hell was continuing to break through and attack them. So far, all she'd done was toss a lot of stupid theories at him. Nothing he could actually work with. Besides that, she hadn't shown up this morning, not a call, not a note, nothing.

He couldn't stop thinking about the taste of her.

He was hard now, thinking of it, and that pissed him off, too. For Jordan, sex over the past few years had been relegated to an occasional one-night stand when he traveled into New Orleans. He favored tourists, women in sundresses and wedge sandals, drunk on hurricanes. The ones who were shy or claimed to be, at least until he cut them from the pack of their squealy girlfriends and took them back to the small, barely furnished flat he kept just off Bourbon Street. Anonymous, brief, nothing but two bodies—or three, and once four—writhing and grinding until there was nothing but pure mindless pleasure. It was something he did with strangers, some who never even thought to ask his name. It was not something he did with women he ever expected to see again.

But he'd had sex with Monica last night, and he *wanted* to see her again.

By the time lunch had come and gone, Jordan had made his rounds. He checked in on the staff congregating in the small common room outside his office but didn't linger, even though today was Peter's birthday and Karen had brought a cake. Instead, Jordan headed for the perimeter wall, intending to walk the entire length of it to look for any breaks or to repair any damage. Also to check for any signs that the thing attacking the animals had returned. He'd made it all the way beyond the empty tiger habitat when the light scent of feminine soap lilted to him along the breeze. His nostrils flared, but he didn't turn. He could hear her and smell her. That didn't mean he needed to acknowledge her.

"Hey," Monica said from behind him. "Sorry I

missed you this morning. I totally overslept. I never do that."

Jordan had been looking carefully over one of the spots that had been damaged to make sure the repairs were holding. He glanced over his shoulder. "No problem."

She stepped up closer, moving beside him. She pointed. "It came through here originally?"

"We found two holes in the outside wall after the first attack. Both broke all the way through, but this was the biggest, and neither one was big enough to get anything through. Even if *it* could squeeze, you can't squeeze a tiger. The barbed wire—" he gestured along the top of the wall "—had been completely torn away. Whatever it was tried to make it through, and when it couldn't, it went over the top."

"Any signs of blood here? Like something had cut itself?"

He gave her a flat look. "There was blood everywhere. Whatever it was came in and dragged away a full-grown tiger."

"There are a few things that could do that." Without looking at him, Monica moved closer to the wall to run her fingers along the patched section, then took a step back to look upward. "The other hole was smaller than this one?"

"Yeah. I can show you."

Wasn't she going to mention anything about the night before? Was she not going to say a word? She'd come on to him like a freight train, and now she was going to pretend it had never happened?

Fine.

He took her there and watched as she studied the repaired spot. She pulled out her phone, took a few photos. Tapped some notes.

"So," he said, unable to stop himself. "What do you think it is?"

Monica looked up. "I'm still not sure. I came here convinced I was looking for a new breed of chupacabra or something similar, but now I'm thinking this is something else entirely."

Jordan snorted. Monica's brows rose. He shrugged. "Is it really so hard for you to believe in the unknown?" She put a hand on her hip and gave him a hard look he thought was meant to shame him.

It didn't, though it did stir another, baser emotion in his lower gut. Jordan shrugged again. Monica sighed.

"Do you know there are thousands of new species of animals and insects discovered every year? The rain forest—"

"This isn't the rain forest," Jordan pointed out. "This is Louisiana."

"And every inch of it's been explored, huh?" she challenged, moving a step closer. "There are thousands of acres of land, all charted. Nothing could possibly be hiding away from the rest of the world, could it?"

"Nothing like what you're talking about. Something big and predatory would've been discovered before now, that's all I'm saying."

Monica frowned. "My grandparents live in New Jersey. Not Jersey Shore, but up north, close to New York. They have a postage-stamp lot backed up to another postage-stamp lot, with neighbors all around them. You could spit and hit two different highways. And guess what they have in their backyard every night."

"A lot of noise?"

"Smart-ass," she said but didn't seem angry. If anything, he'd made her smile. She shook her head. "Deer. They eat my grandma's garden and make her crazy. It's not a place where you'd think you'd see deer, but there they are, and why? Because they've been driven there. They don't have another place to go."

"You're saying whatever's attacking the menagerie has been driven here?"

"Could be. Land development, taking away territory. Chemicals in the water, changing the food supply. Something we don't even know about, like down in Florida, where those people are dropping off their ball pythons and anacondas that got too big to be pets, and now they're breeding and fighting with the alligators for dominance on the food chain."

"That's not happening here," Jordan said.

Monica gave him a solemn look. "Could be something else, then. Too many gators being taken, maybe this thing normally eats *them*, and now it's hungry. Whatever it is, it's discovered the menagerie, and it's not going to stop coming back unless we stop it." She paused. "Why is it so hard for you to believe?"

"I don't believe in monsters," he said flatly.

Monica laughed. "You're lucky, then. Because trust me, they exist. Or they did and have gone extinct. Or, like in this case, haven't been discovered."

"Maybe it's zombies," he said, deadpan. Scoffing.

She narrowed her eyes. "You mean like voodoo?"

"I mean like 'They're coming to get you, Barbara,'" Jordan said. "Voodoo is a religion."

She frowned again. "I wasn't trying to be offensive. Zombies like in *Night of the Living Dead* definitely are not real, I can tell you that much."

"No? But Bigfoot and the Loch Ness monster are, huh?"

She turned on him, finally, with a scowl. "I'm a cryptozoologist, Jordan. That means I search for the existence of animals whose existence has not been proven. Or things outside their natural realm. Do you know that just last year a half-sized cougar was discovered rummaging in the Dumpsters of restaurants in Hell's Kitchen? A cougar in New York City."

"That's not surprising, I bet there are lots of cougars in the city," Jordan said.

Monica laughed, and he discovered how much he liked the sound of it. "Not that kind of cougar. My point is, it might've been someone's pet that got too big or some kind of inbred cougar that managed to thrive in the urban environment. People had been reporting sightings of it for months before the Crew came in and was able to trap it. But first we had to prove it existed."

"A cougar is still a real animal."

"Yes. But there *are* things in the world we don't know or understand, whether you want to believe it or not. And they're animals, too. People can't turn into something else. No vampires, no zombies, no werewolves. There are monsters, but they're not human."

Not human.

Monica drew herself up and visibly shook herself. "Look, I'm here to do a job, so let me get on with it, okay? What's on the other side of this wall?"

"Bayou."

"I guess that goes without saying," she said. "Dumb question, sorry."

"DiNero put a lot of money into draining his land. Lots of money into landscaping. You wouldn't know there's anything out there besides more grass, I guess." Jordan tried to shrug off her words, but they clung to him, making his skin itch.

"I've never been to Louisiana before, if you can believe it." She gave him a small smile and another of those neutral but somehow assessing looks. She turned back to the wall, then glanced at him over her shoulder. "Can you take me over the wall? I want to see the other side."

Jordan paused. "Yeah. I guess so."

They spent the rest of the day that way. He took her outside the gates and showed her the places that had been compromised. She collected scrapings of the bricks. The soil. The water. She didn't tell him what she was looking for, and Jordan didn't ask. When finally she was satisfied, he brought her back inside. They'd shared scarcely more than a few words, which normally would've been perfect, except that the longer she went without paying attention to him, the more disconcerting he found it. They'd been driving in one of the estate's golf carts, so he pulled up into the small space between their bungalows and waited for her to get out.

What the hell kind of woman seduced a man and then proceeded to ignore him as if they'd never been naked and sweating and...

"Thanks," Monica said.

Jordan shrugged, stone-faced. "It's my job."

"Not everything you did was part of your job," she said. When he didn't answer her, she gave him another enigmatic smile and got out of the golf cart. "See you later."

He watched her go, waiting to see if she'd turn back. She didn't. But he was suddenly so damned hard it hurt to move. It made his hands shake, so he clenched them into fists on his thighs, but the hunger didn't abate. It rose within him, something fierce and unyielding, until all he could think about, all he could do, was get out of the golf cart and force himself to put on a pair of running shorts and go for a run.

Run. And run. And run.

By the time he got back, night had fallen. Golden light welcomed him from the windows of her bungalow, while his were cold and dark. Breathing hard, the coiled snake of hunger still hissing in his belly but low and quieter, Jordan paused to bend over and spit into the grass.

Her door opened. Her silhouette made him groan. She took a step onto the patio and was followed by the waft of something warm and delicious. His stomach growled.

Not human, he thought.

"I made dinner," Monica said. "Come inside."

Chapter 7

She'd begged supplies from the main house, despite the cook's assurances she didn't need to make her own dinner. But Monica liked to cook. It helped her think. While chopping and slicing and sautéing, she could let her mind wander over all the possibilities.

Too bad most of the possibilities had involved going another round with the taciturn and delicious Jordan Leone instead of figuring out what exactly was attacking the menagerie.

There *was* a science to what she did, though you couldn't get most people to believe it. Tracking prints in the dirt or analyzing blood samples or simply calculating what sort of musculature would be needed for something to be able to jump over a wall. What sort of claws could dig through brick, what kind of hide was thick enough to fend off the bite of barbed wire. The Crew kept files. Made reports. She and her peers compared notes. But still, so much of what they did had to be based on speculation. When you couldn't prove something, that was all you could go on.

Vadim had sent her down here thinking she might be looking for a chupacabra. Never mind it wasn't killing goats and it was out of the normal territory associated with that beast—there weren't many things that could do whatever *this* thing was doing. Yet after looking over the pictures of the slaughter and having Jordan take her around the estate, Monica wasn't convinced. She'd been on a couple cases hunting chupacabras before, and while they could certainly cause a lot of damage, there'd never been one she'd seen or heard of that could drag away a full-grown tiger or even a half-sized mountain lion, for that matter.

Which meant this was probably something different. Something they didn't know about, hadn't ever seen. The tingle of anticipation had been with her all day long, and being so close to Jordan all afternoon hadn't helped much.

So, she cooked.

She'd never had jambalaya and wouldn't have dared to try it here in the land where it was considered comfort food, so she'd settled on something she knew without a doubt she could pull off. Nothing fancy, just pasta with a fresh tomato sauce and lots of onions, peppers and garlic. Fresh-grated parmesan. The cook had given her a loaf of sourdough bread, which she'd cut into splits and baked with some more parmesan and olive oil. Adding a salad of mixed greens and lots of extra veggies, she had a complete meal. Enough for two, as a matter of fact, which had been her plan all along.

"You didn't have to do this," Jordan said from her doorway.

"I wanted to." She waved him into the small dining area. A table set for two. The plates were white ceramic, heavy and serviceable and far from romantic…but romance wasn't what she really wanted. Was it?

For a half a minute, she was sure he was going to refuse her, but then he shook his head and moved toward the table. He took a seat. Then he looked at her.

"I should… I was running."

"I saw you." She'd watched him head off and return hours later. Sweating. Panting.

"I should shower first."

"Sure," she said. "If you want to."

He didn't move. Monica smiled and set the bowl of pasta in front of him. Jordan fell on it like a starving beast, scooping a huge portion and digging in without so much as a second look. She served herself, eyeing him casually, though in reality she was taking in his every move.

"Good," he grunted around a mouthful of bread.

"You were hungry, huh?"

Jordan paused. Chewed. Swallowed. He reached for the glass of red wine she'd set out and drained half the glass before answering her. "Yes."

"Good," Monica echoed him and set to eating her own portion. She hadn't been exercising as he had, but she managed to put away a decent amount of pasta before she sat back in her chair to rub her belly.

Jordan had cleared his plate, plus the salad and most of the bread, and was looking hopefully toward the kitchen. "Is there more?"

"Yes. Plenty. Help yourself." Monica watched him get up. The view from the back was as nice as the one from the front.

He caught her looking when he came back. She didn't

pretend to be embarrassed. He frowned, settling into his chair.

"I'm not on the menu," he said. "In case you were hoping for dessert."

Monica burst into laughter. "Oh. Was I that obvious?"

"No, actually, you're not obvious at all." He sat back in his chair and gave her a look so stern it made her sit back, too.

"Erm," she said finally when it was clear that was all he was going to say. "Sorry?"

Jordan swiped at his mouth with a paper napkin and flung it down, then got up to pace a little bit. "I mean, what the hell was last night?"

Before she could answer, not that she had any clue what to say, he'd turned on his heel and stalked over to her. He should've been intimidating—and he was, or he would be if she hadn't faced actual monsters, not just some guy with his boxers in a twist. When he leaned to get in her face, though, she did pull back a little.

"I thought you were in trouble," he snapped.

"So you figured you'd save me?" Monica snapped back. "Well, that's noble and all, but I promise you, I can take care of myself."

"I've seen what that thing can do. You haven't, not firsthand."

She put a hand on his bare chest, no longer sweaty. He'd taste like salt, she thought. And fuck, that made her want to lick him.

"I've seen other things, Jordan. I'm not a shrinking flower—"

His hands gripped her upper arms, tight. She was up and out of the chair before she knew it. She thought he meant to kiss her, and she was already opening her

Dark Heat

mouth for it, but instead, he shook his head. His dark hair had fallen over his eyes.

"The next thing I know, you've got me fucking you," he said in a low, rumbling voice. "And that's it. Nothing after that. Not a damned word about it, all day long."

"I made you dinner," Monica whispered, torn between being flattered he was so upset and apologetic for so unexpectedly hurting his feelings.

Jordan let her go and stepped back. He was still breathing hard. Light flashed in his eyes. He turned away from her, shoulders hunched. Fists clenched.

"Why are you even here?" he muttered. "It's ridiculous. DiNero has too much fucking money."

That stung. Monica rubbed at her arms where his fingers had left marks. "Look, I know what I do must seem crazy. But really, there are things out there that people refuse to see."

He swung around to look at her, brows furrowed, mouth curled into a sneer. "Sure. Like a goat sucker?"

"Among others. Yes. You work with animals—is it so hard for you to imagine that there are creatures we don't know about?" She put her hands on her hips. "Something came through that wall. Multiple times. Something killed those animals. And something, if we don't figure out what the hell it is, will come back again and again and continue until everything in this zoo is dead, probably including the people. Because it can, Jordan. It simply fucking can."

"Keeping the animals safe is my job. Not yours."

"Yeah, well, DiNero hired me to figure out what it is, okay? So once I do that, I can tell you what to do to keep them safe. My crew can come in and hunt it down, and if DiNero wants it alive, maybe we can even figure out how to tell you to take care of it. I'm sorry I stepped

on your toes, if I did. And I'm sorry about last night…
No, fuck that," she amended. "I'm not sorry about last
night. I needed you, and you were there. I'm glad you
were. Believe it or not, I appreciated it."

"Great. So I did you a favor?" Jordan's scowl twisted
further.

She stepped closer to him. He backed up. She took
another. This time, he stayed. She'd seen a look like
that before. It turned out she'd been developing a habit
of wounding men's pride, and that broke her more than
anything else had.

Monica closed her eyes for a second. Thinking of
Carl. How much she'd loved him and how long it had
been since she'd felt that way about anyone. Maybe she
never would again.

"I had a nightmare. I was attacked some time ago,
and sometimes I dream about it," she said in a low voice.

"Okay." He eyed her warily. "And that's my problem?"

Oh, he was going to make this difficult. "In the
dreams, I relive the attack. When I wake up, I can't get
out from under it. The only thing that really helps me
is to…fuck."

"What kind of attack?"

"I was hiking with my husband," Monica said flatly.
"We'd gone into some unknown trails, stupid, I guess,
but we thought it would be fun. Isn't that how horror
stories always start? We thought it would be fun at the
time?"

"I don't like horror stories."

Monica laughed bitterly, then shrugged. "Something
came out of the woods. Slashed at him. Knocked me
out next, so I didn't see what happened. It dragged him
into a cave, where it killed him. It took me next. I woke

up next to his body. When it came back, I fought it and killed it."

She said it matter-of-factly, not because the story didn't move her emotionally, but because it was the story she'd told the police and the wildlife officers and everyone else, the same story so many times the words themselves came by rote. It was the only way she could tell that story without breaking down.

Monica rubbed her arms again, this time against the chill of gooseflesh that had risen there. The food in her belly shifted uncomfortably. She couldn't look at him anymore.

"What was it?" Jordan asked.

She shook her head. "They said it was a bear."

"Bullshit," he said.

She did look at him then. Her chin went up. "I don't know what it was. I never figured it out. But I knew it was something, not a bear. It had scales. It could see in the dark. It had claws…"

She shuddered and went silent.

For a moment, neither of them spoke. Then Jordan said quietly, "I'm sorry."

"I'd been studying to become a vet. I decided to focus on figuring out exactly what sorts of thing could have done that to my husband. I'm going to figure out what did this to your animals, too."

"But you still dream about it at night."

She nodded.

Jordan took a step closer. He pulled her into his arms again, this time more gently. Her face pressed against his hot bare skin, and though he might've grumbled about needing a shower earlier, all Monica breathed in was warm male. She closed her eyes. His hand stroked over her back.

"I'm sorry," she said. "I didn't mean to hurt your feelings."

Jordan, typically, didn't say anything. The steady thump of his heart beneath her cheek skipped a beat or so, though. His arms tightened around her.

After a minute, Monica pushed away. She cleared her throat. Jordan stepped back. They stared at each other.

"I need a shower," he said finally. "But after that, if you want to come over so we can talk about what you think this thing out there is…"

She nodded, hiding a smile. Stiffly, he backed away from her. She waited until he'd gone out the front door before she went after him to watch him cross the small piece of lawn between their bungalows. She could not figure him out. Not at all.

Chapter 8

The glass of red wine he'd downed had lit a fire in him that wasn't going to go out. The whiskey wasn't a good idea, not after last night and the wine and the conversation he'd had with Monica earlier, but then again, Jordan didn't always make the best decisions. He downed one shot before getting in the shower, where his cock got hard as soon as he tried to soap up. He took another when he got out. His hair was still wet and he'd barely put on a fresh pair of jeans and a plain white T-shirt before she was knocking on his front door.

"I brought dessert." She held up one of the cook's chocolate cakes. Jordan knew it by the scent of the icing. "I got it from the main house."

"Looks good. C'mon in." He stepped aside to let her pass. He'd managed to tame his dick, but barely. When she brushed his belly with her arm, he felt it stirring again.

They sat at his dining table. He'd put out a box of cheap chocolate doughnuts and made coffee, though the caffeine was going to do a number on him, as well. All of this was. Shit, he was going to need another run.

She'd brought along her tablet to show him some of the things she'd been working on, and before he knew it, they were side by side on his couch while she ran through lists of what she was putting together. She smelled so good. It had been a mistake to invite her here, Jordan thought. He was too hungry.

"But I don't know." Monica shook her head, then tucked a dark cherry curl behind her ear. She flicked her finger along a line of photos she'd pulled up. There was no denying the edge of excitement in her voice. "None of these things match the patterns. I've run through all the databases, and really, just…nothing."

"You love this, don't you? The unknown."

She looked at him. "Love it? I'm not sure. I've always thought of love as something that makes you happy."

"Me, I've always thought it was something that made you miserable," Jordan answered.

Monica laughed. "How many times have you been in love, Jordan?"

He didn't have an answer. He'd been homeschooled since the age of fourteen, when his parents had yanked him out of public school at the first signs of what they both had prayed would never come true. He hadn't gone to the prom, basketball games. Hadn't played in the band. He'd gone to college too wary of other people to trust anyone enough to fall in love.

"I thought so," she said when he didn't answer. "Sure, love can make you miserable. But it also makes you happy. So happy."

For a second, her gaze went faraway. Unexpectedly,

Jordan envied the man who'd married her, the one who'd made her look that way. The one who'd died, he reminded himself.

Monica shrugged off her expression. "Anyway. I have some calls and messages out to some of my colleagues, but at this point, I'm looking at something big. Something strong. Something that lives in the bayou."

"Anaconda? Python? Something like that?" He shook his head. "I know there's a huge problem with that in Florida, but I told you, not so much here."

"Snakes don't have claws."

"Gator?" He laughed at the idea, but Monica looked thoughtful.

"Something like that," she said. "You can laugh all you want, Jordan, but I'm good at what I do, and based on what I've seen and what you told me, I wouldn't put something like a gator off the list."

"Gators can't climb walls."

She smiled. "I said something *like* an alligator. But it's definitely smart enough to figure out how to get through that wall and get what it wants."

He was silent for a moment, thinking. "You really believe all this stuff about things that go bump in the night."

"I believe in things that go bump in the sunlight, too."

He glanced at her to see if she was making a sexy innuendo, but all she gave him was that same blank, assessing look that was starting to make him crazy enough to want to do something to wipe it off her face. He frowned and scooped up another of the chocolate mini doughnuts from the box he'd put out. They were fat coated in fat with another layer of fat on them, but he needed the calories, or else he was definitely going to give Ms. Blackship a surprise she was not going to like.

Her gaze followed the movement of his hand to the box, then to his mouth. Heat filtered through him at the way her eyes lit up, just the barest hint, and the way the tip of her tongue crept out to dimple her top lip.

She caught him looking. "You don't believe in any of this stuff. I know."

Jordan shook his head. "I work with real animals. Real things. You're asking me to believe that some kind of monster is coming out of the bayou and slaughtering them? I'd be more likely to believe some kind of poachers—"

"Except poachers would take the animals alive. If they were going to steal and resell the animals, they'd want them alive. Even if they only wanted the pelts," she added, "they wouldn't slaughter them on-site."

"No," he admitted grudgingly. "I've been thinking about it, and you're right."

She leaned forward a little. "DiNero believes it. That's why he called the Crew."

"Then I guess that's all it matters, huh?" He leaned back.

Monica smiled a little. "Yeah. I guess it does."

They sat in silence for a minute or so that should've been awkward but was only quiet. It had been a long time since he'd sat with a woman this way, without idle chatter and inane small talk, stupid words to cover up the fact both of them were thinking only of how to get in each other's pants with the least amount of effort. He couldn't stop thinking about her flavor.

"Look," Monica said abruptly. "About last night."

"We don't have to talk about it."

"No. We do. I don't want you to think—"

"I don't think anything," Jordan interrupted. "We're both adults. It happened."

Monica shook her head. "But you didn't like it."

"I didn't—" Jordan cut himself off. "What the hell?"

She laughed gently, tipping her face up. "I mean you didn't like that it happened. Not that you didn't like…it."

Jordan scowled. "It was unexpected. That's all."

"It won't happen again."

That did not actually make him feel any better. If anything, the thought that he would never again be inside her tightened a knot in his lower gut. He didn't have words for her, though, just a low grunt.

"I *am* sorry," Monica said. "You were there, and I needed someone."

Jordan gave her a long, steady look. "Gee, way to make a fella feel special."

Monica ducked her head, looking embarrassed for a second, before popping up with the first genuine, full-fledged grin he'd seen on her. It lit her entire face. She was pretty, but that smile, that fucking smile… She was beautiful.

He kissed her.

He could have stopped himself. Years of therapy, of learning self-control, of discipline, of fighting the hunger—he could've done anything but kiss her. She was in his arms the second after that. She opened for him immediately. Her arms went around his neck, her fingers threading through his hair.

He picked her up as easily as he would a bag of feathers. She moaned softly into his mouth. The hum of it sent an arc of electric desire straight to his already rock-hard cock. He settled her on the table and pushed himself between her legs. She moaned again when he pressed his erection against her. She wore a flowing pair of thin batik-printed pants that provided little barrier, but his denim jeans were majorly cock-blocking him.

In seconds, without breaking away from her mouth, he'd yanked open his fly and pressed himself against her again. For a moment, they were at an impasse, but then Monica lifted herself up, fiddled with something at her hip and released a tie he hadn't noticed before. The pants opened somehow in that magic way of women's clothing he'd never understand. She wasn't naked beneath, but a good tug tore her panties away. She cried out, a sharp sound that mimicked pain—except Jordan knew the sound of pain.

He was inside her in the time it took to breathe once, twice. She cried out again, and this time, there was a tinge of true pain in the sound. He wanted to slam deep inside her but eased out, only to have her grab him by the hips and pull him back.

"Look at me," she demanded in a low, urgent voice.

He did and lost himself in her gaze. She took his hand and slid it between them to get his thumb against her clit. She was slick, and his thumb slid easily against her. She bucked and gripped his hips again. Her back arched. Her mouth opened.

"Fuck me," she whispered. Then louder. "Please, fuck me."

The table creaked as they rocked. The hunger built inside him, and the only way to slake it was to take her. Her mouth. The heat between her legs.

"Mine," Jordan heard himself say but as though from far away.

He felt it when she came, her body clutching his and forcing him over the edge into an orgasm so powerful that he saw gold stars flickering around the edges of his vision. He captured her mouth once more, the kiss at first fierce in the last few ripples of his climax, then softening.

In the silence that followed, he heard her breathing shift. He looked into her eyes again, not sure what he expected to see there. Or what he wanted to see.

Monica curled her fingers in the front of his shirt and pulled him to her to brush his lips with hers. "Jordan."

That was all she said. One word, his name, a wealth of meaning in the two syllables, if only he could figure out what it was. Or if he wanted to.

They disengaged. She tidied herself, and he did the same. Neither speaking. She didn't need to ask him where the powder room was, since the layout of their bungalows was the same. By the time she came out, he'd changed into his running clothes.

"Oh," she said.

"I need to go for a run."

"Jordan…"

"What?" he asked roughly.

"What just happened?"

"You ought to know," he told her. "You were there."

"That's not what I mean, and I'm sure you know it."

"What can I say?" he said with a shrug. "I needed someone. You were there."

Chapter 9

Bastard, Monica thought, even though she knew she'd deserved it. Why did she seem to pick only the men who got bent out of shape about what could be pure and simple passion if only they'd let it? She was still bruised and tingling from the ravishment Jordan had so delightfully provided on his dining room table only an hour or so before, but though her body was sated, her mind was anything but. She'd tried to sleep but couldn't, and for once, not because she was afraid of the nightmares.

She'd been watching from the window to catch a glimpse of him coming back, but so far, nothing. Instead, she sat on her uncomfortable couch and made more lists. She'd signed in to the Crew database again to compare what she'd been able to find out with what others had logged in their experiences. So far, not much was making sense. Then again, not much ever did.

Dark had fallen, and with her window cracked, she

could hear the familiar far-off noises of the animals in their habitats and night-active insects. Low-grade anxiety plagued her. A crackle of tension, as though there was an oncoming storm. Or maybe it was simply that she'd been here two days already and hadn't figured out what she was looking for.

Or she was fooling herself, she admitted reluctantly, and her need to pace was directly related to the man who still hadn't come back from his run.

Jordan Leone was trouble. Bad news. Which was probably why she wanted him again, Monica thought with a sigh and a smile so twisted it almost hurt. She rubbed at her face and tried to shake off the lingering feeling of his touch, but all she could think about was the way his mouth tasted.

She wasn't going to accomplish anything this way. No amount of note taking or database studying could help her if she didn't get out there in the field and do her own research. DiNero had hired her for a job, and she meant to do it—because the sooner she found out what had been killing his animals, the sooner she could get out of here and away from Jordan.

She put on a pair of thick khaki work pants with a lot of pockets and her heavy waterproof hiking boots, laced tight over thick socks. Her knife went on her belt, along with several others in different utility pouches. She tucked a notepad and pen sealed inside a plastic waterproof pouch into a pocket. She added a flashlight and a package of matches, both waterproof, and a small wax candle. A couple granola bars and a bottle of water went in another. They weighed her down, especially the water, but she'd spent forty-eight hours in a pitch-black cave, desperate enough to drink just about anything; she never went on any scouting mission without at least a minimum of supplies.

Finally, she pulled her hair into a tight tail at the base of her neck, threw on a baseball cap and shrugged into a denim jacket. She'd be sweating in seconds the moment she stepped outside, but the protection for her arms and upper body would be worth it. She didn't have a map of the menagerie, but DiNero had laid it out to be easily navigated, so it wasn't as if she had to figure out a maze. All she had to do was follow the paths.

She knew how to move quietly, though she wasn't trying to be sneaky. She paused at the first cage she came to, peeking inside at the flashing eyes of the silver fox. It yipped softly at her and came close to the bars of the cage, but Monica didn't reach to pet it. She crooned to it gently, though, watching the fox's ears flick forward and back.

"You're okay, pretty girl," Monica said and moved on.

She wasn't sure what she was looking for, exactly, just that she'd exhausted her resources and needed to come at this from a different angle. She'd worked on a team once that had set a bait trap, something she hesitated to do because it meant sacrificing an innocent living creature. She didn't think DiNero would go for it anyway, at least not with one of his pets. Which meant what, she thought as she walked, waiting for another attack?

Fortifying the walls could work to prevent another slaughter, but it was no guarantee. It also meant they'd never find out what had been doing it, unless the thing showed up someplace else…like a playground, Monica thought with a shudder. Sour bile painted her tongue at the thought of a case where the Crew had successfully managed to chase off a Chimera that had been repeatedly ransacking a poultry-processing plant, only to have the thing show up in the backyard of a nearby day-care center. She hadn't been on that team, but everyone had heard about it. The news had said it was a pit-bull attack.

That was why, she thought as she moved on, people like Jordan didn't believe.

Following the curving brick path, she caught sight of DiNero's house. Lights blazing. The sounds of a party inside. She hadn't been invited, didn't care. She paused, though, to admire the mansion and wonder what it was like to have so much money you could drop a few grand without a second thought. Most of what DiNero was paying her went back to the Crew to fund travel and other expenses, but she got her fair share. It wouldn't buy her a mansion but it was enough, as Carl would've said, to keep her in Cheetos and beer.

For a moment, grief rose in her throat, choking her. Her husband had been full of sayings like that. Most of them had made her laugh, even when his tendency to try to make everything a joke was making her angry. Suddenly, fiercely, but not unexpectedly, she missed him with a deep and wretched longing that would slaughter her faster than any monster ever could—if she succumbed to it.

There, right there, she almost did. She almost went to her knees on the bricks and wept. It was too hard, sometimes, to keep herself from giving in to sorrow. She had ways to manage the terror that came from the dreams that were really memories, but this…oh, this was something else, and nothing could make it pass but time.

Monica did not go to her knees, though she did close her eyes against the burning slide of tears. At the taste of salt, she let out a low, shuddering sigh. She rode the pain for a moment or two before steeling herself and shaking it off.

Carl had died, and nothing could bring him back. The most she could do was honor him by doing her best to prevent more death. And that was exactly what she intended to do here.

Chapter 10

Jordan had lapped the entire perimeter of DiNero's estate, eyes open for any signs of destruction in the wall but finding none. He'd exhausted himself, sweating, panting and finally aching, before he slowed to a walk. The night air was thick and humid, but he sucked it in greedily. No scent of anything weird, just the familiar mingled smells of the animals and, from farther off, dinner coming from DiNero's house. The guy was having another party, which meant that sooner or later Jordan could expect a call to give a tour. DiNero loved showing off his pets.

For now, though, Jordan walked to clear his head and soothe his muscles. He wanted a hot shower and something to eat but didn't dare go back just yet. He'd managed, barely, to fend off the hunger he'd tried to satiate with Monica.

Monica.

Damn, the woman had managed to get under his skin. He'd been stupid, he knew that, but no matter what she said, he *was* only human. Not even his twisted, tangled combination of DNA could make him less than that.

Still, there was shame, instilled in him for as long as he could remember by parents who'd wanted anything but this for their only son. They'd never tried to make him embarrassed about what he'd inherited; if anything, their staunch and devout insistence that he could learn to control his "condition" had been meant to make him feel better about it. But all they'd ever managed to do was repeatedly underline how different he was. How he could try and try, but he would never be the "same."

That made him want to run again, but there was no getting away from the past. He'd learned that long ago. No way to run away from himself. The best he could do was learn to control it, the way his parents had taught him. To keep the hunger at bay.

And still he felt it constantly, always under the surface. Waiting to rise to something as simple as a steak or a beautiful woman or a thousand other things that tempted him to give in to his baser impulses. Not human, Monica had said, but she had no idea.

No matter what happened to him, Jordan thought grimly, he was always a man. Nothing could take that away from him. He wouldn't let it.

For a moment, he leaned against the wall to feel the heat left from the earlier sunshine. It felt good, heat upon heat. It slowed things down. Made him languorous rather than agitated. He let himself press against it, then took a seat in the soft grass DiNero had spent a fortune to grow and maintain. If there was one benefit to his condition, it was that the night bugs left him alone.

Dark Heat

If he stayed here a little longer, maybe she'd be asleep by the time he got back. Her windows would be dark. He wouldn't be tempted to go in and see her... Jordan's eyes drifted closed.

"Maybe we'll be okay," his mother said to his father when she thought Jordan couldn't hear. "His birthday was last week. He's fourteen now. Surely if it was going to happen, we'd know about it by now."

Jordan had been sneaking into the kitchen for a late-night snack, his rumbling stomach making it impossible to sleep. Summer, school out, nothing but the possibilities of a whole three months of freedom ahead of him. He had plans with Trent and Delonn tomorrow, video games and a bike ride to the gas station, where they might try to talk to some girls. Maybe. At the sound of his parents' hushed whispers from the back porch, though, he stopped. He hadn't turned on the light, so they had no idea he was there.

"It's going to be all right, bébé," his father said.

Jordan froze. Dad never called Mom that unless they were arguing about something and he was trying to make up to her. Had his parents been fighting? The soft sound of sniffling made his stomach twist. Mom was crying?

"I just want him to be all right, Marc. I'm so worried..."

His father made a shushing sound. "I know. Me, too."

"We should have been more careful." Now his mother sounded fierce, angry. "We knew the risks. We were stupid. Arrogant and reckless!"

"Hush, bébé, don't. You're going to make yourself sick."

"I *am* sick," his mother said. "Sick with worry. Jordan's the one who will pay the price for us being careless… My sweet boy. Oh God, Marc, what will we do if he has it?"

"We'll love him anyway," his father said. "What else could we do?"

The sound of his mother's sobs should've chased away any lingering hunger, but Jordan's stomach only ached more. What were they talking about? If he had what?

Last year, Penny Devereux had been diagnosed with leukemia. She'd had to miss almost the entire school year, and when she'd finally come back, she'd worn a scarf to cover her bald head. She'd been thin and pale, and she still laughed a lot, but she wasn't quite the same.

His parents had gone silent, but Jordan caught a whiff of smoke. That was bad. His mother only lit up when she was superstressed. She'd been trying to quit. Now she was smoking, right there with his dad, who hated it. Something was very wrong.

It didn't stop him from going to the fridge, though. It was as though a phantom hand pulled him, actually, an impulse he couldn't fight. He was so hungry he thought he might faint from it, that and the anxiety from overhearing what he knew they didn't want him to know.

He'd come down hoping to snag a piece of leftover birthday cake or some of his mom's homemade tapioca pudding, but what his hands pulled from the fridge's bottom shelf was the plastic-wrapped platter of uncooked burgers his mom had put together for tomorrow's dinner. Without thinking, Jordan tore the plastic off. Handfuls of soft ground beef went in his mouth. He barely chewed, shoving the food past his lips and licking his fingers. He couldn't get enough.

The lights came on. His mother cried out. Jordan turned, as guilty and embarrassed as if she'd walked in

on him in the shower or doing what he'd just discovered
he could do under the tent of his sheets late at night. No,
this was somehow worse, because somehow he knew it
was related to what his parents had been saying.

Something was wrong with him.

"Put that down!" his mother cried, but she wasn't
angry, as she ought to have been. Fear had widened her
eyes. He could hear it in her voice.

He could *smell* it on her.

"Jordan, give me that." Dad was calmer, pushing past
Mom, who clung to the doorway and burst into tears.

No. Mine. The thoughts rose unbidden, and though
Jordan would never have dreamed of disobeying his father, he backed up still clutching the platter. His mouth
hurt. He tasted blood, and not from the meat but from
his own gums. He ran his tongue along his teeth and
felt the burn and sting of a wound opening—he'd cut it
on something sharp.

His own teeth.

Mine.

The thought rose again, but this time, he tossed the
platter to the floor. Raw meat splatted on the linoleum,
and he backed up with his hands in front of him. There
was more pain. He clenched his fists. More cuts, fingernails long, sharp. There was blood.

He would carry the scars on his palms for the rest
of his life.

"You're going to be okay, son. It's all going to be all
right," his father said, but the look on his face told Jordan that nothing was going to be all right.

Not ever again.

Jordan woke with a startled gasp, hands in front of
him. He'd clenched his fists and winced automatically

at the expected sting of his nails pressing his flesh, but the years of self-discipline had worked. He wasn't going to run off into the night and start making mayhem.

Still, he got to his feet with the memory of those long-ago burgers coating the inside of his mouth. He spat, then again, but he could still taste them. He still wanted them. He would always want them, the way he'd always want to run and punch and break and devour.

With a low groan, he closed his eyes and breathed deep. He focused. Not full-on meditation, which he did every day, but still a forced pattern of breaths that was supposed to relax him. A minute passed. He opened his eyes.

At fourteen, everything had changed for him. His parents, recessive carriers of a set of genes that had combined in him to make him different, had never planned to have children. And if he'd been a girl, he'd never have ended up this way, since only males manifested the condition.

Monica had said werewolves did not exist, but Jordan could've told her otherwise.

Chapter 11

Monica had just decided to turn back and head for home when the first muttered cackling reached her ears. DiNero kept a bunch of peacocks that were allowed to roam freely over the estate. They weren't particularly exotic, not compared to the big cats or rare Russian foxes, but they were pretty. And they screamed, Monica discovered when the sound rose.

She didn't think twice but ran toward it, changing direction when another scream came. Her boots pounded the bricks, but then she dodged off the path and ran through the grass, past several habitats and into darkness. There was light from the house in the distance but she had to blink rapidly to try to get her night vision working. It didn't happen fast enough. She tripped over something and went sprawling.

It was a dead peahen, its throat slashed and long runnels carved into its body. Just beyond it lay another, a carcass rather than a bird, most of it missing. Monica rolled with a small groan and pushed up from her hands and knees, already expecting something to rush at her from the darkness.

Instead, she heard another chattering set of screams from the distance. She didn't want to run with her knife in her hands—that was a good way to end up stabbing herself. The best she could do was hope that whatever was killing the birds wouldn't see her before she saw it.

The menagerie hadn't been set up in grids or blocks, so she had to circle around one of the habitats, this one with a tall, domed cage. Inside it, small gray monkeys screamed and chattered. None of them appeared hurt and she couldn't see any breaks in their cage, so she kept going. She was heading for the exterior wall, heart racing, when something hurtled at her out of the darkness.

Something growling. Something with eyes that flashed red and sharp teeth that snapped at the air in front of her, coming so close she felt the breeze of it on her eyelashes. Claws raked her side, pulling the blow at the last second so she could roll away with her shirt flapping in shreds. Pain stung her, but she was still able to get her hands up to push away the thing on top of her.

Too dark here to see more than shadows. All she could do was twist and turn, getting an arm up to keep the snapping jaws from getting at her throat. Monica screamed, anticipating the crunch of teeth on her forearm, but it didn't come. She kicked upward and out, connecting.

The thing, which smelled of grass and dirt, growled but didn't retreat. It fell on top of her again, crushing her into the ground. She felt hair and limbs and another press of teeth, but by then she'd fought her knife free of the belt sheath. No hesitation, Monica slashed

upward. Her aim was off, but she still connected. Her
knife stuck and she pulled it free. This time, the thing
howled and backed off.

She needed light, but back here close to the exterior
wall, she was in a giant blind spot. Her head spun from
hitting the ground, and bright sparks of pain made everything a blur anyway, but she did see a shape, a head and a
half taller than she was. She smelled blood. She slashed
again, her grip weaker this time, but the thing smacked
her knife from her hand.

Whatever it was hit her in the face, not claws but a
curled…fist? A hand? All she knew was the crisp feeling of hair on her face and the solid thunk of flesh on
hers. The blow drove Monica to her knees. She rolled,
and the next hit her shoulder hard enough to drive her
face forward into the ground again.

This time, she didn't get up.

*She was in the cave again. Pitch-black. The stink of
death. Rattle of bones. Carl was dead; she'd seen him
in the last flare of her light before it had been smashed.
Her husband was dead, and she would be next, unless
she fought.*

She fought.

*Fists and feet and teeth. Her knife. Slashing. Blood,
pain, screaming.*

Everything blurred.

She woke up screaming, throat raw. Something held
her down and she writhed, fighting it until she realized
it was the soft weight of a comforter. She'd been sweating beneath it, wearing only panties and the tank top
she'd gone out in earlier. Her hair had come free of the
elastic and tangled over her shoulders.

For the first few seconds, Monica still didn't know where she was. Then it came to her—the bungalow at DiNero's menagerie. She'd gone out, then she'd heard something...the peacocks, screaming. She swallowed hard at the thought of the beautiful birds being torn apart.

She'd gone to find out what had happened. Something had attacked her. She had to get up.

She winced and cried out softly when she swung her legs over the edge of the bed. Her head pounded, the back of it tender and swollen where she'd hit the ground. A stinging line on her throat had come from the thing's teeth, she remembered that much. Another set of four slashes on her side hurt, too, but they'd been cleaned and bandaged, so she couldn't see how bad they were. They didn't feel deep enough to be terribly serious, she thought and wondered why on earth she hadn't been torn to ribbons.

The thing had been big and strong and angry, and yet it had not actually tried to kill her. It couldn't have. She'd have been dead if it had. She was certain of it.

As it was, her entire body ached. When she got up and went into the bathroom, her reflection showed a pattern of bruises already gone black. She eased up the tank top to look at the bandages, which had been expertly applied. Gauze and medical tape, not adhesive bandages. The edges glistened with antibiotic ointment. She pulled her shirt back down and turned to go back to the bedroom—and let out a shriek.

She'd punched Jordan twice, first in the nose and then in the throat, before she could stop herself. He stumbled back with a shout, and Monica muttered a stricken apology.

He watched her warily, his eyes watering. She hadn't

made him bleed—at least there was that. She might've laughed at the look on his face if everything didn't hurt so bad and if she weren't so freaked out by what had happened. That and the dream. Always the dream.

A strangled sob had forced itself out of her throat before she could stop it. She found herself pressed against him, though if she'd reached for him or he'd pulled her close, she didn't know. What she did know was that his hand stroking her hair felt good, as did his arms around her. Even the pressure of his body on her aching bruises lessened the pain.

When he picked her up and carried her to the bed, she expected him to lay her down, but instead Jordan sat on the edge of it and held her on his lap. Monica was no small woman and had never been fond of being made to feel delicate, but something in the way he cradled her only made her bury her face against the side of his neck.

"How did I get back here?" she asked against his skin.

Jordan hesitated before answering. "I found you. What the hell were you doing out there by yourself?"

She bristled at his tone, but when she tried to pull away, he held her close. "You're hurting me."

"Sorry." He loosed his grip, but not enough to let her go. "You're going to be sore for a while."

"No shit," Monica said. "Something attacked me."

"You shouldn't have been out there alone," Jordan said.

"I can take care of myself," she snapped.

Jordan slid his hand to the back of her neck and buried his fingers in her hair, tipping her head back hard enough to make her gasp—and yes, it made her body ache, but that wasn't why. His eyes narrowed.

"Obviously, you can't," he said in a low voice.

Monica didn't try to struggle. Part of her knew he was right. Her role here had never been to hunt down the creature on her own, but to determine what it was so the Crew could come in and work together on it. Still, she pushed at his chest, though she couldn't get away from him.

"I was out walking, trying to think. Then I heard the peacocks screaming," Monica said. "What did you expect me to do? Not try to see what it was?"

His mouth was very close to hers, though how it had happened, exactly, she couldn't say. He was going to kiss her, and yes, she was going to let him. Because that was what took away the pain and the fear, and because in his arms she could forget that she'd gone up against something that might've killed her, and this time, despite how hard she'd fought, she had not killed it. Something had saved her, and it had not been herself.

She couldn't think of it. And he wasn't kissing her, so she pulled his mouth down to hers. She gave him her tongue. At his soft groan, Monica pressed herself against him, writhing and ignoring the pain.

He pinned her wrists suddenly and held her away from him. "Monica. Don't. You don't really want this."

"Want? Maybe not," she said. "*Need*, Jordan."

And she did need it. Needed to fuck away the memories and the pain and the fear, the anxiety. She shifted, twisting, to straddle him. He still held her wrists, keeping her from pushing against his chest, but that didn't stop her from grinding her crotch down on his.

"I don't want to hurt you," Jordan said.

Monica slowed but didn't stop the steady rocking of her hips against his hardening cock. "I can handle it."

She leaned to flick her tongue along his lower lip. He didn't release his grip on her wrists, but he did soften. Then he pulled her toward him. He kissed her, hard, until she gasped.

"I'll hurt you," Jordan said into her ear, then slid his teeth along her throat.

His tongue stung the cut there, and she hissed. He gave a low growl and nipped her. Monica jerked, the pain so mingled with pleasure she couldn't be sure which she felt more of.

She shoved him back onto the bed. Still kissing him, she pushed up his shirt, ran her hands up his sides. He jerked when she did, and that was when her fingers encountered the soft padding of gauze bandages.

Head spinning, confused, Monica sat back. "Jordan? What…?"

Oh God. Oh my God. She tried to stumble back, to get off him, but he'd again grabbed her tight. Panic flooded her.

The smell of grass and dirt, the flash of red…the same as she'd seen in his eyes. She'd used her knife against the thing that had attacked her, and now here he was with wounds in the same place… She fought him, but he held her tight. His breath covered her face, and she closed her eyes instinctively, waiting for the press and sting of teeth, this time slashing her throat open instead of nibbling.

"Monica, look at me."

"What the hell are you doing?" she cried. "What are you?"

He let her go so fast she fell back, but they were still tangled together, so she had to fight her way free of him. Panting, dizzy, she backed up from the bed, trying to think about what she could use to defend herself against him, but all Jordan did was sit there.

"What are you?" she asked again in a low, strangled voice.

Jordan shook his head, shaggy dark hair falling over

his eyes for a moment before he gave her a grim look. "Why don't you tell me?"

He'd seen the looks before. Disgust, fear. His parents had tried to shield him from most of it, but that hadn't been much better. Isolated from friends and even family, Jordan's high school years had been lonely and full of self-doubt. It had taken him years to learn how to keep the hungers at bay—for food, for sex, for violence. But he had, and damn it, he didn't deserve to be treated like some kind of serial killer for something he couldn't control.

"I don't know," Monica said in answer to his question.

He thought she meant to bolt, but for now she was staying still. Fists clenched. Every muscle tense. He could smell her anxiety, and it made his stomach hurt.

"No?" he asked, deliberately snide. "Here I thought that was your job."

Her eyes had been wide, but now they narrowed. "Are you the one...?"

"No!" Angry that she'd even think it for a second, Jordan got off the bed. It stung to see how she moved away from him, so wary. Her gaze flicked to the knife he'd laid on her dresser.

He was on her before she got even two steps toward it. He could've hurt her if he'd tried, but he wasn't trying. She didn't struggle. She looked up at him instead.

"You attacked me," she said.

"I didn't know it was you. It was a mistake." The excuse sounded lame, but it was the truth. "I heard the peacocks screaming, the same as you. I thought I could find what was killing the animals. I thought I could..."

"Kill it? With your bare hands?" Beneath his fingers, Monica's arms stiffened, and he let her go. She stepped back from him, but only a step.

Jordan's fingers curled, the tips pressing the faded scars on his palms. "I could've tried."

"This is crazy. It's crazy," she repeated and continued almost as though she were talking to herself, "People don't become things. It doesn't happen. Lycanthropy is a mental disorder, sure, but it's not…real. You can't really be…"

"I'm real," Jordan said flatly and pushed past her toward the door, where he paused to look back at her. "I've got a fucked-up genetic disorder that makes it hard for me to control my impulses. It forces physical changes, and most of the time, I can stop them, but sometimes I can't. Sometimes I don't want to, like last night, when I was thinking I could finally get whatever's killing the animals. But I am real, Monica."

She shook her head. "I don't… I can't…"

That was it. He'd had it. This woman had blown into his life like a fucking hurricane. He'd never asked for it.

"Fuck this noise," Jordan said. "All I ever wanted was to do my job and be left alone. You can believe in monsters, but you can't believe in me?"

He didn't realize how much he'd wanted her to answer him until she didn't, but all she gave him was her silence. His fingers curled again, pressing old wounds before he could force them to open. Then without another word, Jordan left her there alone.

Chapter 12

"It's reptile, we're pretty sure of that." Ted pushed his glasses up on his nose and waved expansively. "Based on the blood samples you gave us and some of those markings, I compared it with a case Boris and I were on last year in Miami. Rangers had found a bunch of gators slaughtered, figured poachers, of course, but we hunted what turned out to be a monstrous fucking… Hell, it was a dinosaur, I'm telling you."

Monica couldn't sit still. She had Ted and Vadim in her bungalow, both of them chowing down on the deli platters DiNero's cook had sent down, but she couldn't take even a bite. Not with Jordan mere steps away in the next bungalow.

You can believe in monsters, but you can't believe in me.

"You're sure it's reptilian?" she asked finally. "It couldn't possibly be something else? Something we haven't seen before?"

Vadim looked up from the sandwich he'd been piling high with meat and cheese. "What is this? You have something, Monica?"

She opened her mouth to spill it all, but at the last moment, her jaw shut with a snap of her teeth so hard on her tongue that tears sparked in her eyes. Secrets tasted like blood, she thought. She poured herself a glass of DiNero's whiskey and sipped it, relishing the burn.

Ted shoveled a handful of chips into his mouth and kept talking. Monica liked Ted a lot, but right now with him misdirecting Vadim's attention from her, she kind of loved him. She pretended she hadn't heard Vadim ask her anything at all.

"The patterns are almost identical," Ted said. "It could be something else, I guess, but I think we should go in armed for dino."

"What happened to the one you went after in Miami?" Monica asked.

Ted sighed. "It went down in the swamp, sank like a stone. Gators were on it before we could even get close enough to try to net it or anything. But it only took a couple shotgun blasts. Thing looked like a raptor of some kind. It wasn't much bigger than a gator—I mean, I've seen ones that were a lot bigger. But it stood on hind legs and worked with its front ones. Definitely smart enough to work at a lock. I could've kicked myself for not trying to tranq it, but when something with teeth the size of your fist is coming at you…"

"That's the nature of our work," Vadim put in. "If it were easy to prove what we find, we'd be out of our jobs, eh?"

He gave Monica a long, steady look that she had to pretend she didn't notice. Everything in her world had turned upside down. She couldn't stop turning it over and over in her head. Jordan, his touch, the sound of his voice, the way he'd made her feel.

There'd been more than a few men after Carl. She'd lost herself in physical sensation to keep herself from feeling anything else, and it had worked, in the short-term. But Jordan had been the only man so far who'd entirely chased away the remnants of the memories, left nothing lingering behind.

Sex was only sex, though.

"Monica?"

She tore herself away from memories of Jordan's hands on her and faced Vadim. He'd been there for her, too, in many other ways that had saved her. He and the entire Crew had believed her when nobody else did. They'd helped her find a purpose to her life. Their work, their passion, was hunting myths, and here was one practically right in front of them. She could offer up living, breathing proof of something Vadim had told her wasn't possible. But what would he do with that knowledge?

Would he hunt Jordan?

Chapter 13

"They're going after it," DiNero said, no mistaking the excitement in his voice. Like a kid on Christmas Eve. He knuckled Jordan's arm, then punched the air and did a little shuffle. "C'mon, man, this is awesome!"

Jordan bent back to the silver fox, who'd been cowering in the corner, frightened by DiNero's antics. "Shh, little girl. Hey. Calm down, okay? You're scaring her."

DiNero looked chastened. "You're putting her in with the others now?"

"Yeah." Jordan lifted the fox, who nestled into his armpit, hiding her face. "I think she'll be all right there."

DiNero couldn't have cared less about the fox. He was all about the thing Monica's team was here to hunt. He'd ordered Jordan to start construction on a new habitat—never mind they had no clue what the thing needed to survive, much less if they could even capture it alive. It was a bad idea, all around—that was what Jordan thought, but DiNero hadn't asked him his opinion.

Jordan hadn't seen Monica in three days. Not since the night she'd figured out he was something other than what she'd thought he was. He kept waiting for the Crew to show up on his doorstep with lit torches and a silver bullet. Not that it needed to be silver to kill him, he thought grimly. A regular bullet would do it.

Leaving DiNero behind, Jordan took the silver fox to her new habitat. There he sat with her for a while as the others, a sweet red fox and another couple of silvers, sniffed them both carefully. All of the foxes in DiNero's collection had come to the menagerie tamed and socialized, but that didn't mean they couldn't reject a newcomer. Jordan sat quietly while the foxes checked out the new girl. He'd brought treats. He relaxed, not wanting to transmit any anxiety toward them. Eventually, the red one came over to investigate again, and he scratched it behind the ears.

"Does he have a name?"

Jordan didn't turn at Monica's quiet question. "DiNero doesn't name them. I just call him Red."

"Of course. Can I come in?"

He shrugged. When she sat next to him, he didn't turn to face her. The silver fox had ventured off his lap, and at Monica's entrance, the others ran away, too. She didn't say anything at first.

"Are you going to tell them about me? Your crew. Am I going to show up in your database?"

She made a soft noise. "No. I don't know."

"DiNero thinks he's going to keep this gator thing you're hunting."

"Ted would be happy not to kill it if it means he gets to study it," she answered.

Jordan looked at her. "It killed a tiger and mountain lions. You really think you're going to take it alive?"

"No. I don't know that, either," she added. "Maybe. I haven't been able to think much about it."

He studied her, thinking he wouldn't ask her why, but the words came out anyway. "Is that so?"

When she moved toward him, he didn't recoil. Something in his expression must've told her how he felt, though, because she sat back. She looked tired.

"I'm sorry if you thought I was cruel, Jordan."

"About what? About using me to get over some kind of trauma, or about reminding me my life's a fucking mess, or what?" He tossed a treat toward the new silver fox, who took it with a small yip.

"About everything. I did use you, and I'm sorry. And I do believe in…you."

He looked at her. "Sure. Like you do in Bigfoot."

"No. Like I believe in you. A man who cares very much for those he's vowed to protect." She tipped her chin toward the foxes. She touched her side, briefly, where he'd slashed her. Her gaze met his, frank and open.

"I didn't mean to do that," he said in a low voice.

"I know you didn't. But I did mean to do it to you."

"You were fighting for your life, or you thought you were. I could've hurt you really bad. I could've…" He swallowed, hard. "I could've killed you."

"But you didn't."

He shook his head. "I'm not an animal. I do know what I'm doing. Even when the hunger gets too big."

"Do you actually change? I mean…"

"Do I turn into a wolf?"

She looked a little embarrassed. "Yeah."

"No. Not like in the movies. My teeth are sharp. My nails grow fast. If I don't shave twice a day, I'm a fucking lumberjack by midafternoon. I'm strong all the time. Adrenaline spikes it. Certain things trigger me. And then it can be hard not to just—" he shrugged "—rampage. Gorge and destroy and fuck."

She made a small noise. He looked at her. She bit her lower lip as though struggling for words.

"I work with myths and mysteries," she told him. "It's in my nature to want to know more."

Jordan looked at the foxes playing. Not at her. "I'm not the only one, you know. It's a family thing. My parents were both recessive carriers. It's a nasty secret we keep. You want me to spill out everything about myself? About my family? I hardly know you."

"I know that." Her soft intake of breath told him his words had hurt her, but he forced himself not to care.

"Just because I fucked you doesn't mean I owe you any damned thing." Jordan got to his feet.

That was when all hell broke loose.

Chapter 14

Ted and Vadim had set a trap and caught themselves a dinogator. Six feet long on its hind legs, talons like razors, teeth sharper than that. A hide so thick handgun bullets bounced off it, but Ted had come prepared with tranquilizers this time, and a dart to the underbelly had felled the creature. DiNero was out of a prize, though, because much like in Miami, the moment the thing went down, it was surrounded by gators that swarmed to devour it.

"Nature's way of cleaning up her messes," Ted said morosely to Monica as he and Vadim packed up their van. "I've never seen alligators act like that."

"Pheromones. Something like that. Put them in a frenzy. Hell if I know." Vadim shrugged and shook his head. "But where there's two, there must be more. You'll get another chance, Ted."

DiNero had been disappointed, of course, but it

seemed he was consoling himself with moving forward on purchasing an elephant instead. Monica didn't think that was the smartest decision the man could've made with his money, but it was probably better than trying to keep some swamp monster in captivity. The upward bump in her bank-account balance was all she really cared about anyway.

Well, that and something else.

"You're sure you don't want to ride back with us?" Vadim gave her a curious look as he shut the van's back doors. "Road trips can be fun, eh?"

Ted waggled his brows. "I have a great playlist. And I convinced Vadim to spring for three-star motels this time around. Not just two."

"Wow, the offer is so tempting." She laughed. "I think I'll stick with my original plans, though. I've never been to New Orleans. While I'm down here, I thought I'd like to check it out. Drink a hurricane or two. Tour a cemetery."

"Suit yourself." Vadim shrugged. "Don't get suckered into a ghost tour."

Monica snorted soft laughter. "Like I can't do one of those for free just about anytime I want?"

Ted got into the van, and Vadim pulled her closer for an unexpected embrace. Even more surprisingly, she didn't merely allow him the hug but returned it. Pressed to the big man's chest, Monica closed her eyes. She didn't want to cry, but damn if she didn't feel close to tears.

"Sometimes this job can be very hard," Vadim said into her ear. Monica nodded against him. He squeezed her gently. "But remember, we don't fear the unknown. We make it ours. Yes?"

She pushed away to look at him. "Cryptic."

He grinned. "There's more to life than hunting things in the swamps, Monica. But you sometimes have to be as fearless in seeking out life as you are about looking for the chupacabra."

Vadim squeezed her again before stepping back. From inside the van came a loud thumping bass beat. He sighed and shook his head.

"Are you sure I can't convince you to come with us?"

"I'm good." Monica eyed the van. "Especially if that's Ted's playlist."

Waving, she watched them drive off, then headed for the bungalow to pack up her things. A rap on the door had her heart racing; she tried not to act disappointed when she opened it to find DiNero, not Jordan. DiNero didn't seem to notice. He bustled in with the same high energy he'd had the whole time.

"He ran off!"

"We told you there was no guarantee we could catch it alive," Monica began, but DiNero stopped her with a look. "Who?"

"Leone. He took leave. He didn't even give me notice—he just said he's off to his place in New Orleans for a few weeks. He left Karen in charge, but I have a group of guests coming to stay next week, and damn it, I need Jordan here. Nobody can show off my animals the way he can."

Monica frowned. "He…left?"

"Yeah, said he needed a vacation." DiNero shook his head. "I think it's because he doesn't want me to get the elephant."

"Maybe." She paused, wondering if she ought to offer him something to drink. It was his own booze, after all. DiNero put his hands on his hips, staring at her. She tried to think of what to say. "Um…"

"Well, it's a clusterfuck, that's all. I need someone who can really handle the animals. I mean if they're sick or whatever."

"Hasn't he gone on vacation before?"

"Yeah, but I…" DiNero looked her over. "He always gave me notice, and I brought in another handler until he came back. And he was only ever gone a few days before. Shit, what will I do if he doesn't come back?"

Monica didn't have a lot of patience for people who worked themselves into a lather for no real reason, but now all she could do was shake her head. "He'll come back. Why wouldn't he? He loves his job here. He loves working with the animals. He's…happy here."

She wasn't sure if that was true, actually. He'd seemed content enough, here out of the way. What had he said to her? All he wanted was to do his job and be left alone.

Shit.

She'd chased him away, she was sure of it. "Where did you say he went, exactly?"

"He has some place in New Orleans that he keeps. I don't know exactly where." DiNero sighed. "And you're heading out, too? Great."

"My job's done. You don't need me here."

DiNero gave her a long, assessing look that left him about three seconds away from getting a knee to the nuts. "Now that you're off the clock, so to speak…"

"Don't even." Monica shook her head and put up a hand. "Do not."

DiNero grinned. "Worth a shot, huh? Can't blame a guy for trying. I mean, I know I'm no Leone, but I have a lot going for me other than brooding good looks and sex appeal."

"I'm sure you do, but what makes you think I'm even interested in him?" Monica crossed her arms.

"Shit, girl, you almost set the bayou on fire every time you looked at each other. You think I didn't notice?" DiNero shook his head and shot her a grin. "I've never seen that man give anything that much attention in all the years he's worked here, including every animal I've ever owned."

She frowned. "That's just…"

"He's got a place near Bourbon Street," DiNero told her. "And I'd like him to come back. It's worth another donation to your vacation fund if you can convince him."

"I don't hunt people," Monica said flatly. "If he wants to come back, he will."

DiNero held up his hands, looking apologetic. "Fine, fine. Again, can't blame a guy for asking. I guess I'll just have to beg him myself."

"No," Monica said. "You know what… I'll see what I can do."

Chapter 15

Long days. Long nights. Booze and women and the rich copper taste of rare steaks.

Jordan had glutted himself on all of it. Sex and meat and all the things he tried so hard to deny himself because giving in to the hunger only made it that much harder to deny it the next time. He'd smashed the mirror in the bathroom, and now he took slow, lingering satisfaction in the way the glass glittered on the floor because he hadn't cleaned it up.

There were other things he could've done, too. Crashed a car. Robbed a bank. Gotten in a fistfight with a motorcycle gang. The possibilities for mayhem were endless and alluring, and fuck it all, if he hadn't had any sense of conscience, he'd have done all of it. Run wild in the streets, howling at the moon.

Instead, he wallowed in his small sins, all he allowed himself to indulge in. Tonight it was a glass of very expensive wine and a steak the size of his head, with all the trimmings. Later, he thought, he would find himself a woman or two or three and spend the night's last hours reveling in naked flesh.

Except there was already a woman on his doorstep when he got home.

He knew her at once by her scent, and his lip curled. His dick got hard, too, immediately, and he hated himself for that. And her a little, too.

"How long have you been here?" he asked.

She shrugged. "A few hours. Where were you?"

"Eating an enormous dinner. Drinking too much. How'd you find me?"

Monica stood when he came closer. She seemed to have been waiting a long time. She stretched, and fuck if watching her body move didn't make him want to take her right there against his front door.

"I hunt down mythical beasts for a living," she said. "You have an address and a credit-card statement and utility bills. You were easy to find."

"What do you want?" He was a little drunk, not so much from the wine and the food but from seeing her again. Smelling her. He wanted to taste her with a real and physical longing.

"You," she said simply.

Jordan heard his own low rumble in answer. She would think he was an animal for sure at that sound, he thought, but he couldn't take it back now. Monica took a step closer.

"You," she whispered again, offering her mouth.

He wasn't going to kiss her. But there she was, soft and curvy, and that hair, that fucking hair spilling down her back and over his hands, and then she was in his arms and her mouth was on his and his knee pressed between her thighs, and in another second or so, he could be inside her, if he only…let…go.

"No," Jordan muttered without moving away from her.

Monica pressed herself against him. "Take me inside. Fuck me. Then feed me. Then we'll talk."

It was the finest offer he'd ever had, but he hadn't spent so many years learning to control himself to give in now, just like that. "What the hell do you want, Monica?"

She linked her fingers behind his neck. "I can't stop thinking about you. I still dream, Jordan. And when I wake up, I reach for you. Not just anyone. You. I don't know why."

He reached behind her to unlock the door and push them both inside. He had a moment to feel ashamed of how he'd let the place get filthy. Maybe she wouldn't notice in the dark.

"I'm not just a curiosity," he told her. "What do you want to do, study me? Put me in a collection the way DiNero does with his pets?"

She shook her head, following him into the small kitchen, where he poured them each a drink. "No. If I wanted to do that, I'd have told Vadim about you."

"You didn't?"

"No. You're not a freak or a curiosity. But I do want to learn more about you. Not just how you are in bed, which is very, very good, by the way." She leaned to kiss him again, but briefly. "Jordan…you're special."

"Sure I am."

She put her hands on his hips and pulled him closer to her. "Maybe it's just sex. Maybe it's only that. Or maybe it's something else. I'm willing to see if there's more to us than that. The best you can do is try."

He backed her up against the kitchen counter but stopped himself from putting her on top of it and ripping her panties off, pushing up her skirt. Sinking into her heat. He shivered from the thought of it. Made a low noise.

"DiNero sent me here to find you. See if you'd come back." Monica hopped up on the counter and drew him between her legs. "I told him I'd see what I could do."

"So that's why you're really here." He slid a hand between them, his thumb rubbing her through her panties. This time, she was the one who made the noise.

Her back arched a little. Her voice became raspy. "I know you love working there. Maybe not the guy himself, but the job? You love it. Don't let me take that from you."

"You think you could take anything from me?" He bent to nip at her neck, angry in a way but also so turned on he could barely think straight.

When she took his face in her hands and held him still so she could look in his eyes, the entire world shifted. "I don't know about taking, but I'm hoping you'll let me try to give you something."

His throat dried. "What's that?"

"Me," she whispered and kissed him again. "It's really all I have."

There was no holding back then. Her skirt went to her waist, her panties torn free. He was deep inside her right after that, and her nails raked his back through his shirt. They fucked hard and fast, rattling the cupboard doors. Her body clenched around his, sending him over the edge, and she cried out his name.

Breathing hard, Jordan blinked, a realization flooding through him. He shook his head, not sure what to think. What to do.

"What?" Monica asked him.

"It's... I'm not...hungry. Anymore."

She gave him a curious look, then one of understanding. She pulled his mouth to hers again, her hand cupping his chin to hold him there for the kiss. Her other went behind his neck.

"I understand," she told him. "You feed me, too."

Later, after a shower and cleaning up the glass and another meal, this time of fresh pasta and salad and bread, they sat at the table together. She'd been quiet, mostly, and that was fine with him. He was still trying to think about where this was going, or what it meant. She'd made him an offer. Just try, she'd said. But could he?

"I didn't think you'd want this," Monica said, indicating the plates in front of them.

He looked at her. She wasn't meeting his gaze, and he thought he knew why. "No?"

"You said you'd had a big dinner. I didn't think you'd want to eat again," she said.

He waited for her to look at him, and when she did, he took her hand and pulled her onto his lap. "There's something you should know about me, Monica. Something that might make a difference in what you asked me."

She looked solemn, slightly frowning. "Okay."

He kissed her hard enough to make her gasp. "Even if I'm not hungry, I can always eat."

It took her a second or two before the light of understanding filled her gaze, but when it did, she laughed. She kissed him, softer than he'd done. She nuzzled his neck, making him shiver.

"So let me feed you," she told him. "And we'll see how the rest of it goes."

* * * * *

DARK DREAMS

Chapter 1

Stephanie Adams wasn't going to wake up.

Not if she could help it anyway, even with the low bleat of her phone alarm begging for her attention. It would get louder. There'd be another. She'd set a total of six alarms on her phone, each progressively closer together. She also had an additional four alarm clocks, the old-fashioned windup kind, set to sound at similar intervals. One of them had been designed for hearing-impaired users and featured a blaring white light that was supposed to sear her eyeballs into opening.

She was *not* going to wake up.

Not now, not so close to this, the end of things, and surely it had to be the end, didn't it? Almost six months of work, she'd come so close, and now she was finally going to find him. Crouching low on the dark and shifting carpet of pine needles that were part of her anchoring spot, Stephanie curled her fingers in the prickly coolness. She breathed in, out, each breath a conscious effort because here in the Ephemeros, she didn't really need to breathe. She sipped at the air instead.

She could smell him. She didn't know his name. Hadn't seen his face. All she had was the softly drifting scent of him, not a cologne or a soap or any sort of perfume. It was the tang of sweat and blood and dirt; it was something else all tangled up with that and woven into a tapestry of sight and sound, left behind every time she'd managed to get close.

Everything worked together here in the dream world. Tasting sounds, seeing smells. That sort of thing. For the lucky ones who could control what happened to them and around them, too, the dream world was a playground. For those who couldn't, it could sometimes be less fun.

"Where are you?" Stephanie murmured as she let her fingers draw patterns in the gritty soil before she stood to dust off her palms on the seat of her leather trousers. Leather—she'd have laughed at herself if she weren't concentrating so hard on staying here instead of being pulled into consciousness. In the waking world, Stephanie would no more have worn leather than she would've slapped a baby. "Come out, come out, wherever you are."

The buzz of her alarm threatened to pull her from the dream world, but she forced herself to stay here. Damn it, why had she come so close to catching this creep now, when she'd had to schedule an early meeting that couldn't be missed? It was the only reason she'd set the alarms in the first place, so she'd be sure not to oversleep.

She'd spent months tracking the shaper who'd been wreaking havoc, using information he'd gleaned here from unwitting shapers in the Ephemeros to empty their bank accounts and run up credit-card debt in the real world. Of all the cases she'd worked, it was far from the worst or most dangerous trick a power-hungry shaper had pulled, but Vadim had been adamant that this was a problem for the Crew to solve. You couldn't have people taking advantage of what they could do in the dream world. It messed with the balance of things in a way Stephanie would never pretend to be philosophical enough to understand.

Again the alarm pulled at her awareness, but she fought off waking. Here in her anchoring spot, where she was strongest, she was able to hold on to her dream self a lot longer, but even so, the edges of the world had started rippling. Stephanie had spent too many hours asleep and dreaming when she could've been living to let go of this now. She had to find him and stop him, before he caused any more trouble.

She sent out a small push of energy to reshape the landscape around her. Out of her forest, into what she thought of as the dark desert. Ringed by black mountains, the sky permanently the color of tar, this space was as close to emptiness as she could manage to shape without losing herself in the void. Just beyond the mountains, which would always be miles out of reach no matter how fast she ran toward them, blue-white lightning sliced apart the sky. Once, she'd seen a face peering through the cut in the atmosphere. Big fingers, pulling apart the edges. Fathomless eyes. Just the once, but that had been enough, because she'd never been able to convince herself she had not glimpsed the face of some god.

Now Stephanie pushed again, a nudge, sending out small tendrils of her will to draw the rogue shaper closer to her. Like a flower tempting a bee, she thought as the next steady, blaring throb of an alarm began pounding her ears. *Come closer*, she thought. *Come and find me.*

She'd flown in this world. Leaped high and floated down. She'd sunk to the bottoms of oceans without fear of drowning. She hadn't faced much in the Ephemeros that scared her, and yet her heart now beat faster as at last she felt the answering push-pull of the other shaper. Anticipation, not fear, though she clenched her fingers into a fist and straightened her back, squaring her shoulders. Ready to fight.

The dreamers who'd faced him in their nightmares had described him as various entities. Vampire, werewolf, dark wizard. He'd played upon their fears to wrangle their personal data, which he'd then used in the real world to access their bank accounts, credit cards. Identity theft, and nearly untraceable because he hadn't actually hacked into anything. He simply forced them to give him what he wanted to use, and in the dreams, they did.

"Come here," Stephanie whispered again. She shaped a park bench. A stone path. A tree. She sent out small and seeking threads of her will and felt the Ephemeros respond around her.

And then…there he was.

A shadow. Tall, lean, but unmistakably male. No features that she could make out, but he wore an outfit that looked similar to hers. Leather pants, jacket with a flare at the tail, or maybe it was a shirt with a vest. Hard to tell against the black of the mountains behind him.

Stephanie straightened. "Come here."

"Who are you?" The voice, low and raspy and rumbly, sent a vibration straight to the core of her stomach and then upward to the pit of her throat, making her feel sort of sick.

He wasn't trying to push her or even to shape anything around them. Stephanie let her forefinger make a small circle, sending a spiral of sand spinning into a dust devil that danced toward him but fell apart before it made it even halfway. The other shaper, the one they'd been calling Mr. Slick, didn't even move.

So, he wasn't threatened by her. Okay, then. Well, she'd faced worse than some dude with a boner for charging up other people's credit cards to keep himself living in style. She'd faced shapers who killed the sleepers they attacked in dreams. This guy was going to be a piece of cake.

Chocolate cake, thick with fudge frosting, a cherry on the top, ice cream nestled in the layers, whipped cream, candy, French fries, no, soft pretzels, pretzel sticks dipped into the sweetness, salt and sweet, and oh my God, she was so hungry, what was this in front of her, a plate, a tray, a trough, and Stephanie was going to dive face-first into the decadence and eat and eat and eat and…

White light blasted her eyelids, painting them with a reverse sort of lightning. She woke with a start and a low cry, her hands moving to shove her mouth full of all that delicious food, which of course was not really there. She sat up in bed, the blankets tangled at her waist, and let out a muttered curse.

"Bastard," she said. "What a dirty trick."

Then she let out a long series of sputtering laughs, because damn. How had he known exactly how to push her so she wouldn't know she was being pushed? That hadn't happened to her in a long, long time.

Sitting up, she swung her legs over the bed with a

small groan. Then, scrubbing at her face and yawning, she stretched. Her phone rang and she glanced at it, thinking she wouldn't answer, but it was Vadim.

"Hey, boss."

"Terry says there were ripples last night. Are you just getting up?"

Terry was working a case in which the shaper was killing sleepers in the dream world. It didn't always kill them in the real world, though it caused comas, heart attacks and strokes. If there were ripples, Terry would be sensing them, for sure. But Stephanie's case wasn't nearly as serious—it was important, as they all were, but it wasn't going to kill anyone.

"I got close. Saw him. Spoke with about six potential victims who said they'd been approached by, in turn, a scary clown, a ventriloquist dummy, a shark, a vampire, and two said it was their ex-wives." She laughed through another yawn. "Funny what really scares people."

"Did they give up their information?"

"The frightened husbands did." She chuckled again. "I'll add it to the data sheet. I have a meeting with Kent this morning. I have to get going."

They signed off. Stephanie scribbled down the information she could recall from her dream. She'd have to tell Kent she'd gathered this data from "sources" and let him think it was something to do with computer searches and stuff, but that was the nature of her job. It wasn't as if she could stroll into his office and tell him she'd met these people in a dream, after all. He'd think she was nuts.

Chapter 2

Kent Gordon woke with a start, just before the sound of his alarm. He rolled with a groan to turn it off, then buried his face in the pillows. He did not want to get up. He wanted to stay in bed all day long.

Wallowing.

In the bed that had been theirs? With another groan, he swung his legs over the side of the bed and got himself moving. Carol had been gone only a week, not even long enough for the scent of her to vanish from the sheets, although he'd washed them. Twice.

In the shower, Kent bent his head beneath the spray and let the hot water pound away at the knots in his shoulders. In the kitchen, he made himself a cup of terrible instant coffee because Carol had always been the one to get the first pot brewing. He grabbed a frozen egg sandwich, nuked it and burned his tongue.

"Shit!" He spit the mess into the sink and stayed there

for a long moment with both hands on the stainless steel, head bowed. Waiting to...

What? Grieve? Mourn? Celebrate?

Whatever he was supposed to feel about the end of his four-year relationship, he wasn't feeling any of it. All Carol's leaving had done was point out to him how empty he'd been for a long time, and probably how empty he was going to stay for a lot longer.

It was not the best way to start the day, that was for sure, but a glance at his calendar when he got into work made it a little better. He had an appointment with Stephanie in about twenty minutes. Just enough time to grab a cup of marginally better coffee and a stale doughnut from the break room before getting back to his desk and pretending as if he wasn't just waiting for her to walk through his door.

He'd been working, on and off, with Stephanie Adams for the past six months. She was one of the investigators on the fraud cases that had been plaguing Member's Best for close to a year now. It had started with a few random account issues. Unauthorized withdrawals or transfers. Charges to the credit union's debit or credit cards, stuff like that. The incidences had started becoming closer together and for greater amounts, which was when the board had called in an outside team to check for security breaches. They'd found no evidence of hackers. Nothing could be traced. It was becoming a real problem for the credit union, which had more than twenty branches throughout Pennsylvania.

Kent was not technically supposed to deal with stuff like this. His job was to oversee the general management of all the credit union's branches. The board had decided that also meant liaising with the investigator to coordinate data regarding the thefts. Which meant he'd spent a lot of time with Ms. Adams over the past six months…and spent a lot of time ignoring that he liked her. Because, Carol.

Who'd left him.

Today Stephanie wore a pair of slim-fitting dark jeans topped with a black mesh sweater that hung off one shoulder. Black Docs on her feet, accented with a set of sparkly pink shoelaces. She slung her thick parka over the back of one chair and took a seat in the other, already pulling out a notepad from her shoulder bag.

"Morning," Kent said mildly.

She looked up, a small crease in her brow fading as she smiled. "Hi. Morning. Sorry, I'm a little distracted. Got some news."

"Bad news?"

She paused, then settled her notepad on one knee while she looked at him. "No. Why would you think…?"

"Sorry." He shook his head, feeling dumb. "You meant news about the fraud. Not personal."

"Oh. No. Nothing personal. But thanks for asking, in case it was." Again she paused to look him over. "You okay?"

"Yeah. Sure." Kent forced a smile and leaned back in his chair.

Stephanie shook her head. "You don't seem okay. Did something else happen? Another account hacked?"

"Not so far today," he said. Then he blurted out, "My girlfriend left me."

"Oh, good! I mean, goodness," Stephanie said. "Goodness me."

It was such an odd thing for her to say, spoken in such a brightly robotic tone, that Kent laughed. Loudly. "What?"

"Oh, I just… That sucks, Kent. I'm sorry. Um…" She coughed, not meeting his gaze.

For a long few seconds of awkward silence, he simply stared at her while she fussed with her notepad. Good, she'd said. Good…as in…she was happy he was single, or what?

There'd been more than a few times in his life when Kent wished he was not so easily led by the ideas his little head got, despite what the one on his shoulders tried to tell it. Today was one of those times, and he cursed himself for it—he'd been single for, like, six freaking days, and even though it had been more like six weeks since he'd last gotten laid, that was no excuse.

Even if Stephanie did have the biggest, bluest eyes he'd ever seen. And that great laugh, coupled with a smile that would've made a priest say hallelujah and not because of a sermon. She was smart, too, on point with everything they'd ever worked on, even if she hadn't yet been able to figure out who was stealing from the Member's Best accounts.

"Right," he said slowly. "So…should we talk about your updates, or…?"

"Right, right." She coughed again, still not meeting his gaze as she fiddled with the notepad. When she did look up, she seemed uncomfortable to find him staring at her.

It of course made Kent feel like an ass to have been caught, so he looked away and it was a comedy of awkward silences and half-started sentences for the next minute until finally Stephanie laughed and shook her head. She cleared her throat.

She slid the notepad across his desk. "I've put together some possibilities of what's been going on. See, at first, the perp was just taking small amounts out of accounts here and there. Nobody even noticed, or they chalked it up to some glitch, right?"

"Yeah." He leaned to look at the names, dates and numbers on the pad.

An hour passed while they talked and Stephanie outlined what she'd been working on. How she'd been trying to connect the dots. She'd scooted her chair around to his side of the desk and was pointing at the notepad.

"Find the pattern," she said. "If we can do that, we'll find the douchecanoe who's doing this, and hopefully before he really hits anyone hard."

We, she'd said, and Kent hadn't missed that. Not that it meant anything beyond the work relationship, of course. But still. It was nice to hear.

"Hey, I'm going out to grab some lunch," he said with a glance at her. Sitting this close, he imagined for a moment he could feel the brush of her hair on his cheek. "You want to come out with me? We can keep looking for patterns."

She tucked a strand of her dark hair behind one ear as she looked at him now, a small smile curving her lips. "Sure. I have some time. Where should we go?"

"How about The Gold Monkey?" It was a quiet little Middle Eastern place around the corner.

"Perfect." She grinned at him, not moving away. Their eyes met. "I'm starving."

Chapter 3

"It wasn't a date," Stephanie told her friend Denise on the phone as she got out of her car and headed into the Morningstar Mocha to pick up a couple bags of their specially blended herbal tea. She was a coffee fiend, no doubt, except when she was working a case that meant she had to spend more of her time sleeping than any one person should've been able to.

Denise handled scheduling and travel arrangements for Crew members who needed, as Stephanie had, to relocate in order to pursue cases. Stephanie had known her for years, though this was the first time she'd ever been assigned close enough to hang out with her in person. It had made the Pennsylvania winter a little more bearable for California girl Stephanie.

"He told you his girlfriend left him, then he asked you to an intimate little venue for fondue. Fondue is not work-related material, Stephanie." Denise's voice dipped low for a second, crackling, before getting clear again. "Sorry, I've got someone on the line waiting for hotel reservations in Moscow. My Russian's pretty rusty. If I break off with you, it's to deal with that."

"I can let you go. I don't have any updates or anything. I mean, yeah, he's cute. And now he's single. But so what? I'm out of here as soon as I bust whoever's doing this stuff, and I'm back to Los Angeles. And he'll be here. So." Stephanie shrugged, though Denise couldn't see her. "I mean, anyway, he's a normal."

"Hey. I'm a normie!"

"You are so not normal," Stephanie said with a laugh. Denise had no paranormal talents, true, but she'd been working with the Crew for long enough to have seen some seriously strange stuff. That left marks.

Denise rattled off a long string of something that sounded like Russian before saying, "I have to go. Fill me in later!"

"There's nothing to—" Too late—Denise had disconnected.

Inside the shop, Stephanie ordered two bags of the tea, then leaned on the counter to wait. She pulled out her phone. No messages, not that she was expecting any. No new email, either. She casually thumbed open a Words with Buddies game, but it wasn't her turn to play any of the rounds.

She people-watched instead.

She'd made the Morningstar Mocha one of her favorite stops, so she already knew a few of the regulars. Carlos was still tapping away on his novel over there by the windows. Tesla worked the counter, her spiky blond hair tipped with bright purple now. Her boyfriend, Charlie, had stopped in to bring her something in a brown paper bag that made her giggle, and watching them

kiss, Stephanie had to turn away because that was a
story that didn't need her to make anything up about it.

There was another face, a kid of about sixteen, sitting in the back corner with a laptop open in front of
him. The back of it was adorned with stickers from
indie bands Stephanie had enjoyed a few times herself,
mostly courtesy of her older brother, which made it a
little strange to see them as decoration for someone at
least ten years younger than she was. Still, it was going
to be a few more minutes before her tea was ready, so
Stephanie wandered over to take a closer look.

"Oh, wow," she said. "Bangtastic Frogmen? Really?
I didn't think anyone else had ever heard of them."

The kid, pale, eyes faintly circled by shadows, looked
up at her through the fringe of black hair. A girl, not a
boy as Stephanie had first assumed from the thin frame
and baggy clothes. The girl gave Stephanie a blank look.

"Huh?"

"The…sticker." Stephanie gestured. "Bangtastic
Frogmen?"

The girl tipped the laptop's lid to look at the assort-
ment of stickers, then closed it firmly and put her hands
on top of it. Her fingernails were bitten to the quick,
so raw in places that Stephanie winced. "It's… Yeah.
They're great."

Great was not how Stephanie would've described
the group, which had prided itself on being actually
awful. Out-of-tune instruments, mumbled and inco-
herent lyrics. They'd made one album, so far as she
knew, and while it had been played to death for a few
months in her circle of middle-school friends, it had
quickly been replaced by something a little more boy
band. She eyed the girl.

"Front of Desperation? You listen to them, too?"

The girl began to put the laptop away, keeping her gaze from Stephanie's. "Look, I just have the stickers, okay. I'm not a fan or anything. I just liked the way they looked."

There was a ceramic mug on the table, one of the refillable ones. You could spend all day in the Mocha on a $2.99 cup of coffee, if you were so inclined. This girl had that sort of look. Come to think of it, there was something familiar about her, as though Stephanie had seen her before. Yet when she tried to remember if the girl was a Mocha regular, she somehow looked less familiar.

"Okay, no big." Stephanie tried on a smile the girl didn't return.

Behind the girl, on the wall, a large clock spun its hands. Frowning, Stephanie glanced at the menu pinned to the bulletin board next to it. For a second, literally one, the letters jumbled and merged, making it impossible to read. Automatically, Stephanie tapped her wrist three times with her forefinger, a trick she'd learned long ago to determine if she was awake or dreaming.

Awake.

But... "Hey, wait a second," she said to the girl, who was now slinging her laptop bag over her shoulder and trying to inch past her.

"Tea's up!" came a voice from behind the counter, and Stephanie turned. That was her order.

When she turned back, the girl had slipped out the front door and disappeared. Stephanie looked again at the clock and the menu, but both were fine. She was standing in the Morningstar Mocha for real, not in the Ephemeros, and she was drawing curious looks. She shook herself, just a little, and turned to the guy behind the counter.

"Who was that?"

He looked past her toward the door's jingling bell overhead. "Who?"

"That girl. The one who was sitting there, in the corner."

The guy shrugged. "I don't know. There was a girl?"

"She must've been sitting here for a while. She had a refillable mug." Stephanie pointed toward the table where the girl had been sitting but then let her hand fall to her side. "She had a Bangtastic Frogmen sticker."

That earned her a weird look, so she took the bag of tea and peeked inside. She didn't really like the way it tasted, but it did wonders for putting her to sleep when her body fought it. "Thanks."

"I love the Sleepytime. Puts me right out." The guy grinned.

Stephanie returned the smile absently, still thinking about the kid in the corner. Out on the street, heading for her car, she tried again to look and see if she could find the mysterious teen, but nope. The girl had vanished.

He had no reason to call her. They'd already had a meeting. Work related. Lunch had been a nice gesture; it didn't mean anything.

He wasn't ready to date. For sure. Right?

Grumbling to himself, Kent forced his way through a lackluster microwaved dinner and some bad TV, ticking off the seconds until he could make it into bed and give up to unconsciousness. If he were a drinking man, he'd have taken a few shots to help him along, but he made do with counting sheep.

He found himself unable to stop thinking of Stephanie instead.

When his phone buzzed, he snatched it up off the nightstand, thumbing the screen before he really paid attention to who was calling him. "Oh," he said. "Carol."

"Just calling to check in on you."

Kent frowned. "I'm fine. Thanks."

"I wanted to tell you that I'll be sending someone to pick up the rest of my stuff that I left in the guest room. I'll be at my mom's for a while." She paused. "How are you, really?"

He closed his eyes, thinking of the brightness of Stephanie's laughter and how nice it had been to sit with her at lunch, enjoying the moment without any resentments hovering between them. No bad memories and all the possibilities of making good ones. How long had it been since he'd felt that way?

"Carol, I'm fine."

"If you're sure." She didn't sound convinced.

That, finally, pissed him off more than her sneaking away while he was at work had. "Look, I'm sure you think that I can't survive without you, but the truth is, I think this is going to be good for both of us. Great, in fact."

She didn't have much to say to that. He took little satisfaction in her silence. It felt more like a standoff than anything else, and he was pretty damned tired of that feeling.

"Good night, Carol," Kent said finally. "I'll make sure to have your stuff by the front door for when the guy comes for it."

"You know, you can call me…" she began but trailed off as though waiting for him to jump in with an answer.

This time, he didn't say good-night.

This time, Kent said, "Goodbye."

Chapter 4

Girls' Night In. Denise had brought a bottle of wine and they'd watched a couple chick flicks, chatting most of the way through them. By nine o'clock, though, Stephanie knew it was time to get to work.

Just one problem. She wasn't tired at all. The wine had worn off, which was good, since she needed to be on top of her game in the dream world if she wanted to make sure she got a lead on this creep.

"Can't Vadim prescribe you something?" Denise had never been able to shape anything in the Ephemeros, though she knew and believed it existed.

"He could, I guess. But I don't want to rely on sleeping pills or anything to get me under. Makes it too hard to wake up if I have to, for one thing. But it also affects me inside, just the way it would out here. I mean, it makes me dream, but it interferes with the shaping." Stephanie dragged a chip through the remnants of the queso dip and crunched it with a sigh. "I could try a food coma, I guess."

Denise laughed. "Sure. But what else works? Booze?"

"Same as pills. Sure, it puts me under, but it makes it hard to work. And then there's the hangover to deal with."

"Ew. Gross." Denise's nose crinkled. She looked at the clock on the wall. "It's early, that's all."

"Yeah, I know, but this guy's targeting the elderly. A lot of them are asleep by now and then up at the odd hours."

Denise nodded. "My grandma's like that. She'll be asleep in her chair by seven, but then she's up at three and can't get back to sleep until six or seven in the morning."

"Yeah." Stephanie crunched another chip, then sat back on the couch with a sigh. "Anyway, there's no telling who this guy will target next, of course, but I'm having better luck earlier in the evening."

"I guess I should let you get to it, then." Denise slapped her knee and stood with a stretch and a yawn. She looked down at Stephanie with a slow, wicked grin. "I have a tried-and-true way I use to fall asleep when I can't. But I'm not sure I should tell you what it is."

Stephanie got up, too, to follow her friend to the front door. "No fair. What's the secret?"

Denise shrugged into her coat and tied her scarf around her neck, then gave Stephanie an arched brow. "Sex."

"Yikes. Well, I guess I'm out of luck on that front," Stephanie said. "Seeing as how it's been a long dry spell for me."

"Orgasm," Denise clarified. "Surely you can have one or four of those all on your own."

Shit, she was blushing. Actually blushing. Stephanie cleared her throat. "Um…well, sure, I guess I could…"

"Don't tell me you don't…" Denise paused, clearly surprised. "Stephanie! Really?"

Awkwardly, Stephanie shrugged. "I do. Sure. Sometimes. I just…haven't. In a while."

"Shew, if I don't get off every other day or so, I'm a raging bitch. I have to keep my portable boyfriend charged at all times." Denise shook her head.

"I like sex," Stephanie said. "I've just been…busy."

"Never too busy for a little self-maintenance," Denise declared and pulled her scarf tighter around her throat as she dug for her gloves. "And I bet it will help you fall asleep for sure."

It was an idea, Stephanie thought as she put the few dishes they'd used in the dishwasher and went around checking the locks and turning out the lights. She'd had some of her best sleep after sex, that was true, even though it had been too long since she'd actually had any. As for self-maintenance, she thought as she went into her bedroom to put on her pajamas, well…it had just started to seem hollow after a while. The seduction of her hand or even the vibrator she kept in her bedside drawer was fine, but it couldn't beat kissing and being kissed. It couldn't replace lovemaking.

Still, the more she thought about it, the better the idea became. Except, just as she wasn't particularly sleepy, she also wasn't particularly turned on. Maybe she should just try to do some non-dream-world work, she thought as she settled against her headboard with her laptop on her knees. That boring stuff would surely help her into sleep, wouldn't it?

In minutes she'd pulled up the data files on her current job. The dates, times and amounts of withdrawals from the accounts, along with the interviews she'd done with the victims. All of them had admitted to sharing their personal financial information with someone in a dream and had been hit a day or so after.

This was about the least sexy thing she could think of doing. At least until she scrolled through her files and pulled up one more. This one had a photo included. His pertinent information, including his contact numbers and his Connex account. She hadn't connexed with Kent Gordon, only because she didn't bother much with social media sites, but she could stalk him a little bit there on what he'd made public.

She did.

It was harmless, Stephanie told herself as she clicked on his profile-picture photo album. It wasn't as if she were showing up beneath his window blasting a song from a boom box. She wasn't hurting anyone or anything by taking a casual peek at... Oh, shit.

"Shit," she breathed.

The photo was nothing anyone would notice as special. In it, Kent stood with his hands on his hips, his shirtsleeves rolled up to the elbow—those forearms, God. Stephanie let her cursor drift over the photo as she let out a long, hard sigh. She had such a thing for forearms. And big hands. And steel-rimmed glasses. And hair going just the tiniest bit gray at the temples...

Damn it, she had a thing for Kent Gordon, that was just the sad truth, and had for months. Since the first time she'd seen him, as a matter of fact, though the fact he'd had a live-in girlfriend had made him off-limits. Her name was Carol. She was blond and blandly pretty, and she posted inane memes and pictures of her lunch, which Stephanie knew because she'd also creeped a few times on Carol's Connex account.

Except now Carol and Kent had broken up.

It was still harmless, Stephanie told herself, logging out and putting the computer on the nightstand. She turned out the light and sank into the pillows, her hands flat on her belly. Everyone did it. Creeped around on social media sites, looking at pictures. That was why she didn't have any accounts.

Her internal clock ticked, loud as any she could've hung on the wall, and the passing minutes began to annoy her. The harder she tried, the less likely it was going to be that she could fall asleep. She should get up. Clean something. Pay some bills. Hell, she could do a little workout.

Or, she thought as her fingertips ran lightly across her belly, then lower, over the thin fabric of her boxers, she could try something else.

Oh, it had been too long, she thought with a sigh as her fingers slipped into her bottoms and she found her soft curls. A little lower, deeper, she delved inside. With a small gasp, she slid another finger in. Her thumb pressed her clit. She stayed that way for a moment, listening to her body. Gauging her response.

Her nipples had hardened, and she tugged her shirt up to free her breasts to the chilly night air. She kept her bedroom cooler than the rest of the house out of habit from California's much warmer temperatures, but in Pennsylvania, February meant it could be downright cold. It wasn't the temperature that had tightened them, though. It was the thought of strong male forearms sprinkled with dark hair, exposed by rolled-up shirtsleeves.

She couldn't do this. Couldn't get off to a real person, a guy she was working with. A guy with a super-recent breakup, Stephanie scolded herself, even as her fingers moved a little faster.

Okay, so she wouldn't think about Kent. She would imagine someone else, another lover with long legs and broad shoulders, dark hair. Lean features. Glasses.

God, how could she have passed up this pleasure for so long? She was wet now, fingers easing in deeper before slipping out to circle her clit. Her hips bumped upward when she stroked herself.

One hand on her breast, squeezing her nipple. Eyes closed. Hips rocking. Fingers stroking. The pleasure built, higher, stronger. Fierce. She slowed the pace, wanting to make this last.

Unbidden, she drifted into fantasy. Not a dream—she was still awake—and though she tried a tentative push to see if she'd perhaps fallen asleep without realizing it, no handsome man appeared at the foot of her bed with his cock in his hand. She opened her eyes to peek again, to be sure, but nope. Nada.

He would, though, she thought. He would crawl up the bed and cover her with his body. He'd kiss her. Slowly at first. Then harder. His hand would slide beneath the back of her head to twist in her hair. His other would slide between them to stroke her clit, the way she was doing now.

"Oh," she breathed. "Oh, fuck. Yes."

A little faster now. A little harder, deeper, her fingers curling. Oh, she wished she had thought to invest in some penetration toys, something that would fill her better than her hand. It felt so good, though, she didn't want to stop. Couldn't stop. Not when each wave of pleasure was cresting. Pushing her to the edge.

She thought of him again, though she refused to let her mouth shape the sound of his name. She couldn't stop herself from imagining his lips on her. Those big hands. He would cover her entirely. He would fill her.

Fuck her.

Hard.

Fast.

With a small gasp, she came, writhing in the tangling sheets. Her back arched. A low, stuttering groan hitched out of her. It felt so damned good she didn't stop stroking, feeling the pleasure build again. Sending her over the edge one more time while she muttered a long, mumbled string of fucktalk that would've been embarrassing except she was alone.

At the end of it, breathing hard and sweating, blinking away the final remnants of her fantasy, she was all by herself.

She did, however, fall asleep.

Languid, relaxed, Stephanie felt soft warmth under her fingertips and smiled before she opened her eyes. She was in the Ephemeros. Still on her own bed and in her own room, but where the walls of her bedroom should have been, there was only empty space.

She sat up and swung her legs over the edge, shaping the forest. Birds chirped, far off, just the sound of them. She didn't put much effort into creating the birds themselves, which was the only way there'd be any. Animals dreamed, but they had their own Ephemeros to play in, so far as Stephanie could tell.

She drew in the scent of pine. Sun dappled its way through the branches and speckled the fallen needles. This was her favorite entry point, built from a childhood memory of the smallish patch of woods behind her grandmother's house, and she worked on it a little bit more each time she entered the dream world so she could keep it as her anchor.

She didn't have a lot of time now that she was on a case, so she quickly focused on shaping a bit more of the curving path. A few more trees. She took another lingering breath and stepped onto the path.

Naked?

With a startled laugh, Stephanie looked at herself. She almost always represented in the same outfit when she was working a case. Slim-fit black leather trousers, black silky T-shirt that clung to her like a second skin, a black corset-vest. Sure, it made her look like a Goth girl, but it was practical, served as armor and didn't impede her movements if she ever had to run— and she often did. The last thing she wanted to worry about when she was hunting down a perp was having to change her clothes.

But now, naked, she stepped with bare toes on the springy needles of the curving path. She lifted her face to the pine-scented breeze and closed her eyes for a second. It felt good to be naked here. Free. And, in the aftermath of the dual orgasms, she still felt sexy.

She was pushing it, too, she realized after a moment or so when the birdsong trilled and yet the forest began to fade. Someone was coming, beckoned by the unsubtle throb of her fading arousal. She was broadcasting sex, and it was going to pull in some unwanted attention if she wasn't careful.

Unless that was the way to catch this thief, she thought for a second as she concentrated just hard enough to shape herself into her regular outfit. Lure him in with sex? He'd been targeting the elderly, both genders, but that didn't mean he wouldn't be immune to a little good old-fashioned catfishing, right?

Maybe she needed to make herself seem a little more…vulnerable.

Gone in a second was the leather, the kick-ass attitude. Replaced by a soft gown with frilly lace at the throat and sleeves. Stephanie shaped her hair longer, to her waist. She kept the bare feet, thickening her soles should she step on anything sharp but keeping the look of innocent damsel.

"Where's your candy house?" she murmured, opening herself to the Ephemeros's shifting, pulsing will. "Let me take a taste."

It was hard to resist the impulse to shape the space around her, but Stephanie kept herself still, curious to see what the collective unconscious was going to build tonight. It turned out to be a Victorian mansion, complete with gardens and a hedge maze and rooms full of people dancing and drinking...and fucking.

So it was going to be that kind of night, she thought as she moved through a room decorated all in red. An orgy. She wasn't shaping any of this, but how much of it had she contributed to, Stephanie wondered as she eased around a naked trio writhing on a velvet couch.

It was tempting to give in to this. The sensuality. The outright sexuality. The steady thrum and throb of music beat through the house. People moved to it. She moved to it.

And there, through the crowd, she caught a glimpse of a lean silhouette in black leather, whispering in a woman's ear. The woman wore a Regency-era gown, though her hair was totally '80s punk rock. She nodded, listening with a rapt expression to whatever the guy in black was saying to her. When he turned his face a bit, the gleam of fangs was the proof Stephanie was waiting for. That was her guy.

She moved forward, ducking around a bunch of people using toys and tools she'd only ever seen on the internet, and although the pull of their will was strong, she managed to resist it. Right before she got to her goal, though, she bumped into someone, hard enough to send them both back a couple steps. Intent on getting to the perp, Stephanie stepped to the side. So did the man in front of her.

She looked up, intending to push a little to get him out of the way and send his attention in another direction, but what she saw stopped her. "Kent?"

Of course, it wasn't impossible for them to meet here. If he was asleep at the same time, as he probably was, and with the strength of what was rippling through the Ephemeros tonight, it was no wonder he'd gravitated toward the orgy. And boy, did he look good.

"I can't," she said by way of apology when he took her hand. "I have…work…"

"You could dance with me," Kent said with a glance around them at the people who were dancing…or naked variations of dancing. "That would be all right, wouldn't it?"

She wanted to. Opening herself to the Ephemeros had left her vulnerable, but it was more than that. It was him.

"I can't," she repeated, threading together a little shield to keep herself from jumping him right there. Over his shoulder she could see the man in black leather bending closer to the woman in the Regency gown. "I want to, but I'm working."

Kent nodded but tugged her hand to pull her a step closer. "Right. Working."

She was pushing up on her tiptoes to kiss him. She wanted it. Wanted him. Her arms went around his neck. His lips, so close she could feel the gust of his breath on her face. Her mouth opened.

"This isn't real," she warned.

"It's as real as we want it to be," Kent said. "Isn't it?"

At the last second, she turned. It wouldn't have been the first time she indulged in a little hanky-panky in the dream world, but doing it with him felt wrong. He wouldn't know what they'd shared, and she'd have to face him across a desk with the memory of his mouth on hers and pretend she didn't know how he tasted.

His hands moved to her hips, nudging her against him, and oh, he was hard against her, and she was going to kiss him, she was going to open for him and let him inside her, and they were going to dance and dance and…

She said his name.

With a gasp, Stephanie forced herself awake. Shit, she'd lost herself. Worse, she'd lost the perp. Heart pounding, sweating, she fell back onto her pillows and licked away the taste of salt on her lips.

She'd been pushed again. Mr. Slick was clever, she gave him that. He'd seen her coming and used what she wanted against her, only this time, instead of chocolate cake, it had been Kent Gordon.

Chapter 5

Kent hated coconut.

He hated the scent of it, the taste of it. He hated the hairy round shape of coconuts and how they sometimes fell out of trees and hit people on the head. There wasn't much in this world that was guaranteed to send Kent over the edge, but coconut would be it. And there it was, tons of it shredded all over the top of his birthday cake.

"Mom," he began, then stopped, because how could he tell her that he wasn't going to eat one slice of that monstrosity, much less take the rest home, as she'd already planned for him to do?

"It's a new recipe." She beamed, all four feet ten inches of her.

Kent didn't have the heart to remind her of his coconut aversion. It would hurt her feelings, first of all, but more than that, would remind her of how precarious her memory had become. Most days they could both pretend that she was simply a little scatterbrained, the way she'd always been. There was going to come a day, he thought, when it wouldn't matter if she was reminded about what she'd forgotten, because she wouldn't be able to remember that she'd ever known what it was in the first place. He didn't want to think of that.

Instead, he patted his stomach. "I'm so full from dinner, Mom. I'll take it home and have a piece later, okay?"

"Make sure to give Carol a piece. It's really too bad she couldn't make it tonight." A shadow passed over his mom's face, and she shook her head. "Oh. No. I'm sorry, honey, I forgot. You two broke up."

Since it had happened only a couple weeks ago, he couldn't really fault her for not remembering. He still sometimes forgot himself, at least until he came home to the empty, silent house and found nobody waiting for him, not even the dog. Carol had taken Lucky with her when she left.

"She wasn't good enough for you anyway," Mom said before Kent could answer.

He shrugged. "Things happen. That's all. I don't hold a grudge."

"No, you never did that. That's a good thing." She smiled again and put the lid on the cake box, which was a relief because now at least he no longer had to smell it. "I'll just put it away for you to take home anyway."

Mom protested when Kent insisted she sit to catch up on her programs while he cleaned the kitchen. It didn't take long. Mom kept a spotless house, even with the enormous meal she'd prepared for his birthday feast. Enough food for ten people. She'd make sure he was sent home with plenty of single-portioned meals to last him for the rest of the month, and he'd take them, because hell if being an unexpected bachelor didn't mean he'd been more apt to indulge in Chinese takeout eaten on paper plates than any kind of healthy food.

Kent put the paper grocery sack of plastic containers on the kitchen table and peeked into the living room to check on his mother. She'd dozed off in front of the television, as he'd expected. It was getting close to 10:00 p.m., well past her normal bedtime, but he'd been late from work and so dinner had been delayed.

"Mom," he said gently with a touch on her arm, trying not to startle her.

"I only have my pension," she said drowsily. "But of course you can have it, if you need it."

Kent paused. "Mom?"

"It's not much, lovey, but I want you to have it. No, really. Yes." Mom reached a hand as though to touch someone. Her fingertips brushed the front of his shirt.

Kent took her hand. "Mom. You're dreaming."

Slowly, her eyes opened. With a furrowed brow, Mom looked at him. Then smiled. "Hello, lovey."

"You were sleeping. Why don't we get you upstairs?" Kent laughed a little. "Must've been some dream."

Mom frowned. "I don't quite recall it."

She didn't struggle to get out of her recliner, though Kent stood by waiting in case she did. Physically, Mom had few issues beyond a bit of arthritis. It might've been easier, he thought as she made sure he'd appropriately packed up all of his leftovers, if she were frail. He could've done something for her to be really helpful, instead of simply suffering through watching her slowly deteriorate mentally.

"Give my love to Carol," she told him at the door as he bent to kiss her.

Kent smiled. "I will, Mom."

In the car, it hit him, though. The long lonely night

ahead of him. A trunkful of food he would eat standing over the sink. A birthday cake covered in coconut.

A night of frustrating, sexy dreams featuring Stephanie Adams.

As far as birthdays went, it had been a pretty shitty one. It got worse when he slipped his phone from his pocket to put in the center console while he drove and saw the missed text from Carol. He didn't want to read it, but he did.

Happy B-day!

It was a nice thing for her to do. To remember. Carol was nice. The life they'd had was nice, at least, Kent had thought so until he came home to find her half of everything moved out and a note on the table telling him that she'd gone to stay with her mother while she looked for a new place to live.

He missed her, of course, but as he pulled up to his driveway and saw the dark windows, he thought that maybe it wasn't Carol he missed as much as simply... someone. They'd been together four years, most of them good, and he'd happily have gone on for four more, or forty, probably. Being with Carol had been easy, not a challenge. It hadn't been much work.

That was the problem. He hadn't put much work into things. That was probably why they'd ended up splitting. You had to put the work in.

Too little, too late, that was the problem. He could think of a hundred ways he might've been able to salvage things with Carol, but none of them mattered now. He could've answered her text, too, though at the moment he saw no point in it. What was she going to do, chat with him about the day? Ask him again if he was recovering without her? That was only going to rub it in about how terrible a birthday it had been.

His stomach rumbled. Dinner at Mom's had been good, but though he'd told her a little white lie about being too full for cake, the truth was he'd left plenty of room for it. And damn it, it was his birthday. Why shouldn't he celebrate it, even if he had to do it all by his loser, lonely self? It was Friday night. He was hungry. The food in the trunk would keep with the temperatures as cold as they were.

Instead of pulling into his driveway, Kent kept on going.

Chapter 6

"I'm not gonna make it." Stephanie held back a yawn as best she could, but no matter how she tried, she couldn't stop it. Her jaw cracked. Her eyes felt filled with sand.

Denise frowned. "C'mon, Steph, wake up. It's not even eleven."

"Yeah, but I've been up since about three this morning." After the sexy dream with Kent, her frustration about losing sight of her target had kept her awake no matter how hard she'd tried to fall back to sleep. Nothing had worked. Now she was tired, angry with herself and cranky.

"Damn. No closer?"

"No, I'm closer. I actually saw him last night." She paused. "But then I got interrupted."

Denise's brows rose. "By what?"

Stephanie definitely didn't want to tell her friend

what had forced her out of the dream. Not only was it an embarrassing failure in her control, but it would let Denise in on the whole crush she had on Kent. Stephanie pressed her lips together.

"Ooh, he was in your dream, huh?"

"He was… A lot of people were…"

"Last night I dreamed I was schtupping my high school biology teacher," Denise said with a chuckle. "In some crazy hedge-maze thing. Man, that was wild."

Stephanie said nothing.

"You were there!" Denise slapped the table and tipped her head back to laugh so loud it earned her several appreciative looks from the guys at the table behind them. "You and Mr. Bank Manager?"

"Keep your voice down!" Stephanie shook her head. "It was nothing. It was a dream."

"Sure it was. Because nothing that happens in dreams is real," Denise said with a deliberately blank expression that quickly shifted again into humor. "Uh-huh."

"That doesn't make it okay. Anyway, I'm beat." Stephanie fought another yawn. "At least tonight I won't have trouble getting to sleep."

Denise sighed and looked around the bar. "Fine. Slim pickings here tonight anyway."

"The job's kicking my ass. That's all."

Denise frowned and leaned a little closer. "What's Vadim say about it?"

"He says keep hunting." Stephanie took a small sip from her beer, letting the flavor roll around in her mouth before swallowing. Last week she'd had a drink in the Ephemeros that had tasted of flowers and chocolate, a combination she doubted would be any good in the real world but which had been almost orgasmic in the dream. "Got a couple new reports that tie in to that same guy."

"You need a break." Denise looked serious. "I know you think of yourself as some kind of lone wolf, but really, you need someone helping you out."

Stephanie laughed. "Lone wolf?"

"You know what I mean." Denise didn't join in Stephanie's humor. "You think you need to take care of it all on your own, but it's dangerous. Too much time in there, and—"

"Yeah, yeah, I know. I might not come out." Stephanie shrugged. She knew it was possible, but she couldn't let it freak her out. She was more likely to end up in a coma from getting hit by a bus than from letting her time in the Ephemeros get away from her.

"Just because you think you're invulnerable in there doesn't mean you are out here," Denise said.

Stephanie gave her friend a grin meant to ease her worries. "I'm fine. I promise. Soon as I figure out who this guy is out here, I'll be done with this case and I can take a vacation."

"Promise?"

"Yes. I promise."

Denise sighed again. "Maybe we can go away for one of those all-inclusive deals. What do you think? A week or so of sun and fun and hot guys in thong bathing suits?"

"Oh. God, Denise, ew." Stephanie laughed.

"What? They'd be European. Totally hot. With accents," Denise added, laughing, too. Her gaze cut away after a second, looking over Stephanie's shoulder, and her giggles became a sly smile. "Oh. Hey. Look who's here."

Stephanie glanced behind her, not expecting to see that familiar long, lean body. Kent Gordon's profile was angular, his dark hair touched just the tiniest bit with silver at the temples. His steel-rimmed glasses flashed as he settled on the bar stool and nodded at the bartender.

Pretty much her ideal guy in every way.

"You should go say hi." Denise nodded.

Stephanie turned away, hoping he wasn't going to turn around and see her there. "Ugh. No."

"Why not? You told me you thought he was cute! You're having sexy dreams with him! He took you on a date."

He *was* cute. That was the problem. "He asked me to join him for lunch. I told you, it was so not a date. And I have to work with him."

"So?"

"So, I haven't exactly been bringing him anything he can use," Stephanie said. "And what can I tell him? That I've been searching for this guy who stalks people in their dreams to steal their money in the real world but I haven't quite managed it yet?"

"You could just tell him you're still investigating. That's the truth," Denise pointed out with another glance over Stephanie's shoulder. "It's not like you work *for* him. He's just your point of contact at the bank. Vadim's the one in charge. He should take the heat."

"Yeah, but I'm the one who has to come up with a plausible explanation for how we're going to nail this guy, something to explain to Kent and the board at Member's Best that doesn't make me look like an incompetent idiot."

"Part of the job," Denise replied unsympathetically.

Stephanie laughed. "Wow, thanks. Yes. Part of the job, but look. You know I can't get involved with a normie."

"There you go with that normie business again. God. I'm a normal, and you like me!"

"You," Stephanie told her friend again, "are so not a normie."

Denise rolled her eyes and tipped her beer toward the bar. "Well, I can't do what you can do anyway. And you never know. Mr. Sexy-Pants Bank Manager might be a shaper."

Stephanie stole another look at him. He'd ordered a beer, the same as her, though he didn't appear to be drinking it. The same as her, really, she thought as she turned the bottle in her hands and felt the slosh of liquid against the glass. She'd been nursing the same one for an hour. It was warm.

She could go up to the bar. Order another. Sit beside him, smile, toss her hair…

"Shit, Denise," Stephanie said. "He really is cute, huh?"

"Yes!"

Still, Stephanie shook her head. "I have to get home and get to work."

"All work and no play," her friend said. "I'm going to run to the restroom. Don't leave."

"Sure." Stephanie stifled another yawn while she waited, glancing up a few minutes later when a figure moved to slide into the booth across from her. "Ready to get out of here? Oh. Hi."

"Hi," Kent said with a small smile. "Your friend told me you were here."

"I am." It was a stupid thing to say, but there it was. Stephanie coughed a little, embarrassed at feeling caught this way. She twisted in her seat to look around for Denise, though she had a suspicion she'd been set up. "Did you happen to see where she went?"

"She left. She told me to tell you she'd call you tomorrow. She…um, she told me you like scrambled eggs for breakfast." Kent echoed Stephanie's awkward cough.

Her jaw dropped. Then she slapped a hand to her forehead, closing her eyes for a moment before looking at him. "That sounds like Denise. Sorry."

"No, it's okay." She'd seen Kent smile before, but not like this.

This smile warmed her all the way to her chilly toes. It spread a flush up her throat and into her cheeks that she sincerely hoped he didn't see. That smile made her want to crawl across the table between them, straddle his lap, take his face in her hands and kiss the breath out of him.

Whoa.

"It's my birthday," Kent said suddenly.

Stephanie's brows rose. "Happy birthday, Kent."

"It hasn't been the greatest," he told her, not sounding as if he were complaining, just being honest. "I'm not usually the guy who makes a big deal out of it, but you know, at least on your birthday you should have cake, right?"

"You didn't have cake? That sucks." Stephanie frowned, holding back another yawn threatening to squeak out of her. She was getting so sleepy that it would've been easy to convince herself she was already dreaming. She shot a quick glance at the menu to be certain she could read the words there. The fastest way for her to tell if she was indeed inside the Ephemeros was that letters and numbers no longer held their places but squiggled all over and refused to be read.

He nodded. "Yeah. My mom made me a cake covered in coconut frosting. She forgot I didn't like coconut."

"That really sucks." Stephanie frowned. The beer

had been a mistake. She should've had coffee or a cola, even an iced tea. Driving home was going to be hard.

"Yeah. She's having some problems with her memory." Kent paused. "Now that I've unloaded my whole sob story on you…"

"It's okay. Birthdays should be fun and special. I don't blame you for being a little cranky about it."

They stared at each other across the table.

"I know a place that makes a killer chocolate raspberry cheesecake," Kent said finally. "Would you go with me?"

Her eyes were full of sand and she wanted to make this table a pillow, but at the sight of Kent's hesitant smile, she sighed. Oh, she was so going to kill Denise later. A little bit anyway.

"Far be it from me to turn down a guy on his birthday."

Kent's widening grin sent another of those disturbing sets of tingles all through her. He got out of the booth and reached for her hand. And, as she had last night in the dream world, Stephanie let him take it.

Chapter 7

It hadn't been much of a date. Or a date at all. Had it? Just as lunch hadn't been more than just, well…lunch… Damn it, now that he was home alone with a stomach full of cheesecake and too much coffee, all Kent could do was overthink things.

Over the past few months, he and Stephanie had met about once a week in the office and had shared dozens of emails, a few phone calls, once or twice an instant-message conversation on the computer to update him on some new developments. She had a terrific laugh. He knew she was originally from California but was renting an apartment locally, because they'd talked about their mutual love for the big fancy grocery store chain that had been putting in a location near his office. He knew she liked punk rock and indie music, because he'd caught a glance at her playlist once when she'd set her phone on his desk. She was smart, quick-witted and kindhearted, and he knew all of that because for the past six months, he'd been pretending he wasn't completely into her.

Now it was all he could think about.

After her friend had not-so-subtly mentioned to him on her way to the bathroom that Stephanie was sitting by herself, Kent had not intended to ask her out. He'd made his way over to say a friendly hello, that was all, but…well. A crappy birthday, a recent breakup, the stress about his job and Mom… Stephanie had given him a friendly smile and that laugh, and he'd been a goner. He'd asked her to join him for dessert on impulse, figuring she'd give him a gentle excuse. It wasn't a workday lunch, after all. She could've easily given him an excuse. Even when she agreed to go with him, he hadn't expected to have such a great time.

Something had told him she'd been surprised, too. They hadn't kissed or anything like that, it not being a date and all, but she'd hugged him. She'd smelled good. She was warm and soft, and she'd pressed her cheek to his at the end of the night in a way that had reminded him of the dream. That kiss. The feeling of her against him.

Ugh. With a groan, he forced himself to roll face-down to press himself into the pillow and try not to pay attention to the semi starting to throb in his pants. He wasn't that much of a creep, was he? But as his dick got harder the more he thought about the way her hair smelled and how she'd felt against him, Kent had to admit that maybe he was.

He wasn't in any good place to even be thinking about dating someone, not with the lingering scent of Carol's perfume still haunting him from unexpected places like the linen closet and the back bedroom upstairs that she'd used as an office. It didn't matter that things had been over with Carol long before she'd walked out. It didn't matter that he'd been noticing Stephanie for months.

"See you," Stephanie had said just before she got into her own car outside the restaurant and drove away.

Had she meant at work or something else? Kent let out a low mutter of frustration. When had he gotten so bad at this? Before Carol he'd certainly been no Lothario, but it wasn't as if he'd ever been afraid to ask a woman out.

"That's it," he said, determined. He pulled out his phone and found Stephanie's number.

Hey, it's Kent, he typed. I had a great time tonight. Maybe we can do it again sometime?

There. Sent. More casual than a call but not quite as impersonal as an email. He glanced at the clock. Just past one in the morning. If she answered him right away, that was a good sign, right?

She didn't, though, and five minutes later he'd begun to regret sending the text at all. Oh, well. Nothing to do about it now except feel like a jerk and go to sleep.

Except he couldn't. Not with the steady pressure in his boxers, his erection straining the front. He ran a hand over the soft material, cupping himself for a minute. Pretending he wasn't going to jack off for about thirty seconds before… Fuck, why pretend when he knew exactly what he wanted.

Well, it might not be what he wanted, but it was what he had. He shucked off his boxers, then stroked himself fully erect. He bit back a groan, arching into the pleasure. Lower, he used his other hand to cup his balls. He set the pace easily, steady and rhythmic. No teasing. Nothing fancy. He was going to get off, that was all.

That was the intention anyway, but as his mind filled with the memory of soft hair, sweet perfume, a lush body pressed to his, Kent found himself slowing. Stroking, languid, then palming the head as he pushed upward into his fist. Fuck, it felt good. Closer, closer, he edged himself.

He'd started off wanting a quick, easy climax, but now he wanted to linger. Savor. He wanted to lose himself in desire and keep himself teetering right there, in that place where nothing mattered but the feeling of flesh on flesh. Where he could let his mind run free and imagine all the things he wanted to do, and tell himself later he was swept away with lust. That it didn't matter.

He muttered, low, a small curse. He fucked his fist a little faster, then slowed to squeeze just behind the head to keep his orgasm at bay for a little longer. With his other hand, he slid his thumb down the seam of his balls, pressing that sweet spot that would not only help him fend off the climax but also make it that much more intense.

Up, up, tighter, twisted. The pleasure built and surged, and Kent rocked with it. Until finally, there it was, that moment of no return. Like that initial crest of a roller coaster in the front car, looking over that precipice before the first screaming, delighted plunge. Ecstasy burst through him. His cock pumped, spurting his belly with hot fluid. Spent, gasping, he let the last final strokes finish him off.

Blinking, Kent stared at the ceiling while his heartbeat slowed. The stickiness on his skin prompted him to roll a little to grab a cloth from the nightstand. Cleaned up, he settled back onto the pillows and closed his eyes. He sought sleep.

When he couldn't find it, he contented himself again with thoughts of Stephanie's laughter and the curve of her smile.

Chapter 8

The sly beep of an incoming text tugged at Stephanie's subconscious just as she was turning around in her usual entry spot into the Ephemeros. She ignored the text. She had only a few hours before dawn, and while she wasn't going to have any trouble sleeping far past that, all of the times she'd encountered the thief had been during local "normal" sleeping hours.

That didn't mean he was actually in her area or time zone, just that he was sleeping during those times. Experience had taught her, though, that it was likely the shaper who was pulling these stunts was in fact pretty close to her. It was why Vadim had sent her here to Central Pennsylvania to find him. She could've worked remotely from California, sure, but it would've meant a fucked-up sleep schedule for her.

Sinking deeper into the dream, Stephanie focused on her representation. She'd worked cases where she'd had

to use a different sort of face and body, even a few times
a different form altogether, and she liked the challenges
of forming and keeping those changes. This case hadn't
required her to be anything other than who she was, at
least beyond the fashions. So far, though, that hadn't
worked out so well for her. The closest she'd come to
getting near the perp was the night she'd represented
in that romantic gown, and look what had happened.

Kent.

What had that all been about tonight? Cheesecake.
Laughter. He'd very carefully not tried anything even
remotely romantic. Should she have been relieved or
offended? Maybe she ought to have been a little more
aggressive. Made the first move.

She didn't have time to worry about that now. She
was going to find out the real-world identity of Mr. Slick
tonight if she had to travel the entire Ephemeros to do it.
Then she'd be done with this job and that would mean
the weird work issue with Kent would no longer matter. Of course, it also meant she'd probably be heading
back to California.

She'd worry about that part later, too.

For now, Stephanie stretched, loving the way her
muscles and bones worked together inside the dream
world. Nothing hurt, nothing cramped or ached. Sure,
she could get injured if she wasn't careful, but she'd
been doing this for such a long time that the only way
she really got hurt was if someone did something to her
before she could stop them, and not something nice like
shaping a platter of dessert in front of her or tempting
her into a kiss she really wanted anyway.

On her last case she'd ended up going face-to-face
with a woman bent on terrorizing her cheating husband into a heart attack while he slept—that bitch had

been righteously crazy, and while Stephanie couldn't blame her for wanting revenge, murder was still murder even if you committed it while you were sleeping. That woman had claimed not to know she was shaping anything, but her innocence had been a farce, proven when she'd turned herself into a mass of seething snakes and launched herself at Stephanie. The bites had been excruciating, leaving scars, but nothing Stephanie hadn't been able to handle. She'd managed to wrestle them into a knot and shove them inside a box, slamming and locking the lid until the woman had begged for release.

Of course, her remorse might not be lasting. That was the problem with punishment in the Ephemeros. You couldn't make it stick, not without doing major harm to the sleeper's real-world body. Putting someone in a permanent coma to keep them imprisoned in the dream world was a last resort, saved for only the worst sorts of criminals.

Stephanie's goal on this case was to find out Mr. Slick's real-world counterpart and then send the information to Vadim. Other members of the Crew would connect him to the actual thefts. It might require some fancy finagling of records or "proof," because it wasn't as though they could go in and explain how he'd been using dreams to manipulate people into giving him their financial information so he could simply take what he wanted without leaving a trace. But it was Vadim's job to assign a Crew member skilled in creating those sorts of tracks, not hers.

Her job was to find out who he was.

When she had, she was going to take a long vacation, just as she'd promised Denise. Someplace warm, with lots of drinks and food and dancing, and she would stay up late every night and barely sleep at all.

Stephanie settled deeper into the dream world with a concerted push of her will. She was aware, as always, of her sleeping body. Her head on the pillow. The weight of the blankets. The white-noise machine. Those things were her touchstones. Her way back in the unlikely event she found herself lost in here. It had never happened to her, but she knew it could.

Every shaper she'd ever met knew the stories of others who'd lost their way and couldn't wake up. She'd never met one, had not in fact met anyone who ever had, but like urban legends about bodies stuffed beneath hotel mattresses and spider eggs in bubble gum, there was always someone who knew someone who'd heard about someone else. Unlike the spider eggs, Stephanie believed in the real truth of being made incapable of getting out of the Ephemeros.

It was also not likely she was going to come across Mr. Slick tonight, it being so close to morning, but she figured she had to try. Where might he be? How about a place where a lot of other people were still clinging to their dreams before the alarms went off. So she opened herself to the push and pull of the collective will that shaped the dream world and let herself be drawn toward… What would it be tonight?

The last time it had been that Victorian mansion. Sometimes it was a dance club, others an amusement park, a shopping mall, a stadium. The places where people congregated in the real world were often represented in the Ephemeros, too, sometimes with bits and pieces of all those sorts of locations all in one. Tonight it was a park, a big one, with green grass and trees and benches and sweetly curving paths on which some people strolled in old-fashioned clothes and others rode bikes or skated on wheels they'd manifested from the bottoms of their feet.

She saw a few people manifesting with wings or horns or tails, a few curious creatures that looked like beasts but that she knew were really people who wanted, at least for a night, to be animal and not human. She saw no sign of her target. Maybe he'd had a run-in with the Crew before now and recognized her, or maybe he was just wily, because he always managed to disappear before she could get to him.

"Hi," said a man from beside her. He was dressed like Bert from *Mary Poppins*, the Disney version. Striped pants, white jacket, pink bow tie. A cartoonish penguin kept step beside him, a part of his manifestation and not a separate entity.

"Not tonight, buddy. Sorry." Stephanie shielded herself from the sleeper's hesitant attempt at shaping her into the matching nanny to his chimney sweep. What sort of dream *that* guy was having, she had no desire to discover. She tried hard not to judge what people dreamed about, but damn, there were some things she really didn't want to know.

He was easy enough to put off. So was everything else going on. She didn't feel any other shapers here right now, at least none who were working hard to mold the Ephemeros to their will. Like herself, they were going along with whatever the collective unconscious wanted. She didn't try to seek them out. She did, however, send out a firm but discreet push.

Have you seen him?

She shaped it as a text message and a photo of Mr. Slick's silhouette, appearing in identical phones in every hand she could reach within the scope of her talents. When no answers came, she moved through the park, shaping and sending without much hope of an answer. She hadn't set herself an alarm, but others clearly had, because one by one many of the locals began fading away. Not all of them, obviously. There were always going to be people sleeping and dreaming all over the world at all different times. But for the most part, those in her part of the world were beginning to wake.

With a sigh, Stephanie sent out one more push. She should wake up, too, so she could accomplish some things in the real world and get back to sleep tonight at a decent time. First, though, she thought she might enjoy herself a bit.

That was when the answer came in, of course, just as she was getting ready to shape herself a warm and sunny spot on a sandy beach. Her phone vibrated in her hand. She looked at it.

I've seen him.

She spotted him at once, a tall man with angular features and the phone she'd shaped in his hand. "Kent?"

He smiled, and while his representation in the dream was slightly different tonight—he was a little more muscular, dressed a little better, his hair a little longer, that smile was exactly the same. "Hi, Stephanie. Did you get my text?"

"You've seen him?"

"Not that one. The other one. The one I sent you earlier, about what a great time I had tonight."

Neither of them had taken a step, but they now faced each other with only a few inches between them. He'd done that, and she'd been so surprised to see him that she hadn't resisted his push. It was the same as it had been in the mansion. Stephanie laughed lightly.

"Oh...no. I'll get that one when I wake up. But thank you. I had a great time with you, too." Honesty was so much easier here, where people might shape themselves to look different but almost never lied about how they truly felt.

"Good. I'd like to take you out on a date," Kent said.

Stephanie laughed again. "Sure. If you ask me, I'll say yes."

"Yeah?" He grinned.

She shrugged, knowing that whatever they talked about in here, he was probably not going to act on it when he woke up. He'd play it off as a dream. Not real.

More important, she had a case to work on. "So. You've seen him. This guy."

She pushed another grainy photo onto Kent's phone. It was the best she had. He looked at it, then nodded.

"Oh. Yeah. He's been around here. What's he done?"

"He steals money from people by making them give up their private account information in the dreams, then uses it in the waking world to access their credit cards and stuff." She tilted her head to study him, wondering if he'd put the pieces together.

Kent in the waking world had seemed like a pretty smart guy, and he maintained that here. "He's the guy who's been hacking into Member's Best?"

"Yes. And probably lots of other places, too. Where have you seen him?"

"He was talking to that woman over there." Kent pointed.

Stephanie looked. The woman was sitting on a bench, feeding a covey of colorful pigeons. Not the most exciting dream she'd ever witnessed, but again, she wasn't going to judge.

"Hey," Kent said as she moved toward the woman. "Wait a second!"

Stephanie glanced at him. "I'll see you in your office on Monday. Ask me out on that date. I'll say yes. I promise."

With that, she moved away from him, heading for Mr. Slick. "Hey!"

He turned. At the sight of her, the fangs he'd been sprouting shrank into his gums. He took a stumbling step back. The woman he'd been talking to made a small noise of relief.

"Can I go? Can I please go? Please, I want to get out of here!"

Without looking at her, Stephanie said, "Yes. Get."

The woman moved away but remained, a shadow standing in silence. Mr. Slick didn't move at all. He had no face, not really, just an amorphous blob of features struggling to rearrange. Into what? Something that would scare her?

"You might as well forget about it," she told him. "I know what's what in here, and you're not going to scare me. So why don't we have a little talk about this business with the bank accounts? What do you say? I promise you, it'll be much better for you if you cooperate."

Mr. Slick's laugh was low and bubbling, like something rising from a mud puddle. A mouth appeared, or the semblance of one. "I know you."

"Do you?" Stephanie kept her gaze on him while she used her will to weave an invisible net, sticky, thinking she might at least bind him in place with it long enough to get some answers.

"Yes. I do. I've seen you before. But you don't pay

attention to me, do you? Just that once. But every other time, I'm just..." Mr. Slick stopped and shook his head. Features formed and disappeared. He grew taller, thin, long arms and legs. Menacing.

"You mean out there? In the waking world?" Carefully, she twitched her fingers to toss the slightly glimmering strands around his ankles without alerting him to the binding. It wouldn't hold him long once he knew about it, but she hoped it would keep him in place a little longer anyway.

"Yes. Nobody pays attention out there. In here, I'm...somebody important. I do things. People give me things!"

Stephanie tugged the binding the tiniest bit tighter. It would trip him up, at the least, if he tried to run. "You steal things. That's what you mean."

"What difference does it make? Out there, nobody gives me anything!" Mr. Slick's voice wavered, getting thin.

The air between them wriggled, like the heat waves coming off a summertime road. Mr. Slick himself grew thin, transparent. Not waking, but definitely disappearing.

"Stay right there," Stephanie warned. "I need to talk to you."

"I don't have to talk to you! You're not my... You're not anything to me!"

Gone was the tall silhouette of the vampire, the werewolf, the slick thief in black leather. Replacing it was a smaller frame—black hair, pale face, dark eyes, a red slash of a mouth—but something nevertheless familiar about it. And then he was pushing her, hard, slamming her with a vibrating force that was not physical and yet might as well have been, because it sent her stumbling back.

She lost hold of the binding. She caught her balance before she could fall on her ass. Her heart raced, expecting an attack, but Mr. Slick only pushed again. Harder this time, sending Stephanie back another few feet.

"You can't stop me! I can do what I want, and I'm not hurting anyone! They can all make more money!"

"You *are* hurting people. You're stealing, and whether or not they can afford it, it's still wrong!"

Mr. Slick pushed, this time slapping a sticky piece of tape over Stephanie's mouth. "Shut up. Shut up."

Stephanie ripped away the tape, wincing at the sting of it. She rubbed her lips and decided to try a different approach. She held out her hands and spoke gently.

"Look, it's not like I can prosecute you for this. You have to know that. If you stop now, I won't be able to trace you in the waking world. You won't be caught. You just have to agree to stop."

For a moment, it seemed as though it might work, but then Mr. Slick shook his head. He'd shrunk, no longer a few feet taller than Stephanie, now a few inches shorter. Slighter. The air around him still shifted and turned, making it impossible to see who was behind the representation.

"I can't stop," he said, almost pleading. His voice had shrunk, too. Grown softer. Sweeter. "Don't you get it? It's all I have, really. When I take stuff from people and get away with it, it makes me feel like at least someone fucking notices me."

And then without another word or hint of warning, Mr. Slick disappeared.

"Shit," Stephanie said, defeated.

Behind her, the woman made another low noise. "I thought it was a soul sucker. Gonna suck my soul."

"Yeah, well. Something sort of like that, sure. What did he ask you?" Stephanie turned toward her.

"My first pet's name and the name of the street I grew up on."

"Did you tell him?" Stephanie asked.

The woman nodded, looking confused. "Was that wrong?"

Stephanie sighed, feeling the pull of morning in her own consciousness. "You should know better, even in a dream. What's your name?"

The woman told her right before Stephanie woke, and she wrote it down. Then she lay back in the bed for a few more minutes, puzzling over everything Mr. Slick had said. Stephanie knew him? From where?

Chapter 9

Kent had not been able to forget about the dream. Here it was, Monday, and he was still thinking about seeing Stephanie in that weird park and how she'd promised him that if he asked her out, she would say yes. Was he really going to do it?

"Hi," he greeted her as she knocked on his office door and peeked around it. "C'mon in."

"Sorry I'm a little late." She shot him a small apologetic grin as she settled into the chair on the other side of his desk. "Traffic."

"No problem." Small talk. Stupid. But he couldn't just blurt out a date request here in the office. "I was just about to go out and grab a coffee, though. Why don't we take the meeting there?"

She gave him an odd, fleeting look but nodded and stood. "Sounds great. I have some updates, but they won't take long. And I could always use a coffee."

"And a piece of cheesecake?" Too much, he told himself, but Stephanie didn't seem to think so.

She laughed. "It's a little early for cheesecake. You could convince me to eat a muffin, though."

"Done."

They chatted, more inane small talk, as they left his office and headed around the corner to the Green Bean, where they both ordered hot drinks and blueberry muffins, then took them to a small table in the corner. Watching her warm her hands on the cup, Kent knew there was no way he was going to actually ask her out, dream or no.

"I think I have an idea of who he might be targeting next," Stephanie said, surprising him.

"You do? How?"

She waved a hand. "Oh. Algorithms. Um…patterns in his previous marks."

That sounded plausible and yet something in the way she said it gave him pause. "Huh. So what do we do about it? Do we let the potential victim know? That could cause some concern. I mean, if we start scaring our customers, they might simply close their accounts. I don't think the board's going to be on…board."

Carol would've rolled her eyes, but Stephanie laughed at his play on words. "No. I agree. We can't warn them. But you can be prepared for any suspicious activity and handle it if it comes up, before the customer even knows."

"But you have no idea who's doing it? No closer to catching him? Or her," Kent added, to be fair.

"Or…her?" Stephanie paused as though considering that. "No. Sorry. Working on that. But I can give you the name of who might be his next target. You can monitor her account."

"I guess if that's the best we can do…"

She blew on her coffee and sipped, then set down the cup to give him a serious look. "I know it's not the best result, but believe me, Kent, we're getting closer. Last night I…"

"Last night you what?"

"I got very close," she said. "Tracking him down."

Kent had never asked how she did that. He'd always assumed it was with some computer program or something, because even though there'd never been any trace of hacking with any of the thefts, that had to be what was going on. He drank some of his own coffee and watched her tear a bite of her muffin.

"So," he said after a half minute had passed and neither of them had spoken, "did you have a good weekend?"

"It started off great," she told him with a grin. "Late-night cheesecake and all."

Kent smiled. "Oh, yeah?"

"Yep." She leaned forward a bit to say, like a secret, "It was nice. Really nice."

"So…" *Do it*, he urged himself. *Just ask her already.* "Maybe you'd like to do it again?"

"Oh, yes. For sure. I said so, didn't I?" An expression fluttered across her face, there and gone so fast he couldn't determine what it had been. "I mean, in the text. I answered your text."

"You…did?" Kent pulled his phone from his pocket to check, but no, there'd been nothing. "It didn't come through."

She smiled, brow furrowing. "No? Huh. Weird. I guess you thought I must've been blowing you off."

"No. I mean… Yes. I figured you were going to pretend I hadn't sent it, that's all. I wasn't going to mention it."

They looked at each other across the table, both silent again but this time smiling. Stephanie's eyes seemed very blue as she looked at him over the rim of her coffee cup.

"Would you like to go out again?"

"On a date?" she asked, her tone of voice making it clear she already knew the answer.

Kent nodded. "Yes. On a real, official date. I'll pick you up at your house and everything."

"Flowers?" Stephanie asked.

This woman was going to kill him, he thought. In all the best ways. Dead as a doornail.

"Flowers, if you like," he told her. "Candy, too."

She laughed and covered her mouth with her hand for a moment. Her eyes gleamed. She leaned across the table, just a little. "You got it. Friday night?"

"Yes," Kent said, and some weird impulse made him add, "You promise?"

For a second, he thought he'd gone too far. Too fast, too creepy. What had felt like flirting might've come across as too desperate.

She smiled, though. "Yes. Sure. I promise."

He had no reason for the feeling of relief at her answer, but it was there anyway. "Great. Pick you up at six?"

They chatted about the details for a minute or so longer before Kent caught sight of the time and realized he had to get back to the office for a meeting he was going to be late for. They parted ways in the credit-union parking lot with a half hug he refused to let himself overanalyze. It wasn't until later in the afternoon that he remembered he had never found out the name of the customer Stephanie thought was going to be the thief's next mark.

Chapter 10

"It's going," Stephanie said in answer to Vadim's question about her progress. "Slowly. I get so close, but this guy... It's like he knows just how to avoid me."

"He's probably been doing it for a long time." Vadim, tall, bald, intimidating, nodded at her from her computer screen. "Do you need backup?"

She shook her head. "No. But if it goes on much longer, more people are going to get duped. I feel bad. I should've figured him out by now."

"All things in their time." Vadim peered at her. "You look tired."

Stephanie laughed. "Gee, thanks."

"You've been spending too much time shaping and not enough time simply dreaming," her boss declared. "You should take tonight off."

"I'm fine," she protested but stopped at his look. "I know the rules, Vadim."

"Everyone needs to dream," he told her. "Without proper dreaming time, your brain does not count the hours you're unconscious as true sleep. And without enough sleep…"

She grumbled, "Yes, I know. You go crazy."

"It's no joking matter, Stephanie. You are too good to lose to madness." Vadim frowned. "I insist you take tonight off."

She couldn't enter the Ephemeros without being aware that she was dreaming, but she could definitely spend more time relaxing and enjoying the dream world rather than actively working it. "Fine, but if I get even a hint of that guy anywhere around, I'm on it."

"Of course. But other than that, take a break." Vadim gave her a small, tight smile. "I am envious of you, of course. To be able to manipulate the dream world. It's a true talent, one I wish I could cultivate."

She didn't blame him. She'd learned in toddlerhood that she could shape and push the Ephemeros and couldn't imagine not being able to control her dreams. With another few minutes of casual chat, she and Vadim ended their conversation and disconnected the call.

Here it was, a full night off. For a moment, Stephanie thought about calling Denise to see if she wanted to head out on the town, maybe for a hump-day happy hour, but then decided against it. She was going to spend the night at home pampering herself, she thought. A couple glasses of good wine she usually couldn't otherwise indulge in, because too much alcohol made it hard to function in dreams as much as in the waking world. A steaming bubble bath. A good book. Chocolate. Oh, yeah, she had a couple pieces of decadent, expensive chocolates she'd been saving for a treat, and if a night off decreed by your boss didn't count, she didn't know what would.

The only thing that would make it better would be a sexy guy joining her in the tub, Stephanie thought as she settled into the apartment's vintage claw-foot with her wineglass and the chocolates on a plate. She hadn't had an orgasm with another person since just before she got assigned to move here, and that had been a rendez-vous with Tomas in the Ephemeros. She and her friend with benefits had been spending quality sexy times with each other, on and off, for decades, though they'd never once met in real life.

She should look him up. Wine, the warm bath, her own slick fingers running over her wet and naked flesh...too many nights without enough quality sleep... She was going to doze right there in the tub. Doze and slip into dreams.

She appeared in the Ephemeros in a warm, bubbling pool of deep-gray-and-blue water faintly scented of lavender. Naked. A little thinner here, a little rounder there, Stephanie noticed with a small chuckle as she stretched in the lovely warmth and let herself float on her back. Above her, a trillion points of light pricked the black velvet of the sky.

Dream, she told herself. Dream, dream, dream.

She did let herself send out some feelers, a little push here and there. Looking for Tomas. When he didn't respond, looking for anyone.

Stephanie had no problem finding sex in the Ephemeros. In here, she could experiment. Take chances she never would while awake. She could be whoever she pleased, do what she liked. It wasn't always emotionally fulfilling to wake up alone after a rampant nightly bout of fucking, but it satisfied her body anyway.

Why should tonight be any different, she thought as she stood to get out of the pool. Her skin gleamed in the starlight. Her nipples peaked at the soft, sighing brush of night air against her nakedness. Why shouldn't she look for a lover here, have her way with him and move on?

Because of Kent, she told herself with a rueful shake of the head. Because she had a date with him in two days, and he was the first real-world guy she'd had any interest in for a long time. Fucking someone else in here wouldn't be cheating even if they were in a long-term relationship, so why, then, did she feel so hesitant to keep sending out her signals into the Ephemeros's vastness?

"Stephanie?"

Turning, she shaped a gauzy dress of ribbons that clung to her wet skin. It did nothing to hide her tight nipples or the shadow between her legs. If anything, a dress like that was meant to draw the viewer's attention to just those places. She'd shaped it without thinking.

"Kent? What are...? Oh. Wow." She shook her head and covered her breasts briefly with her hands. When she tried to shape a different sort of gown, though, one more modest, the pull of his will stopped her. She paused to look at him. "No?"

"You look beautiful."

"Of course I do." She laughed. "It's a dream."

It could be tricky, telling a sleeper they were dreaming. Most of the time, they didn't believe it, and that was fine, unless there was a reason to convince them, like if they were in danger or something. She watched Kent's face carefully to see if he was shocked.

He smiled. "I should've known, right? A woman as beautiful as you wouldn't give me the time of day otherwise."

"That's not true." She moved a step closer and put a hand on his shoulder. He was warm. "I said yes when you asked me out."

He looked faintly surprised, as though he'd forgotten. "Oh. Right. But now I'm sleeping. I have to wait a couple days to see you again."

"You're seeing me right now," Stephanie said with a laugh and let herself sink deeper into the dream.

She could've shaped them into anything or anywhere using the force of her will. Instead, she opened herself to whatever it was Kent wanted to dream about. She had the night off, after all.

And he was very, very cute.

Yet when he moved to kiss her, as she had the first time he tried, she turned her face at the last second so his lips caught her cheek and not her mouth. Sure, wouldn't think of this as real, if he remembered it at all, but she was thinking of Friday and their date and the possibilities ahead of them.

"Wait," she whispered as he pulled her closer. God, he smelled good. He felt good, too. She could've blamed the wine, but no. When he tried to kiss her again, she shook her head. "Wait, I want it to be real. Not just a dream."

He pulled away to look at her, his expression serious. Then he slayed her with that smile again. "Aren't you supposed to get what you want in dreams?"

"Yes." She took a step back. Then another. Crooked her finger to get him to follow. "What you really want is to wait."

"I can't argue with that." He followed.

She took his hand and walked with him through a landscape that shifted and changed with every step. Colors swirled. Neither of them were holding anything in place. Their fingers linked, that was real. Their conversation, words she would not recall in the morning, that was real, too.

"Look," Stephanie said and waved a hand to make a field of flowers grow in front of them. "Try it."

Kent wiggled his fingers, but nothing happened. They both laughed. He tried again, sprouting a dandelion he then plucked for her so she could blow away the seeds. They walked. Night was heading toward morning, and she didn't want to wake up.

They'd been laughing about nothing important when Kent stopped so short that Stephanie kept walking for a few steps before she looked up. "Kent?"

"Hey, I know her," he said. "Who's she talking to?"

She looked to where he was pointing. Her happy, giddy mood vanished when she saw the elderly woman sitting in a recliner, leaning forward to listen as a man in a long black leather coat whispered in her ear.

"Oh, shit. It's him!" she cried and leaped toward them.

That was when the wave came up and swept her away.

She woke, spluttering, her head beneath the water of the tub. Cursing, she got out, coughing. That had been stupid. She dried off and put on some comfy pajamas, her earlier good feelings about the dream with Kent fading. No matter how nice it had been inside, there was never any telling what it would be like for real.

Worse, she'd once again let Mr. Slick slip through her grasp.

Chapter 11

He'd been waiting all week for Friday, but not for this reason. Another account compromised. This time it had been his mother's.

The credit union was insured, of course, but that didn't help make him feel much better when he'd pulled up Mom's accounts after she'd called him questioning why her automatic bill payment hadn't gone through from her checking. Kent had spent all morning trying to figure out where the money had gone, how it had been withdrawn without a trace. His stomach sick, he'd transferred a couple thousand of his own money into Mom's account to cover the rest of her bills. Fortunately, the thief hadn't drained her savings or money-management accounts, and Kent worked quickly to change Mom over to all new accounts, but in the end it didn't make him feel much better.

He'd called Stephanie immediately but got her voice

mail. He hadn't left a message. He'd spent the rest of the day fielding inquiries from the board and sifting through data files to see if he could catch any signs of other thefts. Nobody called to complain, so he supposed everything was all right, but for how much longer?

By the end of the day, his head hurt from clenching his jaw. His stomach churned from the stress. He got out of work too late to go home and shower or change. He was going to be late picking her up.

He wasn't even sure he wanted to.

It wasn't Stephanie's fault, and he knew that. She was one investigator working on a case that Kent could see was unusual. But if she'd done her job by now, his mom wouldn't have had her checking account wiped out.

Sitting in the parking spot in front of her apartment, he pulled out his phone. He should call. Make an excuse. Send a text?

Too late—the curtain of her apartment door twitched, and the door itself opened as Stephanie peeked out. He could see her smile from here. Shit. She waved him in.

He'd make an excuse, Kent thought. Say he was coming down with something, which was what it felt like, sort of, to stand on her front mat and think about telling her he didn't want to go out with her, after all.

He opened his mouth, but before he could say a word, Stephanie pushed up onto her tiptoes to put her arms around his neck. Her cheek pressed to his, she said softly into his ear, "I'm so sorry about your mom. We are going to catch this son of a bitch. I promise you, Kent. I'm going to make it my mission in life to track him down and make him sorry he ever lifted a single cent from anyone."

His arms had gone around her automatically. His eyes closed. He pressed his face into the softness of her dark hair and breathed in the sweetness of her perfume, something light and fresh. Citrus. Damn it, she felt good in his arms, and her words had taken away some of his earlier frustration.

Stephanie stepped back from him, though she let her hands run down his shoulders to rest lightly on his forearms. His hands had anchored on her hips. She looked up at him, her brow furrowed, her mouth thin.

"If you don't feel like taking me out, Kent, I get it."

It had been what he'd been thinking all day long, but when he was faced with her actually saying it, all he could do was shake his head. "No. Look, it's not your fault—"

"It is. If I'd caught this guy before now," she said, "your mom would've been okay. So would all those other people."

His fingers curled a little on her hips. She wore soft leggings and a slouchy sweater, but beneath that, he could feel her curves. "It's not your fault he's a thief."

She tipped her face to look up at him. "I've been on the case for six months. It's long past time I caught him. That's all. You might not blame me, but I take responsibility. So if you don't want to go out…"

"No. I asked you out. We should go out."

Neither of them moved. A flash of a dream came to him, the two of them walking through fields of flowers, hand in hand. He remembered her laughing.

"I…dreamed about you," he said. "Night before last."

Stephanie's smile was like watching a flower bloom. "I know you did. I was there."

Kent shook his head a little. "Okay, this is weird. What's going on?"

He saw the hesitation in her expression and waited for her to give him some lame explanation, but Stephanie drew in a short, sharp breath. She took another step back. Squared her shoulders.

"He's using their dreams to get their information," she said. "And I've been trying to find him in the dream world, but I haven't been able to yet."

Stephanie had told only three people in her life about the Ephemeros who hadn't already known about it. The first had been her high school boyfriend, her first love. She'd had a vulnerable moment after the night she lost her virginity and spilled her truth to him. He'd broken up with her the next day.

The other two had been strangers on a train. Both had been sleeping and had shown up in her world because of the proximity. They'd woken, startled, and given her guilty glances very much alike despite their not knowing each other any more than they'd known her. Her explanation of why the three of them had been having the same dream had spilled out of her on a whim. Rodney and Darryl had gone on to become a couple. They sent her Christmas cards every year.

Now she sat across from her kitchen table with Kent staring at her, and she waited for him to get up and walk out. Call her crazy. Tell her to never darken his doorstep again.

Instead, he said, "Can I do it, too?"

"A little, yes. More than that, I don't know. I mean, everyone shapes their dreams—it's just a matter of if they know it and can do it on purpose." She got up to refill both their mugs of coffee. She'd pulled a frozen cheesecake out to serve, too. Funny how she'd never have bothered to pick up a cheesecake at all before last week, but it had ended up in her cart because of him.

He nodded but said nothing. He leaned forward to

put his elbows on the table, then pushed his glasses up on his nose. "Huh."

"Yeah." She laughed. "Crazy, right?"

"So when I dreamed about you…"

"The dream world is a real place. It's called the Ephemeros," she told him, picking her words carefully. "What happens in it can affect people in the real world, though most of the time, it doesn't. When we met there, it was because we were both asleep at the same time, and though geographical proximity is not at all required, it's usually a factor in who meets up. But you can dream about anyone, anytime. It doesn't necessarily mean that actual person is in there with you. It just means you've shaped them, or that you've put out a…well, like a signal. And someone who can shape not only themselves but also everything else comes along and helps your dream be whatever it needs to be."

"Someone like you?" Kent asked.

She nodded. "Yes. Someone like me."

"You can make dreams come true?" His smile tipped a bit on one side, rueful. Contemplative.

"Yes. I can. There are people who do it all the time."

He wrapped his hands around the coffee mug. "Hmm. Why?"

"Because dreams are important," she said. "Without them, without living out whatever it is we do inside them, well…we go mad. I mean, literally crazy."

"I want to try it."

Stephanie dug her fork into the cheesecake and let herself savor a bite before answering. "Okay."

"Okay?" Kent seemed surprised. "Just like that, okay?"

"Well, sure." She shrugged. "It's not like there's a

secret club that you have to apply for membership to. You either can or you can't."

"Can you teach me?"

"I don't know." She thought about that for a few seconds. "I know it's possible to practice shaping and to get better at it. But I'm not sure you teach someone to do it if they can't already. Kind of like telling a good story. You either can or you can't."

"The other night, in the field. I made a flower, didn't I?"

She laughed. "Yes. You did."

"On purpose."

"Yes." She hesitated. "The other part is knowing you're dreaming. Have you ever had one of those dreams, where you knew it?"

"Yeah," he said, sounding eager. "Once, I dreamed I was being chased by a shark, but I knew it was a dream and I turned around and punched it."

"Yikes. Brave," she said with a grin. She let out a small breath, then said, "I know you were angry at me about your mom. I really am sorry."

"It just makes me all the more determined to catch this jerk. And this is your job? I mean…you do it all the time?"

"When needed. Yes. I shape in dreams to help sleepers along, to help them reach their goals in the dreams, whatever they are, but that's not my job. It's a responsibility." She shrugged. "I'd been doing that without really knowing why for years before Vadim approached me about joining the Crew. The money's good. The work isn't usually hard. And this really shouldn't have been that difficult for me. I guess I… Maybe I wasn't trying hard enough."

"I'm sure you take your job seriously, Stephanie."

"I like being here," she said suddenly, as though daring him to challenge her. "I like working with you. I think maybe I didn't try hard enough because I knew that once the job was over, I'd have to leave."

They stared at each other quietly.

"Sorry about the date. I really did mean to take you out," Kent said. "To be honest, I've been thinking about it for a while."

"You didn't bring the flowers," she told him with a small grin. "Or the candy. How about I take a rain check?"

He sat back in his chair. "Deal. So…how do we catch this asshole?"

Chapter 12

"This isn't the first time I've ended up in a woman's bed on a first date," Kent said in a low voice. "But it's definitely not the way I'd expected things to go."

Beside him, Stephanie giggled. She'd lent him a pair of oversize sweatpants and a T-shirt, then tucked them both into her bed. They'd been staring in silence at the ceiling for about ten minutes while he tried to fall asleep by timing his breathing to her steady, even breaths. It hadn't worked.

"You're a little naughty. I like that." She turned to face him.

He rolled, too. Their knees touched. He wanted to touch more than that but kept himself from it.

"I'm not tired," he said. "Sorry."

"Me neither."

"You don't have any tricks?" He settled a little more into the pillow.

"Deep breathing. Um…" Stephanie laughed and pulled the covers up over her nose for a second. "Orgasm?"

It was not what he'd expected, and he laughed even as several muscles tensed in places he hadn't been paying much attention to for the past few weeks. "Um…"

"Sorry, sorry." She laughed a little breathlessly. "It's true, but a little too much. I know."

"I'd be game, if you are," Kent said.

Her laughter eased and she pulled the blanket away from her face. "On the first date, huh? What a player."

"I'm the furthest thing from a player you could ever meet," he told her quietly. "I think you know that by now."

Silence.

"Yes," she said finally. "I know."

Did she move first? He thought so, although he was moving, too. The kiss was light, soft, gentle, the hint of her breath tickling his lips until, oh, damn, her mouth opened and she drew his tongue in against hers with a low groan that got him hard as rock within half a minute.

She broke the kiss with an embarrassed laugh, though she didn't pull away. "I thought it would be good, but I didn't know how good."

"So…how long have you been thinking about this?" He let his hand slide up to rest on her hip beneath the blankets. She wore a pair of lightweight boxers and a man's T-strap undershirt. There was the tiniest bit of bare skin between the bottom of the shirt and the top of the drawers. When he touched her there, she shivered.

"Oh, for about six months." She pressed her face to the side of his neck. "Since the first time I walked into your office and saw you with your shirtsleeves rolled up. I have a thing for sexy forearms. And guys in glasses."

Heat spread through him. He let his fingers trace more bare skin, easing up the hem of her shirt. Then over her belly, pausing at the small dip of her navel. Across her ribs. Higher still, to just below the curve of her breast. He stopped.

Stephanie let out a low, shuddering sigh. "You can touch me, Kent. This is real. We're really here. We can do this."

He wanted to. Everything about it felt right, even if the smart part of his mind, the part resisting the heat pooling in his groin, told him it was probably going to end painfully in the long run.

As if she felt his hesitation, she nuzzled against his throat, nipping lightly with the perfect amount of pressure to make him squirm. "If you don't want to…"

"I do." He pulled her closer so she could feel how much. "I just…"

She moved to look at his face. "It's soon. I know. You just broke up with Carol. I won't be sticking around. It's not something to jump into. I understand. But what if we just look at it as something to try? I mean…no strings, no promises?"

"Is that what you really want?"

Her brow furrowed. "Truth? No, not really. But I'm not saying I think we should jump into something serious right off the bat. As far as sex goes, I'm not exactly a prude about one-night stands and that sort of thing. I don't hop into bed with just anyone, either."

He stroked a fingertip over her eyebrows to smooth the crease, then tucked her hair behind her ear. "I like you a lot, Stephanie."

"I like you, too."

He kissed her again, tasting her sweetness until she gasped and moved against him. She shook a little. She pressed her head to his chest, and he tightened his arms around her.

"There are other ways to fall asleep," she whispered.

He kissed the top of her head. "But that's not really what this is about right now, is it?"

Her shoulders shook as she laughed. Her breath heated his skin through the T-shirt's thin material. When she put her hand flat on his belly below the hem of it, the warmth of her fingers made him draw in a long, slow breath. His cock throbbed. When she slid a hand lower to cup him, he couldn't hold back the small groan.

He didn't move, though. Uncertain if this was the direction they should go, if they both really wanted it, if they'd be making a mistake. It didn't feel like one. It felt like the best shot at happiness he'd ever taken.

Kent was right. This had nothing to do with sleep and everything to do with orgasms. More than that, too. It was something Stephanie had wanted without admitting it to herself for months.

"Sometimes, in dreams, you jump without knowing you have a place to land," she murmured into his kiss as she slid a hand into the sweatpants she'd lent him and found his hard, thick length. She stroked, gratified and aroused at the way he drew in a gasp at her touch. "But sometimes, when you jump, you fly."

Kent pulled her closer, his kiss getting deeper. His tongue thrust against hers as his hips moved, too. She tugged the sweatpants a little lower on his hips to free him, almost too nervous to look at his nakedness now that she had the chance. Then she didn't have to, because they were kissing so hard and fast all she could think about was how good he tasted, how delicious, how his touch was making her crazy.

He rolled them both to get on top of her, nudging her knees apart with his. One hand slid behind her neck to cradle her. The other moved up to cup her breast. He thumbed her nipple erect, then pinched it lightly, making her cry out into his mouth.

He pushed himself up to tug his shirt off over his head; Stephanie pulled off hers while he worked, too. For a moment, she wished for the Ephemeros to give her bigger boobs and a flatter belly. For a second, she shielded herself from his gaze. Kent ran his hands up her ribs, tickling a little, then let his palms go flat on her skin.

"You're gorgeous," he told her.

She believed him.

Arching, Stephanie put her arms over her head to curl her fingers around the headboard's spindles. She closed her eyes, smiling, as Kent let out a low whistle of appreciation. Her nipples tightened at more tickling touches as he moved his fingertips over her.

It was easy to feel beautiful in the dream world. Even sleepers shaped themselves into loveliness. Stephanie had long ago translated her ability as a shaper into confidence out here where it wasn't so easy to whittle away a few extra pounds or to add curves. Even so, it would've been easy to worry, this first time, if her nakedness pleased him.

Kent gave her no reason for doubt. He bent low over her, whispering compliments in her ear as he traced her body with his fingers, then, moving lower, his mouth. Over the curves of her shoulders, down her arms. He placed kisses on the tender insides of her elbows and her wrists. He kissed her palms and curved her fingers over wetness he left behind.

He kissed her belly, murmuring her name and words

of awe. Sending her higher. Over her hip bones, each one, pausing to nibble while she wiggled. Her thighs, her knees, her ankles. Kneeling over her, he took each foot and kissed her toes, laughing while she protested. Then he slid the sweatpants all the way off and knelt between her legs, fully naked.

Kent put a hand on his cock, lightly stroking. She pushed up on one elbow to get a better look. It was her turn to compliment.

"You work out?" she teased, letting one foot drift up to nudge his hard belly. "Mmm, abs."

"Good genes," he told her.

She arched again, offering her body to him. "Kiss me, Kent."

He did, but not on the mouth. Again he bent to trail his lips and tongue over her thighs and belly, pausing to blow sweet, hot breath through the lace of her panties. Automatically, her hand went to thread through his hair, the silken feeling of it tickling the back of her hand as she lifted her hips to meet his mouth.

He'd slipped her panties off before she knew it, then knelt again between her legs. Gently, he parted her to his questing tongue, which flicked lightly over her clit before he pressed the flat of it to her and stroked. Kent settled onto his belly between her thighs, both hands sliding beneath her ass to lift her to his mouth as he feasted. It was not what Stephanie had expected.

It was so much better.

"Oh," she said. "That's…"

"Good?" he said against her, looking up with a smile. He kissed her there, softly. Then again. He found her clit and sucked it gently before ducking back to the steady, slow stroking that was edging her closer and closer to going over.

She could've resisted, tried to make it last, but when she wriggled and whispered his name, the sound of his groan made it impossible for Stephanie to ask him to wait. She needed this, and him, and oh, fuck, he was giving it to her.

Hovering on the edge, Stephanie rolled her hips, mindless with the pleasure. Kent eased off, blowing soft puffs against her clit until she let out a frustrated gasp that became a laugh. Then a sigh. She looked down at him, her fingers toying in his hair.

"So close," Stephanie whispered. "It feels so good."

She touched his face. Eyebrows. Cheek. She stroked a finger over his lips. He closed his eyes for a second, his gaze hazy when he opened them again. He bent back to her.

Stephanie let him take her away. All the way. Up and over, pleasure coiling inside her so tight she thought she might surely break from it before it could explode. She came with a low cry, then his name. Her body moved; she came again, each wave throbbing through her while she clutched at the sheets so fiercely she pulled them free of the mattress. She fell back, panting.

Silence.

Stephanie licked her lips and breathed. She blinked as the world came back into focus. Kent hadn't moved from between her legs, though he now rested his cheek on her thigh. One hand had moved from her ass to cup her pussy, the warmth strangely comforting and still arousing, even if she didn't think she'd be able to go another round. At least not right away.

"Wow," she said after a few more seconds of quiet broken only by her still-ragged breathing. She moved a hand over his hair, tugging briefly before letting her touch land on his shoulder. "That was…"

He laughed and pushed up on his elbow to move over her body. He kissed her mouth. He covered her with his weight, his cock thick and hard against her thigh.

"That was amazing. You were so… God, Stephanie. Fucking out of this world." He stopped and looked concerned for a moment. "This is real, isn't it? We didn't fall asleep. I'm not dreaming."

She'd have laughed except she could tell he was serious. She pulled him to her for another kiss, then sat up a little to point at one of the clocks on her nightstand. "No. See that? The clock. Can you tell the time?"

"Yeah."

"Time, clocks, words, numbers, those things generally don't work right in the Ephemeros. The easiest way to tell if you're dreaming or awake is if you can read or tell the time." She snuggled closer to him. "This is real."

Kent pressed himself against her for another kiss. "Good. I thought… Never mind."

She reached between them to take his cock in her hand, squeezing gently but enough to make him shiver. She looked at him. "What?"

"I just thought this had to be a dream, that's all. Because that's how it feels, too good to be true."

If she'd ever had a sweeter lover, she couldn't think about it now. She kissed his mouth, her hand moving slowly. "No. This is real. And it's good. And it's going to get better."

Chapter 13

"I don't know how it could— Oh, shit. Oh. Yeah."

She'd slid down on the bed to take him in her mouth, and Kent closed his eyes, head tipping back at that instant ecstasy. Her mouth was magic, her tongue stroking while she sucked the head of his cock before taking him in deeper. She cupped his balls, fingers stroking that perfect spot, exactly how he liked it best. As if she knew him already.

Stephanie hummed a bit in the back of her throat, the vibration adding a wave of pleasure on top of what was already pretty fucking fantastic. He thrust, then caught himself, not wanting to choke her, but damn, she only made another low noise and gripped him at the base as she took him all the way in. He couldn't stop himself from putting his hands on her head, not trying to guide her or change her pace. He simply needed to touch her.

At his touch, Stephanie paused. Then she took his hand and slid it deep into the fall of her thick dark hair, curling his fingers with hers to give him a good grip. She moaned when he tugged.

"Damn," Kent breathed. "You are so…"

She sucked harder, then slid her mouth off his cock long enough to look up at him and say, "You taste so good."

No woman had ever said such a thing to him. He'd had women who suffered through sucking dick, a few who'd claimed to love it and some who'd refused it outright. Not one of them had ever made him feel as though his cock in her mouth was a delight, a treat. A gift.

She looked up at him with a small smile that hit him right between the eyes with all the unerring and vicious accuracy of cupid's pointiest arrow. This was…more, Kent thought. More than sex. This could be something real.

He wanted to tell her, but when she went down on him again, the best he could manage was a few muttered words that sounded a bit like her name. She did that humming thing, and he lost the ability to even form words at all.

All he could do was relax and let the pleasure wash over him. She eased him higher and higher, then teased a bit until he gasped aloud. Kent would never have believed a woman laughing around his cock could feel so good. It made him laugh, too, not with humor exactly. More like joy.

That was how he felt when he was with her. Filled up with joy. And that was the last coherent thought he had before orgasm flooded him, making him mindless and thrusting and writhing under her skilled mouth and hands.

It went on forever, until spent, he fell back against the pillows and wondered if he was going to catch his breath. When Stephanie crawled up to snuggle against him, her face pillowed in the curve of his shoulder and her hand flat on his chest, Kent turned to kiss her forehead.

There should be words, he thought. He should say

something. Yet in the quiet, filled only with the sound of their breathing, he discovered that at least in that moment, speech was unnecessary. All they had to do was hold on to each other. That was more than enough.

Kent fell asleep before she did, which wasn't a surprise to Stephanie, who'd found that most men did. Especially after a blow job. Contented and replete, she was happy to press her face to his bare skin and feel the slowing beat of his heart under her hand.

She did need to put herself under, though. Time was wasting, and she had all day tomorrow to think about what they'd done and what it meant, or what it didn't. Right now she had a job to do, and that meant using a few of her favorite tricks to get herself into the dream world.

She counted back from a hundred, slowly, breathing in and out. She had to do it three times before finally, on the final count of five, she found herself in the forest. She was alone, as she'd expected, though an easy push-pull of her surroundings sent out seeking tendrils to find Kent. It was the sex, she thought as she stepped through the trees, searching for him. It had connected them in a way nothing else ever did.

"Hi," Kent said from behind her. "Stephanie. Hello."

She turned with a smile. "Hey. You're here."

"I am. So are you." He'd represented in jeans and a denim shirt, rolled up in that way she loved. He tilted his head to give her a curious look. "I feel like…"

"You're dreaming," she told him.

"I'm dreaming," Kent agreed. He reached for her, pulling her close. He kissed her, sweetly. No urgency.

She could get lost in this, but not right now. "We have to find the guy who's been stealing."

"I know. I just wanted to kiss you again. You taste like berries."

She licked her lips. It was true. He'd done that, she thought. She liked it.

"Do you remember us talking about what to do in here? How you can shape things if you try?" She gestured and the forest faded, putting them in a gray fog that would make it easier for him to imprint the Ephemeros with his own desire.

"Yes." Kent nodded, his hands still resting lightly on her hips. "Like this."

Slowly and imperfectly, walls formed around them. Some were made of bars, others concrete. The floor that appeared was of smooth black slate. Lighting overhead came from recessed receptacles glowing bright white.

"It's a vault," he told her with a grin. "With lots of money in it. Where else do you think we're going to find a thief?"

She laughed and went to her tiptoes to kiss him. "Good thinking."

"Now what?" He looked around them as the small details filled in.

He was getting better at this as she watched, and Stephanie added her shaping skills to his, anticipating what he meant to do. Stacks of cash. Boxes spilling with gold coin and jewels. It was the stereotype of every bank vault she'd ever seen in any movie. The question was, would it work?

"We call him," she said. "Concentrate. Think of what he looked like. Push it out there into the dream world. Tempt him in."

Others showed up first. Money was powerful motivation for many people, even those who wouldn't have stolen anything, ever. She saw more than one cat burglar in black masks, striped shirts. Some she didn't see at all, only their shadows as they slipped into the cells of the vault and carried away whatever they felt was important enough to steal.

"I didn't realize it would be so…boring," Kent said. "Or that it would take so long."

Time passed differently, so it could've been hours or only minutes since they'd fallen asleep. Still, Stephanie had to agree. "Yeah. Well…it's a job, you know? Like any kind of job."

Kent looked past her at a couple of women who were casually rifling through a box of tiaras and slipping them into their oversize handbags. "Do you ever get to just dream?"

"Sure. Of course. It's not like there are so many dream crimes being committed all the time, at least not ones serious enough to call attention to themselves." She stretched, thinking that while this had been a good idea, it wasn't going to work.

That was when she saw him, Mr. Slick, complete with black leather trench coat and everything else. He wasn't taking money from the vault, but he was whispering lasciviously in the ear of one of the handbag ladies. It was so blatant she could hardly believe it. She took a step forward, but Kent's hand on her arm stopped her.

"I shielded us," he said.

Surprised, she paused to look at the shadows surrounding them. "You did? Wow. How did you…?"

"I thought it." Kent sounded as surprised as she had been, and he shot her a grin. "I figured we wouldn't want him seeing us, right? At least not until we got close enough to grab him."

"You're so smart," she told him with a kiss that lingered, though she knew better than to mingle work with pleasure. "Let's get this dill hole."

Chapter 14

Kent was dreaming, and he knew it. More than that, he could control what happened in the dream, not only to himself but to his surroundings. It was like working out, though, when you'd never lifted before, never run a mile. He was tired.

Still, how fucking cool was this?

Distracted, he listened while Stephanie laid out what had to happen in order for them to catch the thief—they could bind him and try to get the information out of him for only so long before it would become dangerous.

"Not only to him, because keeping someone held here when they're trying to get out can lead to real-world problems, but to us, too. I'm used to dealing with people in here, but you're not," she explained while they both watched the guy move through the crowd of women who apparently liked to dream about shoplifting. "You've got some measure of innate talent—"

"Thanks," he said.

"Focus, Kent," Stephanie said seriously, then paused to take him by the shoulders and turn him to face her. "You know what, I think maybe you should bow out."

He looked at her. "What? No! That asshole stole from my mother. I owe her this."

"You're so new to it." Stephanie shook her head. "I don't want you to end up getting hurt. And this is my job, not yours."

"And you haven't exactly done a great job at it, have you?" He couldn't believe the words had shot out of his mouth, but once out, they couldn't be taken back.

Stephanie moved away from him a step or two. She didn't seem mad. More wary than anything. "That's fair, and true, but what you don't understand is how easy it is to get caught up in here, and how hard it can be to get out. You feel a little drunk now, don't you?"

It was more like stoned, which he'd only ever experienced a couple times a few years ago when a back injury had kept him laid up on the couch dosing with pain meds. "I'm fine. C'mon, he's going to get away."

The tattered shadows he'd pulled around them tugged at his fingers, a physical pull. It hurt a little, keeping up that shield. He hadn't expected it to hurt. As the shield fell away, the thief turned, focusing on them both.

"Oh, you. I should've known." The thief took a second look, stepping closer, zeroing in on Kent. "Hey. I know you! You're that guy from…"

The thief cut off his own words, but in the next second, the overpowering stench of evil assaulted Kent so fiercely he staggered back. Okay, not evil, but the closest thing to it that he could think of. The reek of coconut. It flooded him, his eyes, nose, ears, mouth, tongue, coating it, the taste of it thick in his mouth no matter how he spat to get it out. He went to his knees.

He was aware, as though from far away, of the sound

of Stephanie's shouts, but he couldn't do anything but try to close himself off to the torture of coconut. It made him want to die. In the back of his mind, Kent knew there was no way real coconut, no matter how vile, could do this to him. It was the dream world. He was being manipulated. Knowing it didn't help. If anything, it made him feel worse, because as he watched Stephanie run toward the thief, he knew he'd failed her.

She'd had enough. More than, as a matter of fact. This punk was going to be very, very sorry he'd messed with her man.

That she'd started thinking of Kent as her man was a thought for a different time, because right now Stephanie was hell-bent on grabbing hold of Mr. Slick and shaking the shit out of him. Her fingers skidded on the leather, catching his sleeve. She yanked him forward, making herself taller as she did. Stronger. Faster. Tougher.

"If you don't stop this right now," she hissed, growing fangs, spitting venom, "I'm going to fuck you up so hard you will never get out of here. You'll spend the rest of your life drooling into your pillow while other people wipe your ass for you, because you will never wake up!"

Mr. Slick had been looking beyond her at Kent, who was still on his hands and knees. Now he looked startled. Almost as though he was going to…cry?

"Okay, okay! God, I just wanted to see if I could get away with it, and I used the money for shit I needed!"

Mr. Slick's features were fading and blending again. This time, though, Stephanie kept her grip tight. She dug deep. She held on, even when Mr. Slick started sending out arcing electric shocks, sizzling and burning.

"Who are you?" Stephanie shouted louder than she'd ever yelled before.

The Ephemeros didn't shake—she had nowhere near

that sort of power. It did rumble, though, with a hum and buzz like a hundred thousand angry wasps, stingers poised to attack. It surprised her as much as it did Mr. Slick, at least until Kent got to his feet and strode toward them without so much as a single stumble. His eyes looked red rimmed, his brow creased with pain, but he pushed forward with both his hands in a single shoving gesture that knocked Mr. Slick backward into one of the vaults, where the barred door swung closed and clicked.

Locked.

"You can't do this!" Mr. Slick's panicked voice echoed throughout the vault, which Kent was shaping to look less like a bank and more like a prison. The sound of metal on metal rang out through the vault—Mr. Slick had made his hands into iron bars.

Stephanie had gone against talented and powerful shapers before. This kid was strong, talented but untrained. And he *was* a kid, she realized as a wave of high school–era anxiety washed over her. He was projecting, and hard. She stepped up to the bars, looking in.

"We *can* do this," she said. "You knew there'd be consequences, didn't you?"

Mr. Slick shrank before her eyes, features blurring. He was having trouble holding on to his representation. "I didn't think I'd get caught."

"Well, you did," Kent said.

The entire vault faded around them. So did Mr. Slick. The rush of anxiety that had reminded her of all those times in high school that she'd forgotten her gym clothes or had been ignored by the cute boy she'd had a crush on faded abruptly.

"Shit, he got away," Kent said.

Stephanie shook her head, sagging in the aftermath. Putting the pieces together. She looked at him. "Yeah. But I know who it is."

Chapter 15

Of course the kid tried to run as soon as she saw Stephanie entering the coffee shop. They were ready for that, though. Kent was waiting outside the door, and he snagged the girl by her hoodie and kept her still. She squirmed but didn't scream.

"I didn't do anything. You can't prove anything," she said.

Stephanie glanced behind her into the shop to see if anyone was watching, but as she'd guessed, nobody ever seemed to notice this kid at all. "How do you do it?"

The girl stopped wriggling and gave Stephanie a narrow look. "Do what?"

Stephanie gestured for Kent to take the girl down the street toward the riverfront. They found a park bench, and Kent sat the girl on it. Stephanie stood in front of her, hands on her hips.

"Make yourself hard to see," she said.

"Nobody wants to pay attention to some raggedy

kid," the girl said. She clutched her laptop bag against her chest.

Kent shrugged. "That must suck."

The girl gave him a startled look. "What?"

"It must suck," he repeated conversationally.

Stephanie sat next to her. The girl shrank away. "What did you do with the money? Did you spend it all?"

"Not all. I just used some to eat. Pay for a hotel room. I needed it," the girl said with a lift of her chin, defensive. "Believe me, I could've done a lot worse, you know. I could've taken lots more."

"It was still stealing, even if you only took a little bit," Stephanie told her. "You're going to have to stop."

"Or what?"

"Or I'll make sure the police find you," Stephanie said quietly. "Or worse."

"What's worse than the police?" The girl sneered.

Stephanie's smile tightened. "People who can do the sorts of things you can do, only better."

"I'm not scared." But her voice trembled a little.

"Look, kid. What's your name?"

"Destiny."

Stephanie nodded. "Destiny. What if I told you I could send you to a place where people would notice you. And teach you, too. How to use the talents you have. Here and in the dream world, too."

"What, like some sort of high school for mutants? No thanks!" The girl got up, but Kent was there to stop her. She sat again, her fierce gaze going back and forth between them before she looked defeated. "Fine. I'm listening."

"The money you took will go back to the account holders," Stephanie said. "And I'm going to send you to talk to a friend of mine. His name is Vadim, and he lives in Florida. He'll be able to help you with a lot of things. And in a few years, when you're ready, he'll probably give you a job."

"Why are you being so nice? Why not just call the cops? Or whoever else you said you'd call."

Kent sighed. "Because, and you know it, we can't prove it was you. There's no real-world tie. Nothing to trace."

The girl laughed. "I know, right? Fucking awesome."

"And because I think you have potential to be something more than a petty thief," Stephanie said.

The girl's laughter faded, and she looked at Stephanie warily. "You don't even know me."

"I know you have good taste in music," Stephanie said lightly and touched the laptop bag.

The girl's face fell. "That was my mom's. She left it behind when she ran off. It's all I have of hers. I don't even like Bangtastic Frogmen. I think they suck. Their songs make no sense and they sound like pissed-off cats in a bathtub."

"See? Excellent taste in music," Stephanie said. She leaned forward a little. "Let us help you, Destiny."

At last, the girl nodded. She still looked wary and defensive, but at least she was listening when Stephanie told her all about the Crew and what sorts of jobs they took. About Vadim, how he could help her and how Destiny could get herself to him.

"Think she'll actually go?" Kent asked as they watched the girl walk away from them without looking back. "She might take that train ticket and vanish."

"She'll go. I remember what it was like to find out I wasn't as weird as I'd thought I was," Stephanie told him.

Kent tugged her by the wrist until she was pressed

against him. "Are you about to reveal to me that you had a lifetime of crime before I met you?"

She laughed and kissed him. "No. I was a huge nerd. A real Goody Two-Shoes. I never even kissed a guy until I was in my early twenties."

"You got really good at it," he said against her mouth.

The kiss lingered, getting deeper. Breathless after a minute, she pulled away to look up at him and felt the creep of heat in her cheeks. "Kent…"

"Yes," he said. "It's real."

"I didn't even ask…"

He kissed her again. Then once more. His hands on her hips anchored her against him. His mouth moved from her lips to her throat to press against the pulse beating there.

"Yes," he said again. "It's real."

* * * * *

DARK FANTASY

Chapter 1

Jason Davis did not want to look inside the closet. Something disgusting was inside it—he could tell that already by the smell. The odor, a toxic mix of garbage and unwashed human body, was strong enough outside the closed door to make his eyes water.

"Think he's alive?" his partner asked. Reg Bamford had drawn his gun, ready at Jase's back.

"Hope so, or else this case just escalated." In the past month they'd been covering a spate of freakish attacks and injuries that seemed to be related, but none yet had resulted in a death. Jase pulled his knife, ready for whatever happened.

Reg shot him a grin. "On three?"

"I don't think we need to kick it down, Reg. Maybe just open it slowly." Jase gave his partner a raised eyebrow, knowing how much Reg wanted to go in full force.

"Fine." Reg didn't holster his gun. He gave Jase a nod. "Go."

"Hey, buddy?" Jase eased open the closet door, bracing himself for the stink. Shit, it was bad. Worse even than he'd anticipated. He put up a hand to cover his mouth and nose. "Hey, guy. You in here?"

Nothing.

Reg moved a step closer. "Careful, Jase. He could—"

Something launched itself out of the closet. Hulking, reeking, arms flailing. Fortunately, it wasn't very strong, and a double one-two attack from Jase and Reg got it on the ground with Reg's gun pressed to the back of its head.

"Please," the thing said. "Please, don't hurt me any more."

Chapter 2

He'd stalked her for days. Weeks. Watching her through the windows. Following her to the bus and then to the train, where he sat several seats behind her and counted the number of pages she read in the book she carried with her everywhere. He wanted to touch her hair.

He wanted to cut off her hair and keep it in his pocket, where he could touch it whenever he wanted.

But when he came up behind her and tried to touch her, the woman turned. Fists clenched. Teeth bared. She fought him, hard, in a way none of the others ever had, and he found himself on the ground with a mouthful of blood before he knew what had happened.

Chelle Monroe paused, her fingers lightly resting on the computer keyboard. This book wanted to be dark and fierce, edging toward the gory side. The problem was, she hadn't started out to write a serial-killer novel. She wanted to write a romance.

Shit.

There was a satisfaction in writing this, though. The guy at the bus stop *had* been a creep. She didn't think he wanted to keep her hair in his pocket, but you never knew.

It figured the only male attention she'd had in the past few months had been from some wild-eyed dude who'd thought flirting meant standing too close and breathing on her neck while she waited to catch a ride to the bookstore. Or in the form of the random dick pics she got every so often in her inbox, though she hadn't updated her profile on the LuvFinder site in forever. Dating had started to seem like so much freaking...work.

Yet here she was, trying to write a romance novel, and why, when her heart seemed more inclined to come up with stories about serial killers or creepy clowns or natural disasters? She had bunches of those stored away in her files, unfinished, as all the other pieces were at this point. It had been a long time since she'd gone on a date but longer since she'd actually finished writing something she felt was good enough to submit to a publisher. Grant would've pushed her, probably until she got annoyed, to stop screwing around and just finish something already. But Grant had left her behind a long time ago.

"C'mon, Chelle, get to it," she said aloud, working her fingers open and closed before settling them back on the keyboard. "Write the damned book."

With a sigh, she opened a fresh GOLEM file. The usual prompts came up—character, plot, research. There were places for her to add photos for inspiration. A word-count calculator. The program had been designed to make plotting and brainstorming a story as easy as possible. The only thing it couldn't do was actually write the damned book for her.

She tried again, typing a few words, but they came out sounding like a really awful late-1980s soft-core porn movie. She erased them. Tried again. Nothing.

The problem could be that she'd been suffering a distinct lack of romance in her own life for the past couple years and, in fact, had probably stopped believing in it. At least the hearts-and-flowers kind of romance you were supposed to read about in novels. Nope, for Chelle, love had come with a lot of baggage. She knew she wasn't alone in that, obviously. The world didn't go around without a whole lot of heartbreak along the way. It made writing about falling in love difficult, though.

Then again, she didn't believe in monsters or aliens, and she'd written horror and science-fiction stories that had gotten critical acclaim, if not a lot of money. Romance shouldn't be so hard, right? At least at the end you could be guaranteed a happy-ever-after, and that was something to aim for. Bringing a little joy into the world, even if it lasted only as long as it took to read four hundred pages or so.

It took staring at the blank computer screen for five solid minutes without typing a word before she gave up and opened the Works in Progress folder where she'd been keeping all her false starts. She'd tried a murder mystery, a comedy of errors, an experimental novel written entirely in iambic pentameter—that one she was proud of, actually. She'd made it to five whole pages before giving up on it. Not because the idea sucked, but because honestly, who the hell would sit through an entire novel written in iambic pentameter?

Chelle sighed, then clicked out of the folder and

toodled around a bit online, but it was a lost cause and after a few minutes of being sucked into reading click-bait articles, she thought maybe the future lay in writing deliberately misleading headlines attached to lists that tried hard and usually failed to be clever. Oh, and stock photos, she thought. You had to have a sort-of-appropriate stock picture to go along with the list.

"C'mon," she said aloud again. "You got this. You can do it. You've done it before—you can do it again."

Except what if she couldn't?

With a frown, Chelle put her computer to sleep and pushed away from her desk. She wanted chocolate but would settle for a seltzer water and some grapes. She'd been spending more time in her chair than running, and it was going to show up on her ass if she wasn't careful.

Come to think of it, a good run might clear her head, inspire her and tire her out enough to get a good night's sleep. She changed into her running gear, grabbed her tiny iPod that strapped to her arm and tucked a twenty in her pocket. She'd head for the coffee shop, and if the universe meant for her to have a cinnamon bun, there'd be one left just before they closed. Usually Derek gave her a discount if she was the last customer of the night, but it had been a few weeks since she'd made one of these late-night trips. The weather had been too bad for running.

Outside now, though, Chelle breathed in the faint scent of spring. Snow and ice still collected in piles from the hard winter, but the steady sound of drip-ping off every roof proved the weather was warming. She couldn't wait, frankly. Winter in Delaware, with its early darkness and chill temperatures, always took something out of her soul. She and Grant had often talked about moving permanently to where it was warmer, but he'd gone off to Arizona alone.

Veering to the left as she exited her quiet neighborhood, all the houses mostly dark even though it wasn't yet nine o'clock because this was the off-season, she ran for a half mile along the highway. In the summer, traffic on this road would make it impossible to run along here, so she usually ran along the beach instead. But then there wouldn't be coffee and a cinnamon bun as a reward, only the chilly ocean spray and sand in her socks.

She hadn't always liked running. It had been Grant's thing first. He spent so much time in front of the computer that he'd made it a point to take up a hobby that would keep him fit. He'd never pressured her to join him—that wasn't his style. She'd merely found herself picking up the habit because it meant spending more time with him. When their relationship had unraveled, she'd kept up running, not because it was any sort of tie to him, but because she'd ended up craving the mindless rush of pushing herself to the point where all she could think about was one foot in front of the other.

Her sneakers slapped the pavement. She dodged a puddle. She ducked into one of the side streets to take a turn around another neighborhood, this one almost completely dark, as well. She pushed herself a little harder to make the turn through the cul-de-sac. She still wanted to get to the coffee shop before it closed.

The bike came up out of nowhere, no lights, not even a glimmer from a reflector. Chelle screamed, breathless, and dodged, but the bike clipped her on the hip and sent her tumbling forward. She landed on her hands and knees, her running tights torn and her palms a stinging mess of scrapes.

The guy on the bike ended up in a tangle of limbs and spinning wheels. He let out a string of curses, all directed at her, including an incredibly offensive insult about her gender. And her weight. And her ancestry.

Chelle got to her feet, feeling for anything broken. She was going to ache later, for sure, but nothing seemed out of place. "Are you all right?"

"Watch where the fuck you're going!"

"You were riding on the wrong side of the street," she said and weathered the next barrage of insults before saying, "and I'm wearing a reflective vest!"

"Fucking moron," the guy said as he got up and lifted his bike. "You'd better hope nothing's wrong with my bike. I should get your name and number, make you pay for it."

"Sure, let's do that. Let's trade information," Chelle shot back. "I'll send you the doctor bill."

That shut him up anyway. Still muttering curses, he got back on his bike and rode it toward one of the condos at the end of the block, where he went inside. Chelle had paused to catch her breath and make sure she was really okay before she started running again, this time at a much slower pace. She was closer to the coffee shop than to home by this point, or she'd have turned around.

By the time she got to Waves, she was really hurting. Both knees, both palms, something in the small of her back. She limped into the coffee shop five minutes before closing, already apologizing.

"What the hell happened to you?" It was a surprise to see Bess there, since as the owner, she didn't often take the closing shifts. The older woman, brow furrowed, came around the counter to pull out a chair for Chelle. "Sit. Wow. Are you okay?"

"Some jerk hit me with his bike." Chelle winced as she sat. "Then tried to say it was my fault!"

Bess shook her head. "Wow. Thank God it wasn't a car."

"I think he was drunk," Chelle said. "He smelled like it anyway."

"Let me grab you a coffee. You want something else? I have some scones left. A piece of coffee cake." Bess frowned again, looking her over. "How about some ice packs?"

"Yeah. That would be great." Chelle pulled apart the torn edges of her running tights to look at the damage. No blood, but she'd bruise plenty.

Bess brought her a hot mocha latte and a plate of coffee cake, as well as two ice packs from the back. She sat at the table across from Chelle with her own mug of coffee. She asked for a few more details about the crash, though Chelle didn't have many.

"I couldn't tell if he was a local or a renter," Chelle said. "It's early in the season, but I don't want to think someone local would be such an asshole."

Bess nodded. "Yeah. That sucks. I'm sorry. Hey, can we give you a ride home? Eddie's going to be here soon to take me. You shouldn't try to run back."

"Oh. Yeah. That would be great, thanks." Chelle had met Bess's husband a few times. He owned Sugarland, the Bethany Beach fudge shop downtown. She tested out her legs, one at a time. Both hurt.

Bess excused herself to finish closing up while Chelle finished her drink and the coffee cake. Eddie came through the door with a greeting for his wife, stopping to double-take at the sight of Chelle. Bess explained the situation.

"Are you going to file a report or anything?" he asked, concerned.

Chelle shook her head and got to her feet. Everything still worked, but she was definitely grateful for the ride home. "Nah. I'm all right. Anyway, he'll get what's coming to him, I'm sure."

"Let's hope so," Eddie said.

Chapter 3

"He said it was King Kong." Reg craned his neck for a moment to look into the next room at the victim. "Big fucking gorilla."

Three days ago, Stan George had allegedly been attacked in his own living room. That he'd suffered some kind of attack wasn't in question, although the manner of it was suspicious. Not that everything they ever dealt with wasn't in some way weird. That was their job, after all.

Jase looked at the notes in front of him. Reg had done the interviewing while Jase checked out the rest of the house for signs of forced entry. None. Signs of paranormal activity. None of the usual. It was the same as the other four cases they'd been investigating, some dating back about six months without a clue as to what had caused them.

"Guy was online, surfing for…appliances?" Jase looked up. "So, porn."

Reg laughed low, dark eyes sparkling. "That's what the browser history shows, yeah. But then, whose wouldn't."

"So he's online, surfing for wank material. King Kong comes in, tosses the laptop, wrecks the room, beats the guy up." Jase shook his head. "How'd Vadim find out about this guy?"

Vadim, Jase and Reg's boss in the Crew, had a network of people around the world dedicated to reporting in on the strange and fantastic. Sightings of strange creatures, hauntings, that sort of thing. Jase didn't usually ask how Vadim found out about the cases; he went where the boss told him to go and did what the boss told him to do. In the last case, they hadn't even known there'd be a guy in the closet until they got to the house. They'd been called in to investigate what someone had claimed were flying monkeys. So far, they hadn't found any evidence of winged apes, but now here was this guy talking about a giant gorilla.

"I'm seeing a simian similarity," Jase said.

Reg laughed. From the other room came the sound of angry shouting at the television. "Dude's got anger problems," Reg said in a low voice.

Jase leaned back in his chair to take a peek into the living room, then looked back to his partner. "He filed a police report? Or did it come from the hospital?"

"We've got one of the EMTs with us," Reg explained. "He's the one who called it in. Said the guy's injuries weren't that severe but that he kept ranting about King Kong."

"Think the cases are related?"

Weird things often were.

"Let me go talk to this guy. You look around, see if you can find anything we can use." Jase went into the living room, where the guy had propped his casted ankle on a footstool. He was nursing a glass of what appeared to be a very fine whiskey, though he hadn't offered Jase or Reg so much as a shitty light beer.

Jase helped himself from the decanter.

"Hey…"

"So, did the big monkey do that to you?" Jase gestured with the glass toward the guy's ankle.

His name was Stan, Jase recalled. Stan scowled.

"Nah, that happened because some dumb bitch ran into me while I was on my bike."

Jase sipped. Not as fine a whiskey as he'd thought, actually. The guy had money, that was obvious, but his taste left a lot to be desired. He put the glass back on the table.

"So tell me again when King Kong decided to show up."

"I know you think I'm making this up," Stan said. "So fuck off and leave me alone."

"You sure the booze didn't have anything to do with this?"

For a moment, Stan looked guilty. Then angry again. "A giant fucking ape came into my fucking house and fucked me up—you think I just imagined it?"

Jase did not, in fact, think the guy was making it up. He did, however, think Stan George was an asshole. "So, this woman ran into you while you were on your bike. She was in a car?"

"No, man, she was just jogging along!"

Jase paused. "So really, you ran into her."

"No! She was… It was dark. She was…" Stan scowled again. "Look, I gave that other guy this whole story already. I know it sounds crazy. But it's the truth."

"Jase," Reg said from the doorway. "C'mere."

"Let yourselves out," Stan called after Jase as he left. "Close the door behind you."

On the front porch, Reg showed Jase the last glittering remnants of something glowing beneath the black-light wand Reg had been using. It disappeared as they watched. Reg shrugged and slipped the wand back into his bag as the glow faded. "Same as the other case."

"Not ectoplasm."

"No. I don't know what it is. Lots of stuff glows under the black light," Reg said with another shrug. "But it stays glowing—it doesn't fade away."

"Did you send it to the team?" Jase ran a finger along the wooden porch railing, expecting to feel something. Sticky, gooey. Something gross. All he felt was softly splintered wood.

"Yeah, I took some videos and a few pictures. So far, nothing. Eggy and Burt are working on it, but Eggy said she'd never seen anything like it, either. And if Eggy hasn't seen it—"

Jase nodded. "Yeah, it's not in the database."

"So it's something new," Reg added. He grinned. "Great!"

Jase laughed at his partner's enthusiasm and clapped him on the shoulder. "Yeah. Great. Let's go grab a drink and something to eat. Did you get any info on the woman he says ran into him?"

In the car, Reg read off what Stan had told him. "Says she was about five-six, dark hair, he didn't know her. Referred to her as 'dumb bitch' several times."

Jase put the Challenger in gear and pulled out of the cul-de-sac, heading for the Cottage Cafe. It was one of the only places open in the off-season down here at this time of night, unless they wanted to head into Ocean City. Since they were staying in one of the

Crew's condos in North Bethany, he didn't want to make the twenty-minute trip in the opposite direction.

"Yeah, he's a real winner. Any police reports? Anything from the EMT about a woman with matching injuries?"

"Nope. If she got hurt, she hasn't sought treatment. From how it sounds, though, that asshole really bowled her over." Reg tucked his notebook away. "Maybe he'll get another visit from an angry giant gorilla, teach him a lesson about riding drunk. He lost his license, you know. That's why he was on his bike in the first place. Asshole. But I still haven't figured out the tie between him and the guy in the closet, or any of the other cases reported in the past six months. Other than they both seemed kind of like dicks who deserved to get the crap beat out of them by imaginary monkeys."

"Arguably," Jase said, "nobody really deserves that."

"No," Reg answered with another grin. "Some people deserve worse."

At the Cottage Cafe, they grabbed seats at the bar, ordered a couple drinks. Talked about the latest case a bit, though there wasn't much to say about it, since nobody from the home office had gotten back to them with any idea what the glowing stuff was. Reg ordered some wings and rings, and Jase got a burger to go.

"They have great burgers," said the woman to his left at the bar. She hadn't taken a seat but stood waiting for her own take-out order. "I should've ordered one of those instead of a salad."

"It's never too late," Jase said, taking in the fall of her dark hair and a flash of greenish-blue eyes. She had a great smile, though it was hard to tell what the rest of her looked like under the baggy sweatshirt and matching sweatpants.

Her smile widened. "You know what? You're right. Hey, Mitch. I'll also take a Cottage burger to go. Fries and slaw."

"Much better than a salad," Jase said as he grabbed his to-go bag and started to follow Reg out of the bar.

"Yeah, thanks!" She gave him a little wave.

Jase gave her one more look over his shoulder as he went out the front doors. Yeah, she was checking him out. For a moment, he considered heading back in to chat her up, but then Reg said something to catch his attention. When he looked back again, she'd turned away. Opportunity lost.

Not that he had time for it anyway, Jase told himself as he headed out to the car. Not while working a case. And in a month or so, less if he and Reg got themselves together and figured it all out, he'd be gone anyway.

Still, he looked back again before driving away, hoping maybe she'd be coming through the front doors, but all he saw was glass.

Chapter 4

Chelle woke from a dream about Grant, her heart pounding. Breath catching. She'd made a tangled mess of the sheets. Sticky with sweat, she pushed the blankets off and swung her legs over the edge of the bed. For a moment, the world tilted, and she closed her eyes, although the room was so dark it didn't matter if she had them open or not.

She was sure she'd stumble on her way to the kitchen. End up on her knees, still stinging from her run-in with the bike. She made it into the kitchen without turning on a light, so when she opened the fridge to pull out the jug of filtered water, the brightness made her wince and shield her eyes. She poured a glass and sipped at it, hoping to settle her stomach.

She hadn't dreamed of Grant in months, though she still thought of him almost every day. Almost. It was an accomplishment, she thought as she leaned against the counter in her dark kitchen and let the night soothe her. Making it to almost. In the beginning, she'd thought of him every second. Then minute. After a time, she'd managed to break it down to hour by hour, then day by day.

One day, she would not think of him at all; the thought of this broke her more than anything ever had and was what made her stumble more than any walk in the dark ever could. The glass slipped from her hand into the sink, where, fortunately, it did not shatter the way her heart had already done, over and over again.

Too many times she'd allowed herself to succumb to this sort of grief, but it had been a long enough time since the last that she was no longer used to how fiercely it could sting. There were choices to be made here. She could give in to it, let the sorrow sweep her away like the undertow in a storm-tossed ocean. Or she could force away the pain and refuse to let it drown her.

She could write.

Of course, this reminded her of Grant, too. After all, he'd been the one to code and design the GOLEM writing program, just for her. He'd never made more than the single copy locked into her laptop, and which she'd discovered only a short time ago while cleaning out some old folders. His big plans of making money hand over fist had never been realized. He'd gone to Arizona without her or the program. There'd been many times when she thought of erasing GOLEM—which stood for Genre Originating Laptop Entertainment Machine and had nothing to do with the famous *Lord of the Rings* character. Although she did think of her laptop as "the precious" sometimes, Chelle thought as she slipped into the chair at her kitchen table and opened the computer lid.

Her fingers rested on the keys as she closed her eyes,

letting her mind open up to the possibilities of new words. A story. A…man?

A face flashed through her mind. The guy from the bar. He'd been pretty cute. He'd do, for inspiration.

She opened a GOLEM file.

She started typing.

The man in front of her kneels, head bowed, to accept the garland of flowers his regent is placing around his neck. Roses in shades of ivory and crimson, her colors. She has sometimes wished to dress in gold and violet, in shades of night or summer sky, but no. She wears red and white, because that is what is expected of her.

The scout has been gone for some long turnings; that's what is expected of him. To go away and then come back. They both have their places in this world. He has returned to her with the treasures of a far-off planet, precious metals and gems to fill her coffers.

More important, he has brought her himself.

"Lady," he says and looks up at her with a longing that should not be there in his eyes.

It's not appropriate. Forbidden, in fact. She is meant for another. The fate of their two empires rests upon the union, upon the children who will issue forth to bind the warring regencies. Her wedding to Darten is set for only two turnings from now. She will wear red and white.

It's expected of her.

She cannot think of that now. Not with her scout on his knees in front of her with that look on his face and the soft touch of her fingers on his bristled cheeks. She needs to stop touching him, now, before all she can manage to do is keep touching him. She allows herself one last brush against his face before she sits back in her chair.

"You've done well," she says. "What price have you set as your reward?"

He's entitled to a portion of what he brings her. That is custom. What he asks of her, though, is not.

"A night with you."

A collective gasp reverberates through the greeting room. Anadais, the regent's companion, steps forward with her sword drawn. The scout has done more than overstep.

"You've insulted the regent," Anadais says in her clear, calm voice. "Punishment commencing."

The scout does not move. He has no weapon to draw—nobody can enter the greeting room armed. Still, he could rise and go hand to hand with Anadais, who will surely still slaughter him easily. But he does not move, does not flinch.

He looks into his regent's eyes.

"Wait!" She stands, hand raised.

Another gasp circles the room. She dares not look to see the source of the tittering, the sly glances of her ladies and lords. Those who would see her tumbled from power. She doesn't want to see the sympathetic looks, either, from those few who do not agree with her binding to Darten.

Anadais does not wait. Her sword already raised, it is on its downward slice, primed to take the scout's head from his shoulders. At the regent's shout, the companion barely falters. She would've amputated the regent's arm if the scout had not thrust himself between them and rolled with her onto the dais.

There is no gasp this time. No behind-the-teeth laughter. Silence, thick and severe, covers them all.

"You have touched the regent," Anadais says in that same calm voice. She raises her sword again.

"No!"

The weight of her ceremonial gown makes it almost impossible for her to get up on her own, so the regent doesn't struggle, doesn't make a fool of herself. She holds up a hand for Anadais to take, and the companion lifts her to her feet as easily as if the regent were made of air. The scout gets up, too.

"Regent, he must pay for the insult he's made upon your person."

The regent smooths the front of her gown. "Should I not decide what the insult is, and if he's made one?"

A rippling murmur travels the room. She looks out to her audience, but none will meet her gaze. She knows the rumors, the stories about her, the opinions that she is too headstrong for the role into which she was born.

"There are those in this room who have spoken of removing me from my place," the regent says aloud. "I would think that far more of an insult to my person than anything this scout could ask. This man has brought more wealth to this regency than any other scout. His price is not too high."

The regent lifts her chin, daring anyone to speak out. None will, of course. Not to her face, not here. As regent she has ultimate power. There will be whispers, rumors. Her advisors will meet and tut. She supposes she could be taken to task by her future spouse's representatives. Perhaps there will be repercussions. Maybe the war that has been threatening since her father's time will at last become reality, and she will be written in the histories as the most foolish regent to ever lead. She will risk it, she thinks as the scout takes her gloved hand. She will risk it all, for the chance to spend a night with him.

Chapter 5

The rush of a breeze swept past Jase's face and he rolled instinctively, then landed on the balls of his feet beside the bed, already pulling his knife.

There was nothing there.

He touched the back of his neck and felt the sting there. His fingers came away sticky. Blood? But he'd been on his back, sleeping, though in the dream he'd been on his knees with a blade pressed to his skin.

And then...other things.

"You okay?" Reg asked from the doorway.

Jase stood. "Yeah. Weird freaking dream, though. I was some kind of..."

Not a knight. Something else. An explorer or something like that. There'd been a journey of some kind, he'd felt that. He'd gotten into trouble, though the reasons for it were fading, hazy, back into dreamland. There'd been a woman with beautiful, sad eyes. He'd wanted to serve her. He'd have given his life for her.

That *had* to be a dream, because so far in his whole life, Jase had never met a woman who'd made him feel that way. The feeling lingered even now, that sensation of wanting to protect someone so much he'd have done anything to keep her safe. Sure, he'd worked cases where he had to keep people safe, but nothing like he'd just dreamed. Nothing like…love.

He shook it off.

"Some kind of what?"

Jase shook his head. "I don't know. It was just a dream, man."

"Think someone was fucking with you in the Ephemeros?"

"Nah. Just a regular dream." Though there had been a familiar face in it. The woman from the bar. That could've been his mind shaping her, or maybe she'd simply been dreaming in the same space he'd been.

It didn't mean anything, really, other than maybe he'd left an impression on her, the way she had on him. He should've gone back, chatted her up…but then, what was the point? He'd learned the hard way that a one- or three- or six-night stand always ended up being more work than it was worth.

"You sure?" Reg gave him a curious look. "It must've been some dream. You hollered like you were being murdered."

Jase laughed, stretching his arms and legs, trying to feel if there was any other damage than the now-fading scratchy feeling at the back of his neck. "Just a dream. Sorry I woke you, man."

"Nah, I was already awake. I've been online, working some data. Got a few more leads on some interesting shit that's gone down around here, things that might help us. Bunch of weird sightings, stuff like that, but I just can't quite pinpoint a connection. There has to be one." Reg, with all his banter and fooling around, liked to play at being the stupid one of the pair, the muscle and not the brains. It wasn't really true. Reg, when he got hold of an idea, was apt to hold on to it until he figured out whatever puzzle needed solving.

"Any updates from home base?"

"Nah. Been feeding them data, but..." Reg shrugged. "It could take a while, you know? I'm heading to bed now, though, unless you need me to tuck you back in. Maybe sing you a lullaby?"

Reg shot him a cocky grin, then laughed at the double bird Jase flipped him. "Yeah, yeah, whatever. See you in the morning."

Reg closed the door behind him, and Jase got back into bed. He couldn't fall back to sleep, though. He was suddenly hard as a rock, with no real reason other than it had been kind of a dry spell over the past few months. He tried to ignore it but should've known better. He hadn't been able to pretend away a hard-on since sometime in early junior high. He could wait it out or take care of it, and waiting it out wasn't going to get him back to sleep any faster.

Sliding a hand inside his boxers, he took his cock in his fist. Slow, up and down, he stroked. Lifting his hips, he tugged off the boxers and kicked back the covers. He'd left the window open a bit so he could hear the ocean, and he used the steady rush of the waves to time his strokes. Slick precome leaked, smoothing his grip. He thrust a little, closing his eyes.

Pleasure built, rising until it consumed him. Nothing much to it other than the steady throb of desire tightening in his balls. There'd been times in the past when Jase had edged himself to draw out ecstasy, but tonight he was intent on filling a need, nothing more. Faster, gripping for a second behind the head, then palming it. Fuck, it felt good.

Yet also, somehow, empty.

His grip faltered, until he heard the whisper of a feminine voice in his ear. The soft scent of perfume. The touch of a woman replaced his.

He went with it.

She's had lovers, of course. Mostly courtesans, paid to give her pleasure in the absence of a partner. The regent knows well how to please a man—but she also knows exactly how she likes to be pleased.

"You risked much to be here." She raises her glass of wine. They both drink.

The scout puts his glass aside and takes her in his arms. The suddenness of the embrace causes her to spill sweet red liquid down the front of her, but she doesn't care if her gown is ruined. Not when his lips are on her skin, licking away the crimson fluid.

"Lady, I have loved you since the moment I entered your service," the scout says against her throat. "You're worth every risk."

Her fingers thread through his hair, and she tugs until he looks into her eyes. "You entered my service when you were fourteen and I was ten. Surely you don't mean to say you've—"

"I have. Every second of my apprenticeship and every moment after that. I've loved you." The scout does not smile or make light with his words, though she wants to laugh and push him away.

She doesn't want to believe him. If she does, it might kill her. She's pledged to another, after all.

"Every raid I've made, every world I've plundered,

every bit of treasure I have ever brought to you is a measure of my devotion." He has not yet kissed her mouth, but oh, how she longs for him there.

As she has always done, the regent thinks as she pushes her scout away and walks to the window to look outside at the night. Since she was old enough to understand desire, she has wanted this man. Never admitting it, never allowing herself to believe he could be hers. Because of course he cannot be.

At least not for longer than this single night. Turning, she loosens the ties at the front of her gown and allows it to fall away. Naked, she draws in a breath, lifting her chin, refusing to let herself look away from his face.

"You are beautiful," her scout says, and in that moment, the regent has no doubt that she is.

He's across the room in the time it takes for her to breathe in and out. Then at last he is kissing her, mouth on mouth. Her gasp draws him into her. His tongue strokes hers.

The marble windowsill is cool on her bare skin as he pushes her back to sit, her thighs parted. He kneels between them. With a reverent sound of worship, her scout kisses her again. Not her mouth this time. The pleasure of it, the heat and warmth of his lips against her most private flesh, tips her head back so the fall of her hair tickles her back.

His mouth moves on her. Tongue stroking. Lips tugging the tender pearl of her body, until she cannot stop herself from crying out. When his fingers slide inside her, stretching, she is sent shuddering over the edge.

Without time for the pleasure to fade, her scout stands. He's pulled himself free of his trousers and is inside her, so deep the sweet sting of his entry sends another shiver of pleasure through her. Her body clutches him; he groans, thrusting, lifting her legs to wrap around his lean hips.

He kisses her again, harder this time. There's the tangy taste of blood on her tongue, and she loves it, she loves him, she is toppling again into the maelstrom of desire. No holding back.

They might have only this one night, this one time, but it will have to be enough to last for the rest of her life.

Sweet feminine flavor flooded Jase's tongue. He groaned aloud, blinking into the darkness as his orgasm rushed through him. He came so hard he bit his tongue, tasting blood. Shuddering, he let his stroking hand slow until, panting, he let it rest on the sticky heat puddling on his belly.

"Fuck," he whispered aloud. "What the…"

Still blinking, he shook himself and pushed up on one elbow. He'd been back in the dream, only this time, he'd been awake, he was sure of it. He'd been between her legs, lapping her sweetness, making her come. Even now, the memory made his cock twitch, though he was nowhere near capable of getting hard again, not after that explosion.

Something glittered in the air around him.

He sat up so fast his head spun. The edges of his vision sparkled, sort of like if he'd pressed his thumbs to his closed eyelids. Only, this faded and renewed when he tried to focus. Jase hopped out of bed, grabbing a stray T-shirt and swiping at his belly as he did. His black-light wand was in his bag, and he fumbled for it as the glittering lights faded again.

He flashed it around the room and let out a long, slow breath of wonder. The entire room lit up like the night sky. The glow faded even as he watched, leaving behind a few traces here and there, identical to what he and Reg had found on the gorilla guy's front porch.

Shit.

Whatever had happened to those other guys had just happened to him.

Chapter 6

With a short, sharp breath, Chelle lifted her fingers from the keys. Blinking, she sipped in another breath, this one slower. Every part of her still pulsed from the pleasure that had rocked through her while she wrote.

Whoa.

It usually felt good to write…but it had never felt *that* good. Yes, she'd been turned on in the past by something she'd written, but never to the point of an actual orgasm. Chelle sat back in her chair. The first hint of sunlight had started pinking the window over her kitchen sink. She'd been writing for hours. Pages of words…not a full story, but definitely the good start to one, she thought with a rueful shake of her head. Way better than that stupid one about the giant gorilla.

Making sure to save her file, Chelle stared at her computer screen for a few more seconds. GOLEM was more than a word processing program. Grant had designed it as a true writer's dream. She took the time to type a few notes for future plot points. Then she saved again and closed her laptop.

On still-trembling legs, she went to the sink to get herself another glass of water. This one she gulped down, refilled and drank again. She should've been exhausted, but every nerve still jangled. She'd never get to sleep.

Still, she had to try. Not having a day job to go to had to be good for something, even if it meant working all night and sleeping until noon. She took a hot shower first, letting the water beat away some of the stress and tension she still carried with her from being hit by the bike and from the hours she'd spent hunched over the computer.

Cupping her breasts, she let her thumbs pass over her still-sensitive nipples. They tightened at once, and there was an answering pull of arousal between her legs. Chelle laughed a little and tipped her face into the shower's spray, taking in a mouthful of water she spit out in a stream in an attempt at getting her mind off the slickness in her pussy.

She'd had an orgasm while writing.

She wanted to have another one now.

She was no stranger to self-pleasure—that was part of not having a lover, taking care of her own needs. Lately it had seemed her self-gratification had become fairly utilitarian, though. Fast, steady, she got off within minutes as a way to ease the buildup of arousal, though she hadn't found herself particularly turned on. When you were bored fucking yourself, she thought as she turned to let the hot water pound her back, that was bad.

She was turned on now, though. The story. It had filled her head as if she were watching a movie. She'd been immersed. The words, flowing the way her blood pumped now, swift and fierce.

Chelle let out a small groan as she slipped a hand between her legs to stroke her clit. Despite the water from the showerhead, she still found herself so wet that her fingers slipped easily against her folds. Then inside. One, then two. She put her other hand on the shower wall to keep herself steady as she fucked into herself, slowly. Her thumb pressed her clit.

God, it felt good.

How long had it been since she'd really felt this way? Months? Shit, had it been years?

Nipples tight, pussy clenching, breath coming fast. Her belly muscles leaped and jumped as her hips pumped forward. She circled her clit, then tweaked it. Her entire body convulsed with the first twinges of pleasure, building, unbelievable and delightful and yet also somehow desperate.

Her mind filled with the images from the story. The stoic regent, yearning for the touch of the man she loved. The steadfast and inappropriate lover who risked everything for a night with her.

She thought of the man she'd seen in the bar, the one whose face she'd appropriated for her hero. With another small groan, Chelle tried to turn her thoughts to someone else. A celebrity, a mishmash of features, something, anything but that real man who had turned back to look at her. It was useless. Her body had already started the inevitable journey to climax, and she couldn't hold it back any more than she could've stood up against a tsunami.

She gave in, letting the pleasure take her. So good, so fucking good, maybe even better because of that twisted twinge of guilt. Her fingers slipped on the wet tile as she pressed her forehead to the wall. Her body shook, racked with desire. Her pussy throbbed against her fingers and she gave her clit another slow circling tweak before cupping herself.

The water was starting to get cold, but Chelle stayed under the spray for another minute or so, relishing the chilly sting on her overheated skin. When she started shivering, she turned off the water and got out, toweling off and wrapping the towel around her hair to walk naked from the bathroom into her bedroom, where she fell down onto the bed and spread out her arms and legs to stare up at the ceiling fan taking its slow and inevitable journey round and round. Hypnotic.

She let it seduce her into sleep, which was jumbled and fraught with strange dreams, but when she woke, the sun hadn't yet angled into afternoon, and she was ravenous. Over a sandwich and iced tea, she typed some more notes into GOLEM. Nothing seemed as if it would spill into a full-length novel, but she thought she had the kernel for a few short stories, maybe.

On her front deck, she stretched out in the sunshine and let herself drift for a bit. Part of the creative process was refilling the well. Downtime. Grant had teased her that most people couldn't write off napping or daydreaming as part of their job, but he'd never been the sort to take a break. Grant had two speeds: on and off.

She didn't want to think about Grant now. It never led to anyplace good. She supposed one day she'd be able to just put all the memories of him aside, or at least face them with more dignity, but for now, it required a lot of wrestling with herself not to dissolve into grief at the thought of him.

So, she put it away.

She scribbled a few more notes, mostly junk, then

went inside to grab her phone. She dialed her best friend, Angie. "Hey, you. What's up?"

"Ugh. Just finishing up this stupid database. What's going on?"

"Trying to write."

Angie was silent for a second. "How's it going?"

"Bad." Chelle laughed. "Not sure what made me think I could do this."

"You can do it. You've been writing stories since you could write. You'll get it. Anything from the editor?"

They talked for a while about work, family, television, shoes, gossip about a couple former classmates. Best-friend talk. It ended with an agreement to meet for drinks and dinner.

"I need this like you wouldn't believe," Angie said. "I want to make out with some random cute guy and just…ugh."

"Ugh, indeed," Chelle said with a laugh, already looking in her wardrobe. "It's the off-season. We'll be lucky to find a cute guy."

"It's the big sports-show weekend. There will be guys there. Cute, I don't know about. That's what vodka's for!"

Chelle paused. "Oh Lord. That kind of night?"

"If you're lucky," her friend said. "I'll pay for the cab, too. Don't argue with me about it."

Chelle wasn't going to argue. There wasn't any use in it—her friend would simply refuse to take any cash. Besides, it all worked out in the end between picking up the tab for drinks or dinner or any of the other things they did together—they'd been friends for so long that neither of them was ever going to be up on the other.

She spent the rest of the afternoon cleaning her house and taking care of some errands. Another few hours…

yes, hours…getting ready for what was not promising to be a particularly "lucky" night out. She'd shaved her legs, after all. That was almost a guarantee that she wasn't going to hook up with someone.

Oh, the thought of it, though. A small shiver sent a tickling tremor up and down her spine when she remembered the new project she'd started. Her time in the shower. The guy from the bar… He'd been cute, Chelle admitted to herself as she pulled out dress after dress and put them all away before taking them out again. And if there was one cute guy around, she supposed there'd be more at Oceanside, especially, as Angie had said, since the sports show was going on in Ocean City.

The two of them hadn't gone out in forever, so it was more than past time, but damn if her wardrobe wasn't reflecting just how long it had been. Chelle held up a dress, finally, with a shake of her head. It would have to do.

"Pretty as a peach."

The voice, warm and sugary, nudged her ear and sent her a step toward the mirror. Eyes wide. Mouth open.

She turned, but of course there was nobody behind her. She was alone, the way she'd been since moving into this house, nobody to share this space. This bed. Her bedroom, all her own, decorated to her style and nobody else's.

Chelle closed her eyes for a moment, taking a long, deep breath. She'd imagined the voice. Grant's words, the compliment he'd always paid her. When she opened them, she lifted her chin and gave her reflection a long, hard look.

"You're going out tonight," she told herself. "You're going to have fun. And you're going to make out with a cute guy, if it kills you."

Chapter 7

"Why so...cereal?" Reg pointed at the bowl of frosted wheats in front of Jase.

Jase dug his spoon into the mess of milk and soggy mush. "Nice one."

"Seriously, man. You've been in a shitty mood all day." Reg pulled up one of the bar stools and gave Jase a long, steady look that wasn't going to be easy to ignore.

Jase shrugged, not wanting to admit that he'd had a... Well, shit. What had happened anyway? A weird kind of dream? An out-of-body experience? Whatever it had been, it might be tied to the rest of this case or it might not, but either way, it had happened to *him*, damn it, not some random asshole who probably deserved a little roughing up from an imaginary monkey. He didn't want to compare himself to guys like that, but the truth was, that weirdly fantastic dream and the aftershocks of glittering color had made him more than an investigator in this case. They had made him a victim.

Jase had not been a victim for a long damned time.

"The dream I had last night," he began and stopped.

Reg looked curious. "Yeah? What about it?"

"I don't think it was a dream. It was something else. Like a hallucination. But with physical results." Jase grimaced, remembering the exact nature of those results. He'd had to put the evidence in the laundry this morning.

"Like a giant gorilla beating on some douche bag?"

Jase nodded. "Yeah, but…"

"Not a gorilla," Reg said. "Please tell me you didn't have sex with a gorilla, dude. I mean, you've been with some ugly girls, but…"

Jase snorted. "Fuck you."

Reg crowed a little more about it, teasing him. That was his way, to make light of serious things. It was why they made such good partners. Jase took everything too seriously, Reg sometimes not enough.

"But seriously. It was like a sex…thing?"

"Yeah. But hard to describe. I mean, it was so real, but it wasn't." Jase shook his head. "Messed up, man."

"Too long between lays?" Reg offered, not even joking. "And you're sure it wasn't something in the Ephemeros? Dreams can feel really real."

"It wasn't. And there was all that glittery sort of…"

"Spooge," offered Reg.

Jase grimaced again. "Gross."

"So, we're definitely dealing with something related to the other cases. Spiritual, maybe? It's not ectoplasm. Something like it, maybe."

Jase got up to put his dishes in the dishwasher, then leaned on the counter. "No. But it felt like something close to that. Like…while it was going on, I couldn't have told you for sure it wasn't real, but when I came out of it, I could remember everything that happened but almost like it happened to someone else. Like I'd been watching it in a movie. Or maybe...more like reading it in a book."

"I don't read books," Reg said.

Jase hadn't read a book in a long time, though not because he didn't like to. "When you read a really good one, you sort of get immersed in it. Like whatever's happening to the characters is happening to you. You're still aware that you're, say, sitting in your chair, but you're in it, whatever it is. That's what it was like."

"Freaky. Remind me not to read a book."

"Like playing a really great video game," Jase said.

Reg grinned. "Okay, now I got it. So I guess the question is, why you and not me? And can we make it happen again?"

"I don't want it to happen again," Jase said at once.

"Sounds like it was a good time..." Reg began, then stopped himself at Jase's look. "Okay, sorry. I get it."

He didn't, really. Jase wasn't sure he did, either. Except that he worked cases. He didn't want to become one. Jase never again wanted to experience something like what had happened that long-ago summer when he'd nearly lost his mind and his life.

Not ever.

Chapter 8

Okay, so finding a cute guy to make out with wasn't going to kill her, Chelle thought with a look around the crowded dance club. But it very well might break something. She sipped her vodka Collins so she didn't have to make conversation with the guy who'd been trying hard to catch her attention for the past five minutes.

"C'mon," Angie said and put her empty glass on the bar. She glanced over Chelle's shoulder at the would-be paramour. "No."

Chelle didn't dare look behind her to see his reaction, just set her glass down next to Angie's and let her friend pull her onto the dance floor. The music was thumping, the entire floor shaking, and for a weekend in the off-season, the place was full to overflowing.

"Sausage party," Angie shouted into Chelle's ear with a grin. "We're outnumbered four to one!"

Chelle, being rump-humped from behind by a guy

in a pink polo shirt, could only laugh. "May the odds be ever in your favor!"

Boy, were they ever. Angie's goal had been to make out with a random cute guy? Before another hour had passed, she'd successfully been smooched up on by three guys who appeared to be in a bachelor party. The fourth guy in their group, a little shorter, a little less drunk, though that was relative at this point in the night, hung back laughing. He caught Chelle's eye.

Before he could say anything, though, one of the other guys took a break from twirling Angie to duck close to them. "Hey. This is Steve. He hasn't been laid in a year."

With that introduction, he turned back around to leave an embarrassed-looking Steve to face Chelle, who covered a laugh with her hand. Steve coughed. Chelle smiled.

"Why haven't you been laid in a year?" Vodka asked that question, not her.

Steve leaned a little closer so she could hear him. "I've been…busy? I guess?"

"Don't worry," Chelle said as they both danced a little closer, letting the crowd push them. "I haven't been laid in longer than that."

He put his hands on her hips to keep her from being jostled too much. They moved together easily enough. He was a good dancer.

"How come?"

Chelle leaned in to let her lips brush the curve of his ear. Vodka again, and more than that. The music. The crowd. The idea that the man in front of her hadn't been in bed with someone else in a long time.

"I lost my boyfriend," came out of her mouth instead

of something sexy and carefree, something casual. The truth slipped out of her, followed immediately by regret.

Lost him. As if they'd gone to the park and he'd slipped his leash. Lost, as though he could ever be found.

Steve didn't seem fazed by her admission. He pulled her closer and nuzzled her cheek. He had nice hands, flat and warm on her hips, his fingers curling against her. "His loss."

Chelle wasn't drunk, but when he kissed her, she did feel unsteady and uncertain. He tasted of dollar beers. He kissed too hard, too fast, but softened when she tried to draw back. Over his shoulder, Chelle saw Angie deep in conversation with one of the guys from the bachelor party, not the bachelor himself. The best man, the one who'd told Chelle that Steve hadn't been laid in a year.

She was going to do this, Chelle thought with sudden determination. Make out with a cute random. Have fun. Dance.

Forget the past.

She kissed him this time, and it was better. He laughed when she pulled away. His glasses were a little askew. She straightened them.

"Buy me a drink," Chelle said.

He did. They kissed some more, in a dark corner with black light turning the flecks in his black T-shirt brilliant white. The kissing got better. Steve got handsy, and it felt good to be wanted. To be touched. Dirty, in the good way. The music played on. They danced.

Chelle did not want to go home with him. Home being a room in the hotel attached to the club, a room he was sharing with two other guys. Definitely not her own house, which would require a twenty-minute cab ride and then breakfast in the morning.

"They want us to eat hot dogs with them," Angie said, bright eyes, lipstick worn off, her hair tousled. "Girl, I can't eat any hot dogs at this hour."

"You want to go home?" They'd ducked into the bathroom together, leaving the "boys" behind. Chelle washed her hands and used a damp paper towel to blot away the sweat. She turned to her friend. "We can totally slip out the side. They'll never know. Did you give him your name? Your number?"

"I said my name was Amy, and hell no." Angie laughed. "I wanted to make out, not get married. Let's run. Oh... Don't... You want to go upstairs? Sorry, I should've asked."

Chelle stepped aside to let someone else use the sink. "No. I mean, he's nice and all, but I don't want to go with him."

Angie took her by the shoulders gently and looked closely at her face. "Honey, if you want to go upstairs and kiss up on Steve a little bit more, I'm good with that. I just didn't want you to feel..."

"No." Chelle shook her head, refusing to give in to melancholy. It was that time of night, when the buzz from the drinks and the kissing was wearing off. "Let's get out of here."

In the surge of people exiting the club, Chelle and Angie managed to duck away from Steve and his buddy, whose name Chelle still didn't know. She caught a glimpse of him, looking for her, and guilt prickled through her. Not so much that she turned back, though. All she wanted now was her bed.

In the parking lot, something ugly was happening. Too many drunks, not enough cabs. A fistfight. She and Angie held back.

"God, it's like a pack of zombies," Angie said as they

waved over a cab at last. "You should write that story, Chelle. Two friends go out dancing and get caught up in the end of the world."

"Sexy," Chelle said with a laugh as the cab pulled out of the parking lot.

At home, though, with a couple glasses of cold water in her but a still-unsettled stomach, she wasn't ready for bed yet. She didn't want to think too much about Steve or why she'd ended up passing up the chance for what might've been a few more hours of fun. It wasn't the idea of hooking up—she'd had a few one-nighters, a long time ago.

It had been the way he'd looked at her as the night wore on. Hungry, but something else, too. Something soft and hopeful, which was not what you were supposed to find in the gaze of the random cute guy you wanted to make out with in a dark corner. At least, that wasn't what Chelle had wanted to find.

She opened her laptop, thinking to browse her emails, but instead, she pulled up GOLEM and a fresh file.

Hungry, she typed. Steve had never been so hungry.

Chapter 9

"You have to be fucking kidding me!" Jase pulled his knife from the back of his belt as Reg unholstered his weapon. "That's not... Is it?"

Reg spat to the side. "Sure looks like it to me, man."

The thing in question was a rotting, stinking corpse in tattered clothes. Half its jaw swung, gaping, but it still managed to burble a gargling refrain of complaint. Jase would bitch, too, if he were the walking undead trapped under a Dumpster with a beady-eyed gull aiming to pluck out his tongue.

The call had come in from a couple of drunks who'd gone into the alley to fuck but who'd found this thing instead. Whoever scanned the 911 calls had been quick to alert Vadim, who'd sent them out on this. The cops apparently hadn't done anything about it, and who could blame them? Ocean City at four in the morning had enough other shit going on without responding to a call about a zombie in an alley.

"You want to kill it?" Reg asked. "Splat, punch that effer in the brain?"

Jase was well out of reach of the thing's clutching fingers. "Dude, you know this isn't a real zombie."

"It looks real enough that you could kill it," Reg said mildly. "And shit, it stinks bad enough that you should."

"It's like the flying monkeys, or King Kong," Jase said in a low voice, easing closer. God, the thing did reek. Puddles of goo leaked out of it, so freaking gross. And it wasn't as if he wanted to take a chance on it getting its teeth into him, even if virus zombies had never been proven to be real. The kind raised up from voodoo, yeah, but this guy on the ground was clearly the product of someone's movie imagination. "Shine the light."

Glowing sparkles everywhere. The entire alley lit up with them. Not phosphorescence, and nothing actually present.

"What the hell is going on?" Jase murmured, going to one knee to look the zombie in its desiccated face.

Reg spat to the side. "Just off it."

That would've been easy enough to do. Knife to the head. Would it fade away, the thing, or would it remain as proof of what had happened?

It snapped its teeth at him. Jase studied it. "Trying to find the link between this and the others."

Reg stood behind him. "Same glowing stuff under the black light. That's about it."

"Did it attack anyone?"

"No." Reg scuffed at the garbage spilling out of the Dumpster. "Looks like it wants to."

Another thing shambled around the corner. Identical to the first, but this one upright and moving. It let out one of those disgusting gargles and reached for Reg, who rolled with a shout to escape. Jase, stuck between the Dumpster, the zombie on the ground and this new arrival, ducked its lunge and ended up with his back to the metal.

The one on the ground sank its teeth into his boot; a quick kick thoroughly crunched its face into mush, but it kept going. The walker lunged at him again, and over its shoulder, Jase saw Reg draw.

"No!" he shouted.

Gunfire would attract attention. It would also splatter zombie gunk all over Jase, and he didn't want to get a face full of guts. Instead, he kicked the looming monster in the knees, one at a time, sending it tumbling forward as he rolled out of the way. The thunk of its head connecting with the metal Dumpster was the sound of a watermelon hitting pavement.

"Cool," Reg said.

Jase got to his feet, waiting to see if the thing was going to get up again, but it didn't stir. He waved a hand in front of his face. "God, that smell."

"The smell's kind of the same as that guy in the closet," Reg said conversationally, turning as a couple of drunks stumbled into the alley. "Hey. You. Get the fuck out of here!"

"You didn't need to pull your piece on them," Jase said. "What if they call the cops?"

Reg grinned, but before he could answer, two more zombies rose up from behind the Dumpster. These were faster. Stronger. They didn't fall apart at the first punch or kick. Still, it took only about a minute's effort from both Reg and Jase to send them into a heap with the others.

Barely panting, Reg gave Jase a look. "Okay, so... where are they coming from? Hole in the wall, like rats? What? Did you see them manifest or anything?"

"No." Jase nudged the pile with his foot. "And they're physical, for sure. I don't—"

Four more zombies rose up from the shadows, though it was impossible to tell if they'd manifested from the darkness or had been merely lying in silent wait all this time. Four against two was still odds Jase and Reg could handle, especially against rotten corpses unsteady on their feet. It took more effort this time, and Jase had to use his knife, but they downed all four of the things in a splash of goo.

"Okay, man," Reg said. "This is getting freaky."

Eight zombies.

No more conversation. He and Reg went into battle mode without words, without effort. They slipped as easily into the fight as if they were on the practice field. Fists and knives, still no guns because just around the corner, they could hear the laughter of a few more late-night revelers. The hint of a red-blue light drifted into the alley but faded along with the warning whoop of a police siren.

Sweating, Jase dropped the last zombie and stood over it, watching it writhe for a moment before it went still. Swiping at his face with a grimace of disgust at the goop and stench, he shot Reg a look. The other man was in a similar pose.

"The fuck," Reg said.

Jase shook his head. "Whatever's going on, it's got to be—"

Sixteen zombies. The alley swarmed with them, and they backed Jase and Reg against the Dumpster, ankle deep in dead, rotting flesh. They'd come from nowhere. Slavering, lunging, jaws snapping. A bite wasn't going to turn either of them into the risen dead, but it was going to hurt like hell and might still get infected.

Reg waded in, knife slashing. Jase was right beside him, both pushing, slicing, kicking, punching. Jase brought his knife down, then up. Gore spattered. The zombie in front of him fell apart.

They all fell apart.

They were all gone.

Reg looked at him. "Dude."

The only thing left in the alley was a swiftly fluttering bunch of trash on the ground and the gull, and that flew away with a startled squawk.

Chapter 10

She didn't have to be up at any certain time, but Chelle set her alarm anyway because if she didn't, she'd end up sleeping until ten or so, and then it felt as though she'd wasted too much of the day. Writing wasn't a nine-to-five job, of course. The good thing was that she could do it anytime she liked. It was just that she liked to get a start on her day like a normal person, not like some slug who didn't have the wherewithal to get out of bed.

Even if she *had* been up until four in the morning, she thought as she groaned and turned off the alarm. Maybe if she'd been working on something new and fantastic until that time, she'd have felt more justified about not getting up, but instead, she'd spent a lot of her time fiddling around with stuff she'd already written, cutting and pasting and revising, cobbling together bits and bobs of old things without really creating anything new. GOLEM was an awesome program, but it was also a huge time waster once you fell into the pit of character work sheets and plotting tools.

The zombie story had been promising, she thought as she considered a shower but couldn't quite rouse herself enough to get out of the warm blankets. If only because it had been so darned fun to write. A raging orgy of fluids and flying limbs. Basically the same thing as what she'd seen on Friday night at the club, she thought with a giggle, then felt another small pang of guilt about ducking out on the guy she'd been kissing.

Stretching, Chelle snuggled back into her pillow for a few more seconds. Her eyes felt gritty. The residual aches and pains from getting hit by the bike were always worse in the morning, although her bruises had faded. There was just some remaining soreness in her shoulder and neck, and that could be attributed as much to her terrible posture when she was on her laptop as anything else.

"Get up," she told herself out loud, as though scolding were going to work. "Lazy ass."

When her phone pinged, she twisted to check the message, which turned out to be a reminder that her meter was going to be read. Excitement, she thought and gave herself permission to also check her email while she was there.

"Holy…" Chelle sat straight up in bed, phone clutched in suddenly sweaty hands.

Someone wanted to buy her short story. It was for an anthology, small print press, but there was a nominal advance. Far from what she'd been earning with her nonfiction work, but…it was a sale.

An honest-to-goodness sale.

She was already turning in bed to tell him the good news when she remembered she was alone. Still. Always.

Chelle slid a fingertip across the phone's screen to close her mail and let her hands rest in her lap. She was not going to cry, she told herself. Grant would've been happy for her no matter what had happened between them, and she would remember that, not any of the other stuff. She closed her eyes, breathing in. Breathing out. She was not going to cry.

She'd go for a run instead.

She would run and run and work this out, and when she got back, she'd answer the editor's email, and then she would write more words and maybe even put together something for another submission. She was going to do this, make it happen. She was going to do this.

Up and dressed, she decided against running through the streets. It was light out, but that didn't mean she couldn't get hit by another drunk dude on a bike. Besides, she needed the ocean today. She needed the rush and crash of the salt and sea.

She needed a lot of things, Chelle thought, but she'd have to settle for this.

Chapter 11

Jase had grown up so far from the ocean it had seemed like a myth. He'd been nearly thirty before he'd ever tasted that particular grit of salt water and sand you could get in your mouth only after being tumbled by a wave. Since then, he'd made it a point to get himself into the sea as often as he could.

He'd been up early this morning for a swim. The encounter behind the dance club had left him and Reg working overtime trying to put the pieces together, but though they'd interviewed a half dozen of the people who'd been in the parking lot that night, the ones they could find anyway, nobody else had seen anything except that first couple.

They'd been lucky, he thought as he stretched, bare chested, in the brisk early-morning air. Getting beaten up by King Kong would probably have been a walk in the park compared to fending off a pack of zombies, even if they'd turned out not to be real.

"I get it now," Reg had told him after it happened, on the long, quiet and stinking car ride back to the condo. "I totally understand what you meant, about being inside it but looking back as though it had happened to someone else. We really need to figure this out and stop it, Jase. Someone's going to get more than banged up. Someone's going to get killed."

Reg, for all his joking around, took his job with the Crew really seriously. Jase had never asked his partner what had brought him to the job, but whatever had happened to Reg had left a scar as deep as anything could.

They'd both been working all night but still hadn't been able to draw any lines. Eggy had been researching all kinds of explanations, including solar storms, which she said could cause insomnia and headaches but had never been known to lead to hallucinations with physical manifestations.

"Shit," Jase muttered and scrubbed at his eyes.

He stretched again, feeling ill at ease and with nothing to do about it. This morning he'd already swum farther, ran faster than usual. The cup of joe he normally needed first thing in the morning to even consider feeling like a normal person? Nope. The mug on the railing in front of him had gone cold from lack of interest. He tossed it over the edge now.

And heard a scream.

Shit—Jase looked over the edge to see a woman on the small path that led from the access road toward the beach. He'd completely drenched her, top to toe, with lukewarm coffee. At least it hadn't been boiling, he had time to think before she tipped her face up to see who'd done such an egregious thing to her.

It was the woman from the Cottage Cafe. The woman from the other night. Her dark hair had pressed down over her forehead, coffee running in rivulets over her cheeks. It had stained her white T-shirt and made the fabric cling to her in ways his libido definitely sat up and noticed.

"Sorry," Jase called down to her. "Hey, c'mon up here—let me at least get you a towel."

The woman hesitated, looking wary. "I'm okay."

"If you're sure? Damn, I feel bad. Some paper towels, something. A napkin?" He paused, considering the situation. "You can stay out here on the deck if you're… worried."

That she'd even have to take one second to fear for her safety pissed him off, but he understood it. You didn't need to believe in things that went bump in the night to understand the world was full of monsters. He watched her doubt cross her face, but then she nodded.

"Sure, okay. I could use something to dry off." In half a minute, she'd made it up the wooden stairs to the deck.

Jase had grabbed one of the beach towels he'd hung over the railing to dry. Too late realizing it was still damp and cold from the late-spring air, he first handed it to her, then pulled it back before she could get a grip on it. He looked like an asshole.

The woman laughed. "Um?"

"Sorry, this one, it's… I used it earlier. Let me get you a dry one. You want to stay out here or…?" Now he sounded even more like an asshole.

At that moment, Reg took the opportunity to slide open the glass door and shake his naked ass all over the place.

"Looks like I'm not the only one who needs a towel," the woman said.

* * *

The cute blond guy with the amazing green eyes was Jason. Jase, the other guy called him. Reg, he of the bare-booty shaking and wicked sense of humor. Also Jase's partner, which just figured, didn't it? Chelle thought with an internal sigh. Two superhot guys, of course they'd be together.

"Here, drink this." Reg passed her a mug of blessedly hot coffee. "You sure you're all right?"

"It was cold, I told you that." Jase sounded annoyed. "I already told her I was sorry."

Chelle sipped the coffee with a sigh. "I'm fine. Really. I was more surprised than anything."

Her shirt still clung to her, and the run she'd been looking forward to now seemed more of a chore. The coffee would help with the creeping exhaustion she'd known was going to hit her, but it wasn't going to be enough to get her motivated for a run any longer than it took to get her back home. She wrapped her hands around the mug, warming them.

She watched the two men move around the kitchen with an easy compatibility that made her envious. "I should get going. Thanks for the towel, and the coffee."

Standing, she realized her mistake in sitting. She'd gone stiff and sore again. At the sight of her wincing, Jase moved forward.

"You're hurt?"

"Not from the coffee shower," she assured him as she rotated her shoulder. "Just sore muscles. I'll be okay."

"Let me give you a ride, at least. Shit, I feel like the biggest ass." He shook his head. "At least let me drive you."

She didn't want to say yes. It felt like too much of an

imposition, especially after she'd needed to bum a ride from Eddie the other night. But Reg looked her over with a practiced eye and nodded.

"Yeah, let Jase give you a ride. You look like you feel like shit."

She had to laugh at that, then again at Jase's expression. "Wow. Thank you."

"Reg!"

"No, it's fine." She waved a hand. "But I will take you up on the ride. Sure."

"So…you're local?" Jase asked as she gave him directions to her house. The twenty-minute run was going to be a five-minute car ride.

Chelle nodded. "Yep. Grew up in Millville, then moved away for a while. Moved back down here from Wilmington about four years ago, after… Well, I quit my job to focus on some other things, and I figured the beach would be a great place to do that."

"Other things?" He shot her a curious glance as he made the turn at the square.

"Yeah. I'm… Well, I'm trying to be a writer. I mean, I am a writer. I just am trying to be a different kind of writer." It felt awkward to say it out loud, like admitting something shameful.

Jase looked impressed. "Yeah? What kind of writing?"

"I used to be a journalist. Now I'm focusing on fiction." She pointed. "Turn here. Then the next left."

"Wow. I don't think I've ever met a writer before. Have you had anything published?"

She smiled. "You know, that's the first thing anyone ever asks."

"Yeah. I bet. Sorry."

"No, it's a legit question. The answer is yes, tons of stuff in my old career. I wrote a lot of articles for different newspapers, a bunch of web content, stuff like that. My fiction has been taking a while to get off the ground, but…actually…" She paused. She hadn't told anyone else this, not her parents or sister, not Angie. The closest she'd come was that moment this morning in bed when she'd turned to a man who was no longer there. Taking in a breath, she blurted, "I just sold a story."

Jase twisted a bit to look at her. "No kidding? Really?"

"Just a short story, nothing big. The money's not that great, but it's for a good small press, they're respected and…" She stopped herself from babbling more. "It feels good. Like maybe I'm going to make something of it."

"Doing what you love—that's a real blessing," he told her.

She smiled. "What do you do, Jase?"

"I'm a private investigator. Mostly insurance-fraud stuff," he said casually. "Down here working on a couple different cases. I've never been to Bethany Beach before. It's a great little town."

"Very quiet," she said with a laugh. "If you want any kind of excitement, you really need to go to Ocean City or Rehoboth. Even Dewey."

"Oh, I don't know about that." He pulled smoothly into her driveway. "This the place?"

"Yep. Home, sweet home. Thanks for the ride." Chelle put her hand on the door handle, then glanced at him over her shoulder. He was the guy from a few nights ago at the Cottage Cafe, she was sure of it. Which meant she'd written something sexy about him. And he'd dumped cold coffee on her over a balcony. "Do you believe in coincidence?"

"No," Jase said firmly.

Fair enough. She did. There was proof of it, right

there in the driver's seat. She didn't argue, though, just smiled and thanked him again. Right before she got out of the car, he stopped her with a question.

"Do you run up my way often? I mean, I like to get in a run in the mornings, do a few miles. Reg doesn't run. Sometimes it's good to have someone pushing you, though."

She paused, then nodded. "Yeah. I run up that way, along the beach. I know some great trails through the parkland, too, and you can get to them really easily from your neighborhood. If you want to grab my number, you can text me if you—"

"I'd like that," Jase said immediately.

They exchanged numbers. She got out of the car and watched him drive away with a small wave. It didn't mean…anything, she told herself. Just a running partner. Right? It wasn't more than that?

She didn't have much time to contemplate it further, though, because at that moment, her neighbors' pack of obnoxious dogs began their furious cacophony of barking. There were at least five of the tiny terrors, though sometimes in the summer, when the neighbors had guests, there'd been seven or more rowdy dogs creating havoc. They were supposed to stay in their fenced yard but often escaped to leave presents for her in her…

"Damn it," Chelle muttered. She'd stepped in a pile of poo. She let out a long string of other curses as she scraped the bottom of her sneaker on the driveway stones, then toed off her shoes on the front deck and went inside.

The noise was barely quieter—her house was in the popular windjammer style, with sliding glass at the front and rear. Great for sunlight. Bad for soundproofing.

She'd spoken to the neighbors a few times, but Linda

and Fred were the sorts of pet owners who referred to the dogs as their "fur babies" and who didn't seem to think letting the animals run wild and tear up the neighborhood, creating a noise disturbance in the process, was anything to worry about. She could've called the police. Made a complaint. That would lead to awkward interactions at the annual neighborhood picnic, of course, not to mention having to deal with them across the tiny backyards all summer long. Anytime she tried to cook out or use the outdoor shower or take a nap in her hammock. It wasn't worth it.

She could manage some kind of revenge, however, she thought as she went inside, stripping out of her dirty clothes and tossing them in the hamper. After a quick shower and some breakfast, she thought of her bed, but something else was more compelling.

She sat down at her computer and started to write.

Chapter 12

"A pterodactyl," Jase said. "Really."

"Swear to God," said the woman in front of her. Linda Rogers wore her teased blond hair like a helmet, her matching blue eye shadow like goggles. She was shaking.

Reg, to give him credit, did not laugh. Jase wanted to, but more at the inside decor of the woman's house than the fate of her dog. Four of the remaining pooches were huddled around her feet, all of them shaking, too.

He looked around the kitschy room before focusing on her. "Describe it again, please."

"I told you both already. I'd let the kids out in the backyard to do their doodles, as you do…"

"As you do," Reg murmured.

Jase shot him a look. "And?"

"And I heard them all barking, which they never do, and I looked out the back window, and there was this… giant… Well, it was a flying dinosaur. That's all!" She moaned, rocking, and one of the smaller dogs hopped onto her lap. "It carried off Pipsy!"

It wasn't funny at all. A third case, more of that glowing stuff and, this time, an actual death. Or presumed death anyway. They hadn't actually found the dog's body. Things were escalating, though. That was clear.

They got more information from Mrs. Rogers and left her with assurances that they'd be in touch. Out in the driveway, Reg avoided a few piles of dog crap, all glowing with the black-light wand, even in the late-afternoon sunshine. Jase looked across the gravel toward the house next door.

Chelle's house.

"Hey, go on and take the car," he said, pressing his keys into Reg's hand. "I'm going to say hi."

Reg grinned. "Uh-huh. I'll leave the light on for you."

"It's not like that," Jase said, though of course his protests did no good. Reg was already getting in the driver's seat and giving him two fingerguns of approval. Jase shook his head. "It's just part of the investigation. Maybe she saw something."

"Maybe she'll see a giant anaconda," Reg said with a straight face.

Jase didn't dignify that with an answer. He didn't wait for Reg to leave, either, before heading over to rap on Chelle's sliding-glass front door. He caught sight of her through the sheer curtains and hoped he wasn't overstepping.

Investigation, he told himself. That was all this was. It had nothing to do with that dark curly hair or the bright green-blue eyes or the lush body. It had nothing to do with how easily she'd laughed with him.

Nothing to do with the dream he'd had of being her guard, her champion. Her lover.

"Hi," she said, surprised. "Jase! What a surprise."

"I was next door." He jerked a thumb in that direction. "Um…investigating."

Too late, he realized he was going to have to backtrack to a lie, since he'd already told her he dealt with insurance stuff. What was he going to say now? That he was checking into tales about real-life flying dinosaurs making off with yappy little dogs?

"Linda and Fred? Are they in trouble?"

He wasn't imagining the swiftest glimmer of smug satisfaction rippling over her expression before neighborly concern replaced it. "No. I was just asking them some questions about something else going on."

Shit, what if she asked the Rogers about it? Linda wasn't going to lie about losing her dog or about the two guys who'd come around asking about it. She might not admit to seeing a long-extinct reptile, but you never knew.

He was getting sloppy, which wasn't like him. And for what? A pretty face? Stupid, he told himself as she stepped aside to let him in.

"Can I get you a drink? Coffee, cola?" She'd pulled her hair on top of her head, but a few tendrils had escaped to frame her face. She looked down at her clinging yoga pants and T-shirt, then at him with a twist of a smile. "I was working. I'd apologize for being a mess, but hey, at least I'm not covered in coffee."

"If it makes you feel better, you can dump it all over my head."

She tilted hers to look at him. "There might be a certain satisfaction in it, I'll admit. But nah, I think I'm okay. Do you want to sit, or…?"

"Yeah, sure. I'll take some coffee." He settled into one of the stools lined up along the bar separating the galley kitchen from the living-and-dining area. "Nice place."

She handed him the mug along with a shaker of sugar and some creamers in plastic tubs. "Thanks. It's more of a cottage, really. It wasn't meant for year-round living. But I had it winterized and stuff, so it's all right. And it's just me, so I don't need a lot of room."

He sipped. Perfect. "How long have you lived here?"

"Four years." She leaned her hip on the counter and looked around the space. "I love it down here. How about you? Where are you from?"

"Kansas, originally. Now, wherever I need to go. So, have you seen anything strange around here lately?" Smooth, Jase, he thought. So smooth.

Chelle frowned. "Like what?"

"Just anything."

"They're not supposed to have a shed," she said quietly after a moment. "It's against the homeowners' association. Fred and Linda, I mean. Their shed. It doesn't bother me or anything, if that's what you want to know. Are they getting in trouble for it?"

"No. It's not that."

She hesitated. "I'm pretty sure they have too many dogs."

"You don't like dogs?" Jase asked.

"I like dogs," Chelle answered after a second. "But theirs are very loud."

He decided to come clean, at least a little. "Yeah. They are. And they have one less."

"What?" She looked startled and put her mug down hard enough to splash coffee on the counter.

"Yeah. Something happened to one of their dogs."

He watched her carefully, noting her reaction. "Know anything about it?"

"No," she said too quickly, with a cut of her gaze from his. "Did they have insurance for them or something?"

"Um…sure, homeowners' covers it," he lied easily. "But there's been a few weird things happening around here lately, so. If you've seen anything strange…"

Chelle, biting her lower lip, shook her head, then looked at him with a small, strained smile. "I'll let you know."

Something was off here, that was for sure, but he couldn't figure out what it was. Maybe, Jase thought, something had happened to her, something offbeat that she didn't want to share. That could be one of the hardest parts of his job, getting people to admit to something they didn't want to believe happened.

He drank more coffee. They made small talk. She relaxed visibly as the conversation steered away from the neighbors' dogs and weird things. It turned to her writing.

"My mom and dad aren't thrilled," she admitted. She'd curled up on the couch with another mug of coffee and a plate of cookies on the coffee table between them. "They didn't love that I went to college for journalism, but at least I had a job and was making money. They don't like that I'm living in Bethany Beach, which isn't that far from them at all, but they think I'm… Well, they think I'm kind of destitute."

She laughed, shaking her head, and gave him a slow smile that sent warmth all through him that had nothing to do with the fresh cup of coffee. Jase looked around the house. Small, cozy, but in prime real estate.

"Not many people would think that of someone who

lives in this neighborhood. What are you, a mile from the ocean?"

"About that." She shrugged. "They want to see me settled, that's all. And they don't think I'll be able to maintain myself writing fiction. Truth is, the only reason I…"

She stopped with another small shake of her head and looked away. Jase waited. One thing he'd learned from his work—sometimes the best question to get the answer you wanted was asked with silence.

"The only reason I could afford to buy this house and put this effort into writing this way, without a job, is because I inherited a decent sum of money. They thought I should put it away for the future. But they didn't realize he left it to me so I could make *writing* my future." She cleared her throat, her gaze bright.

"He?" Shit, there was a he.

She nodded. "My boyfriend. We'd been together for eight years. They also thought he should've married me. It didn't matter in the end, though, except to them."

"He…died?" Jase held his mug in both hands, then put it down to take a cookie he suddenly didn't really want to eat.

"Yeah. Sorry, this is a terrible conversation." She put down her mug, too. "What a downer."

Jase shook his head. "No. It's all right. In my line of work, I meet a lot of people who've lost someone special."

"His name was Grant. What we had wasn't perfect, but really, what is? Unless it's in a story," Chelle said with a laugh that broke a bit in the middle. "We'd been talking about moving to Arizona. We talked about a lot of things. And then, suddenly, he broke it off with me. Took his stuff, moved to Arizona without me. He broke my heart. I mean, he shattered it, Jase. Have you ever had your heart broken?"

"No," he said without hesitation.

"Never been in love, huh?" Chelle laughed again, without much more humor than the first time.

He smiled, though the truth was he hadn't been, and that was pretty damned sad. "No. Not that lucky, I guess."

"I don't know about luck. To be honest, I'm not sure what is worse, the fact he broke me apart when he left me, or the fact he did it because he wanted, somehow, to protect me." She took up a cookie and put it on the small plate in her lap. She broke the treat into pieces, but she didn't eat any of them.

"Was he sick?"

"Yes. He had cancer. Fast acting, pancreatic. By the time he found out, I guess it had spread so far they told him he had only a few months." She wiped her fingers free of crumbs and shrugged, then winced, rubbing her shoulder.

"Still hurts?"

She hesitated, then nodded. "One of those things, you think it's going to go away and then all of a sudden you're in agony again."

"Kind of like a broken heart, I guess."

He'd meant it lightly, but boy had he overstepped. He saw that as soon as her eyes welled with tears, and then he felt like shit, all right. He'd had his share of women who used tears to manipulate him, and often the easiest way to get him to turn and run was to start crying, but now at the sight of Chelle's crumpling expression, all he could think about was how he hated that he'd been the one to make that happen.

She pressed her fingertips to her closed eyelids,

visibly struggling. When she opened them, she shot him another stiff smile. "Sorry. God. So lame. But you know, this shoulder will heal. My heart did, too. Or it will. I have to think so, or else what's the use in going on?"

"Not sure I can do anything about the heart," he told her, "but I could try a little something with the shoulder, if you want."

Again he'd overstepped. The startled look she gave him was enough to make him curse himself. He stood.

"Sorry. That was… I'll just go."

She shook her head. "No. Really, if you can get this knot worked out, I'll be so grateful. Honestly."

"Sure. I know a few trigger points." That was true, not just a line he used. That the trigger points were more often the sort to send someone into unconsciousness was a little fact he was going to keep to himself.

Chelle slid around the edge of the L-shaped couch to expose her neck to him, lifting away the weight of her hair to let it fall over the other shoulder. He stopped himself from touching the soft hair at the nape of her neck only because doing that would make him a world-class creep who took advantage of a grieving woman. Yet he couldn't stop himself from thinking about that dream or hallucination or whatever it was.

The one in which he'd been her protector.

He found the spot at once, the knot of muscles tight beneath his trained fingertips. He dug in a little, encouraged by her soft sigh and the way she relaxed under his touch even though it obviously hurt her. Just a massage, he told himself as her low groan of pleasure/pain sent a ripple of desire through him.

Nothing more than that.

Chapter 13

"How's this?" Jase dug a little deeper.

Chelle moaned, softly at first. Then a little louder. He was finding all the right spots. "God. That's perfect."

The soft hairs at the nape of her neck tingled under the gust of his breath as he leaned closer. He wasn't going to kiss her there, but her body responded as though he had. Tight nipples. Parted lips. She held back another moan by sheer force of will. The guy behind her was a real person, not something she'd made up in a story. And he had a partner.

Jase rubbed another minute or so, then let his big warm hands rest on her shoulders. "Better?"

She turned to give him a smile over her shoulder. "Much."

They stared at each other for a long, long moment in silence. Chelle's smile faded, her brow furrowing. She tilted her head to look at him, curious about why he looked so awkward.

"Jase...?"

"So...when you write," he said abruptly, "how do you do it?"

Surprised, Chelle scooted forward on the couch away from him and gestured toward the kitchen table. "I use my laptop. I don't have a desk, so I sit there or out on the deck if the weather's nice."

"No pen and paper?"

She laughed. "Not usually. I have a program, actually. Grant wrote it for me. He was going to try to market it, but he never had the chance. It's called GOLEM."

"Like the clay monster?"

More than surprised this time. Startled. "Yes! Usually people would say like from *Lord of the Rings*, but yes, like the clay monster. You put the words—"

"You put the words in his mouth and he does your bidding," Jase said.

"Wow." Chelle smiled at him. "I can't believe you know what a golem is. Are you Jewish?"

"No. Just full of trivia."

"Do you want to see it?" she asked after another of those strange pauses. "The computer program."

"Sure. Yeah. That would be cool. I barely know how to use a computer," Jase said.

"You're kidding, right?" she asked as she got up and grabbed the laptop to bring over to the couch. She opened the lid and poised her fingers on the keys.

Jase laughed, leaning closer. "Nope. Reg is the one who handles all the computer stuff."

Reg. Right. His partner. It was a good reminder about getting all fluttery about him, Chelle thought as she tapped to open GOLEM.

Too late she remembered that the program automatically opened up the last document she'd been working on.

And that had been more of the science-fiction romance story. The sexy one.

The one that was kind of about Jase.

He has knelt before few, and even when protocol required it, the scout bent out of respect and not obeisance. In front of his regent, his woman, his heart, he kneels to serve her in all ways.

Right now he serves her with his tongue. Her sweet, hot flesh beneath his lips is better than anything he's ever dreamed. When he slides his hands beneath the softness of her rear to lift her to his mouth, she moans. His cock, thick already with wanting her, aches.

He has feasted on her forever and will continue until the suns turn to ash, if only to hear her make that sound again. He flicks his tongue along her folds, dipping inside to taste her honey. Then up to circle the tight knot of flesh that is the center of her pleasure. She bucks under that attention, her fingers finding his hair and tugging, hard, though not to pull him away. She rocks beneath him.

When she says his name, he pauses in his worship of her to press a single soft kiss between her legs. He looks up at her to see her staring down at him. Her fingers loosen so she can pass a hand over his hair, then to cup his cheek.

"You are the true treasure," she murmurs.

Everything inside him squeezes. He has loved the woman in front of him for as long as he's understood what love is supposed to be. The scout never dreamed he might have the chance to make her his, and he's not such a fool as to think that making love proclaims anything more than simple physical pleasure. She is promised to another. She is regent.

"I want you inside me," his love whispers. "Again, again, again."

It's everything he wants in that moment, especially if it's all he's meant to have. They are already naked, and all he needs to do is slide up her body and push himself into her heat. The regent moves upward on the bed, crooking a finger for him to follow. He does, as he always will, her servant, her slave.

But he does not push inside her. Instead, he teases her with the tip of his cock, using the slickness leaking from the head of him to lubricate her. She already glistens from the attentions of his tongue and her own sweetness. There's no resistance as he thrusts against her, only the most delicious friction of his throbbing cock against her swollen flesh.

When she arches, opening herself to him, the scout wants to slide into her so deep they will never be separated again. Yet he wants to tease her, too, until she writhes and cries his name and begs him to enter her. He gives her the tip, pressing just inside her. Not moving. His muscles tense and tighten, and he shakes from the effort of keeping himself from fucking into her fast and hard, pumping until they both shatter.

He gives her only this small part of him, because he wants to give her everything.

When her hands go above her head to clutch at the spindles of the headboard, he can no longer control himself. She is regent and he is meant to serve her, but the sight of her in such submission to him drives him mad with longing. They both cry out when he enters her.

Their eyes meet. She draws him to her, a hand at the nape of his neck to hold him close as she kisses him. She bites lightly at his lips and takes his tongue into her mouth to suck it gently. The pleasure of that intimacy echoes in his cock, equally embraced by her body.

They move together. Slow, slow, then faster. Harder. Deeper. His body slams against hers. They will break this bed with the force of their passion.

They will break the world with it.

Chelle let out a low, embarrassed cough and closed the laptop with a snap. She couldn't look him in the face, not after that. Bad enough to share her unpolished work with a near stranger, but that particular piece...

More than that, how easily she'd lost herself in reading it. Only a few minutes could've passed, but it had felt like hours. She was used to getting lost inside the world she created when she was writing, but this had been different. Almost as though it had been really happening to them.

"What the hell," Jase said, "was that?"

"I'm sorry. It was inspiration. I don't know if you remember, but we passed each other at the Cottage Cafe, and I guess you got stuck in my brain—" she babbled, mortified, only to realize in a second or so that there was no way he could've known by reading that short section of her work in progress that she'd been imagining him as the hero and herself in the heroine's role.

He couldn't know that, but the way he was looking at her said he did.

"It's only a story," Chelle whispered. "It's not real."

"It felt real," he said. "I felt every word."

She swallowed against a strange tightness in her throat and shook her head. "No. That's not possible."

"You felt it, too? It happened to us. That room. Those people," he said. "They were us, weren't they? Tell me I'm not crazy."

"That is crazy," she said sharply. Beyond embarrassed. This was fucking with her head, and she was not about to go there.

Jase kissed her. Hard, deep, his fingers gripping her shoulders so she couldn't pull away. Not that she wanted to. At the first touch of his lips on hers, she was lost. Caught up in a whirlwind of lust and passion, exactly what she'd been imagining and writing about and hadn't found in any random make-out session in a dark corner of a dance club.

Breathless, Chelle pulled away and put a hand over her mouth. Her lips felt swollen. Bruised.

"Shit," Jase said. "I'm sorry—"

She kissed him. Not as hard as he'd done. Hers was softer, exploring. She moved onto his lap, straddling, her knees pressing the couch's back cushions. She rocked against him. When he opened his mouth wider, she took his tongue and sucked gently. She'd written that but couldn't recall ever actually trying it.

Damn, that was hot.

Hotter was the way his hands gripped her hips, pulling her down against him. His moan in her ear when she broke the kiss to slide her mouth along his jaw. The way he thrust upward, grinding his hardness against her when she nibbled.

The rush of it left her trembling, but Chelle forced herself to pull away and cup his face in her hands. "Jase, this is crazy. What about Reg?"

"What about him?" His hands roamed over her back, nudging her closer.

"Won't he care?"

Jase paused, looking confused. The way he ran his tongue along his lower lip drove her crazy. She wanted to kiss him again so much it was like fire, but she held herself back.

"Why would he care?"

"He's your partner," she said.

"Yeah, but he doesn't usually get involved with my… erm…who I…" Jase blinked. "Oh. You think he's my 'partner' partner?"

This was all going wrong. Really wrong. Embarrassed, she tried to pull away, but the way her body had bent in order to fit on his lap made it impossible for her to gracefully extricate herself, at least not without a lot of wriggling. With his erection still pushing against her, wriggling was the last thing she wanted to do. Well, it was everything she wanted to do, she thought with a small, helpless giggle. She was just going to have to stop herself from doing it.

"No," Jase said in a low voice. His gaze burned into hers. He pulled her closer, inch by inch, until their mouths brushed with every word he said. "No, it's not like that at all."

His kiss plundered her again, and she loved every second of it. This was better than anything she ever could've written. She let her head fall back so he could get at her throat, and that was perfect, the press of his teeth and the swipe of his tongue.

He pulled her T-shirt off over her head, exposing her breasts to the heat and wetness of his mouth. Jase tugged a nipple between his lips, and Chelle let out a long, low and grinding moan of pleasure. It had been so long. Too long.

"I want you," she said.

Chelle slammed the laptop lid closed.

Jase blinked. His cock pressed uncomfortably at the

front of his jeans. Heat had flooded him. He could still taste her mouth.

She stared at him. "I didn't... Did I write that...?"

He kissed her. She moved onto his lap, not straddling but twisted to half face him. She fell onto the cushions, but her arms were around his neck, pulling him down to her. He was on top of her, between her legs. He was so hard his dick ached, but he couldn't stop himself from pushing against her, dry-humping like teenagers—it didn't matter. He could only think about touching her. Tasting her.

He moved down her body, pushing up her T-shirt to get at her magnificent breasts. Her nipples were already hard, poking through the sheer lace of her bra. Jase covered one with his mouth, wetting the lace, nibbling her as he slid a hand beneath her ass to lift her against him.

Chelle moaned his name. She moved to let him get her shirt off over her head, then tugged at his to get him bare, too. Skin to skin, they moved on the couch until the cushions flew off. He was still on top of her. Moving. Thrusting.

She got a hand between them, cupping his cock through the denim, and fuck, it was not enough—he needed her to unzip and get inside there, to take him in her hand. Her mouth. Her pussy. He'd never wanted anything so much in his life.

"Fuck me," Chelle said and looked surprised. "Yeah, that is what I want."

He wanted it, too. But their clothes were still a barrier and he couldn't manage to get his pants unbuttoned, and she was moving, pushing at him, sitting up and letting him kiss and bite at her neck, but what he wanted was to dive between her thighs and eat her until she screamed.

"Yes, I want that," Chelle told him, though he hadn't

said a word out loud. "Get your mouth on me, Jase. Get your mouth on every part of me."

Chelle closed the laptop, this time for real, and jumped up from the couch to take a few steps back from Jase, who was blinking, stunned. Not moving. She put a hand to her fast-beating heart, her pulse throbbing as though she'd run a marathon.

"What the hell is going on?" she cried.

Everything inside her was molten, melting, though she couldn't tell if it was from humiliation or arousal or some sickening combination of both. She drew in a breath and then another, waiting to see if he would stand up and kiss her again. Or if she'd kiss him. If they would end up half-naked or all-the-way bare, fucking on her couch like animals.

"Are you all right?" he asked her in a low voice.

She took a second to make sure she was answering honestly before nodding. Still wary, she took another step back until the L of the couch hit her behind the calves. She had no place to run. She didn't want to run. She wanted to tear off her clothes and have passionate sex with this guy.

"I have some things to tell you," Jase said. "About things that have been going on around town. I think you might be part of them."

"What kinds of things?" Her heartbeat had slowed, as had her breathing. When she shifted, she still felt tingly and slick between her legs, but she could see a bulge in his pants even from here, so she guessed he was feeling the same.

"We haven't been able to figure it out yet, but it's what we were sent here to do. Reg and I aren't insurance investigators," Jase told her.

"Reg. Your partner. Who's not your 'partner' partner." Chelle let out a small, strangely gleeful laugh. "Oh my God. This is madness. What is this?"

"I don't know, but I'm sorry I…" Jase coughed and looked away from her. "I shouldn't have touched you that way."

If there was any part of this that she regretted, it was definitely not that he'd touched her in "that" way or any way. "I'm not."

He looked back at her, and the blaze of desire in his eyes glittered a little brighter. Neither of them moved. She licked her lips and watched him follow the tracing of her tongue along them.

"I haven't had a lover in about a year and a half," she told him. "I tried a couple one-night stands, but they never were more than that. I tried going out with my friend the other night, tried to pick up a guy in Ocean City, but I only kissed him. When it came time to go upstairs with him, I wasn't into it. Not like this. Nothing like what just happened."

"You were in Ocean City on Friday night?" Jase ran a hand through his blond hair until it stood on end.

It only made him more attractive, that rumpled look. Chelle ran a hand along her chin, feeling the burn from his stubble there. Her nipples, too, she realized, though she didn't dare cup her breasts to feel the sting he'd left behind.

"Yes."

Jase stood so suddenly his knee hit the coffee table. Cold coffee sloshed, but he ignored it as he moved away from the couch to pace. He ran both hands through his hair this time before turning to face her with a grim look.

"Did you go home and write after? Like two or three in the morning?"

The heat was fading, leaving behind a seminauseated ache in the pit of her stomach. She nodded. "Yes?"

"Shit." Jase shook his head. "I think it's you. It's not just happening to you. You're doing this."

Chelle flinched. "Doing this? Look, I know I wrote that sci-fi story, and yes, I definitely used you as a model for the hero, but it really was just fiction. I had no idea—"

"Not just this thing with us. Damn, I wanted you from the minute I saw you," Jase cut in. "All the other stuff that's been going on around here. Flying monkeys and zombies and shit."

"You did?" She grinned, not sure what the hell he was going on about but not really caring. "That night at the Cottage Cafe, I saw you turn around to look back at me, but I didn't think much of it. Wait. What? Zombies? What?"

"Yeah. I saw you. Yeah, I turned around." His small smile turned tight in a second. "You started writing about me right after that. Didn't you?"

She blushed, more heat, not nearly as pleasant as the sort that had come from his hands on her. "Yes."

"I know. I felt it. The same as what just happened. Only, I was alone. I was that guy, that scout guy."

"And I was the regent?" Chelle asked in a whisper. She had to sit, or she was going to fall. She shook her head, not understanding. By the look on his face, Jase had only a little more clue.

"Yes. You were the regent and I was in love with you. And when I came out of it, there was all this stuff, this glowing remnant of something. It was the same as the other cases. I knew they were connected. I just didn't see the connection until now."

Chelle twisted her hands together in her lap to keep

them from shaking. Chills had replaced the heat, though she was still sweating. She swallowed another rush of nausea. Her head was starting to hurt.

"I don't understand, Jase."

He moved toward her so fast that she let out a yelp and retreated against the couch. That stopped him. He moved slower then to sit beside her without touching her.

"Don't be scared," he said.

She was a little scared, though not of him. She ought to be, Chelle thought at the sight of his expression, which had gone dark and stern. She knew nothing about him except that everything he'd told her had been lies.

"Do you know what's going on?" she asked him.

Jase shook his head, pulling out his phone from his pocket and tapping a quick text. "No. But Reg might be able to put it together. If he can't, someone on the team should be able to figure it out."

"The team?"

He looked at her, then put away his phone. "Yeah. I belong to a team called the Crew."

"And you don't investigate insurance fraud," Chelle said.

Jase's smile shouldn't have sent another glittery slice of heat through her, not with all this other weird stuff surrounding them. But it did. The slight brush of his hand on hers did, too, when he moved a smidgen closer.

"No," he said. "Let me tell you what we do."

"When I was seventeen, my family and I went camping in Yellowstone Park. We'd gone every year for as long as I could remember. Sometimes we had an RV. Sometimes we stayed at one of the lodges. This year was the first time we'd gotten passes to go far back, off the marked trails. Me, my dad, my sister. My mom had stayed home with my younger brother, Corey, who'd broken his leg playing soccer.

"The three of us carried only what could fit in packs on our backs. My dad had camped like this plenty of times. He even served as a guide sometimes during the summer. He was a schoolteacher. Geometry. But he loved being outdoors more than anything else.

"We knew to watch for bears, of course. And there are wolves in Yellowstone, too. But my dad knew how to be careful, how to keep our food locked up in scent-proof containers so we didn't attract anything. We spent the first night hiking as far back off the trail as we could. We made camp right near a waterfall. There was a hot spring there, too, one of the small ones, but still pretty amazing to see. Every so often, it would bubble up a little higher, then settle down. Nothing like Old Faithful, but enough to make the evening entertaining without much else to do but play checkers.

"I beat my sister every time. She was laughing about that when the thing came after us. They would tell us later it was a bear, but I can tell you, Chelle, I saw that thing and it was not a bear. It was about nine feet tall and had teeth like swords. Claws to match. If it was anything, it was something out of the Stone Age, some kind of saber-toothed tiger hybrid that had been hiding out in the wilds forever. Like the Loch Ness monster, like Sasquatch.

"It killed my father and my sister. It left me for dead, and I wasn't faking—I was as close to death as I've ever been, and I've been hurt pretty damned bad since then.

"I lay in the backwoods of Yellowstone for three days before a ranger found us. By then the thing had taken my father's and sister's bodies. They were never found.

It ate them. Everything, even the bones. I don't know why it left me behind. Maybe it was full.

"What I do know is that when I got out of the hospital, a man named Vadim came to see me. He told my mom he was a grief counselor. That's one of those things we learn to do, see. Tell lies in order to get where we need to be so we can figure out what the hell is happening.

"I knew he wasn't any sort of counselor. I didn't want to tell him anything. Nobody would've believed my story, I knew that from the start. If the rangers said a bear or bears had taken my dad and Karen, then that's what I was going to say, too. The nightmares were bad enough without anyone trying to also psychoanalyze me.

"Vadim, though, had a photo of something that looked a helluva lot like what had come out of the trees that night. Blurry—maybe it could've been faked—but as soon as I saw it, I turned and puked into the trash can by my bed. It didn't faze him. He's an unshakable bastard, Vadim. One of the bravest men I've ever known, and that's saying a lot.

"He told me others had seen this thing, close to where it had killed my family. The picture had been found on the phone of someone who'd gone missing, leaving behind that as the only evidence they'd come to harm. He never told me how he got hold of it, but it didn't matter. Once I saw it, I knew I had to help him find it.

"My mother thinks I joined an elite branch of the marines, and I aim to keep her thinking that. She worries about me, but at least I never had to convince her I wasn't insane, not with the sorts of cases I've taken on. Most people can't wrap their heads around it. Hell, there are times I can't even figure it out.

"But I'll tell you this, Chelle. I found that thing that killed my dad and Karen, and I followed it to its lair, where it had a litter of kits, still sucking. No sign of a mate, and we never found out how it breeds, but we know there are more of them out there than we thought. They are real.

"So are a lot of other things you never believed were true."

Chelle had listened, her stomach twisting, to Jase's story. He'd told it without so much as a break in his voice, and it was somehow all the more awful for that lack of emotion. She wanted to hug him. She wanted to run away.

"So...you killed it?"

He shook his head. "No. Seeing it with its young, I couldn't do it. Yes, it had killed my family, but we were in its territory. A bear might've done the same. Wolves. My dad always taught us that entering into nature's realm meant taking risks. That we were the interlopers. I could've killed it, for sure, and its babies. But it was an animal, not some kind of monstrosity bent on slaughtering for the fun of it. Believe me, I've met those kinds of monsters, and they deserve to die. This thing was only trying to feed its children."

It was a more fantastic story than any she'd written, that was for sure. She shouldn't have believed it. Crazy talk, or at the very least, simple lies told for a purpose she couldn't comprehend.

"I've always believed in Nessie and Bigfoot," she told him, not quite sure why she was admitting it.

"They're real."

She bit her lower lip for a second. "I'm sorry about your family."

"Thanks."

They stared at each other again. She reached for his hand and he let her take it. She squeezed his fingers.

His phone buzzed, and he withdrew his hand with an apologetic smile to look at the text. He read it, then looked up at her with narrowed eyes. He looked at the computer.

"This writing program. GOLEM. You say your boy-friend wrote it for you?"

"Yes." She gestured at the laptop, wondering if suddenly she was going to find herself naked on his lap. To her regret and relief, nothing like that happened.

"The night after you went dancing, you wrote about zombies."

"Yes," she said, startled. "How did—"

"You wrote about the neighbors' yappy dogs. A dinosaur? And the woman that jerk ran over on his bike, that was you, too. You came home and wrote out a little revenge on him. King Kong?"

Sickened, Chelle fell back against the couch. "Yes, yes. Oh my God, Jase, what are you saying?"

"Everything you've been writing has come true," he said. "At least some of the things have. And I think it's because of GOLEM."

This was too much. Chelle got off the couch and pushed past him to go to the fridge for some cold seltzer. No, screw that—she needed something stronger. She pulled the bottle of vodka from the freezer and poured two shots, holding up one for him before setting it on the bar so she could toss the other. It went down like fire, making her cough and her eyes water, but she shook it off.

"That's crazy," she said. "I write fiction."

Jase leaned on the bar to take the shot of vodka. "Two

years ago, Reg and I worked a case with a real golem, one made of clay. It had been made by a rabbinical student who wasn't happy with some of the things his rabbi was doing. It killed four people before we stopped it."

"I haven't killed anyone. Oh my God, I haven't, have I?" Chelle put the vodka back in the freezer, though she wanted another shot. She clenched her shaking hands into fists at her sides. "The dog. Oh, no."

"We don't know for sure that it's dead," Jase told her.

It wasn't much comfort. In the story she'd written, the pterodactyl had definitely eaten the dog. There'd been no gore in the story—she'd written it tongue in cheek—but even so. The dog was definitely a goner.

She took a deep breath and forced herself to meet his gaze. "The stuff with us. That wasn't real, then? Or did it really happen?"

"I think it really happened." He touched his mouth, which looked a little swollen, the way hers still felt. "Not the part on that other planet. But at least some of the stuff on the couch."

"Oh God," she whispered and put her face in her hands. "I'm so embarrassed!"

"Hey, hey. Don't." He came around the bar as though he meant to take her in his arms, but Chelle stepped back before he could.

She didn't need his pity, that was for sure.

"Would it be all right if I took a look at the program?" Jase asked after a minute. "Reg's text said he was sending some updates to the data team."

"Yeah. Of course you can look at it. It's not like you haven't already seen the most mortifying stuff already."

Jase shot her a look. "Chelle, don't. I meant what I said about seeing you for the first time. Whatever is happening has nothing to do with how attracted I am to you."

This time when he moved to take her in his arms, she didn't pull away. He didn't kiss her. He hugged her instead, and this simple comfort was enough to burn her eyes with tears she was helpless to keep from sliding down her cheeks. She pressed her face to his shirt. His hands rubbed her back in slow circles until she got herself under control.

"Let's take a look at that program," she told him. "Because if I'm really what's causing this stuff to go on, I want to stop."

Chapter 14

He hadn't been lying when he'd told Chelle he wasn't really that great with technology. Jase wasn't afraid of much anymore, not after facing down the things he'd seen. Comparatively, nothing on this case so far should've frightened him. Yet he hesitated before opening the laptop.

His fingertips tingled as they hovered over the metal. He glanced at Chelle, who'd been watching intently. Her brows went up.

"You want me to do it?" she asked.

"I'm not sure what's going to happen," he said honestly. "Twenty minutes ago, you and I were…"

"Yeah," she said. "I remember."

"If that happens again, we'll have to stop it," Jase told her.

She laughed lightly, a pink tinge climbing into her cheeks. "Yes. I know."

"But first," he said, "I'd like to kiss you again."

Chelle looked surprised. "Why?"

"Because right now we can be sure it's something we both really want."

She ducked her head, smiling. The blush spread across her face, sending a flush down her throat and into the V of her T-shirt. "Just a kiss, then."

"Yeah," he said, sliding closer. "Just a kiss."

He half expected to be taken over by that mad rush of lust again the way he had before, but this time, the kiss was truly just a kiss. If anything that sweet and tempting could be called "just" anything anyway. Her mouth was lush and delicious and everything he'd dreamed of it being, yet nothing like it had been while they were swept up in that previous madness.

"This," she whispered against his mouth, "this is real."

It was, which was more terrifying than anything he'd ever had to face with a knife. He kissed her again, softer this time. It lingered. When he pulled away, she was smiling.

"Are you ready?" Jase asked.

Chelle looked uncertain but then nodded firmly. "Yes. Bring it on."

He lifted the lid of the laptop, tensing. Nothing happened except for the whir of a fan inside the computer's workings. She laughed in relief and he joined her.

"Show me how this works." He leaned to the side so she could get her fingertips on the keyboard. He couldn't stop himself from breathing her in.

She gave him a sideways glance and a secret sort of smile but didn't shift away from him as she drew a finger over the trackpad to move the cursor to an icon in her task bar. She let it hover there for a moment, then clicked to open a small menu that closed the program down.

"It's set to automatically open the last-used document," she explained. "I just closed it totally, so when we start it up again, we should be able to choose which project to open."

He nodded and watched her double-click the icon again. A menu appeared with a list of document names and folders. "Don't open any just yet. Tell me how this works."

"Grant built it to not just help me write and make word count, but to really plot and do character development. Stuff like that." She gave him another sideways glance as her fingertips tapped across the keys. "See, you can start a new document like this."

She showed him, along with the tabs and functions that brought up different databases. All blank in this case, as was the document she'd started.

"He's the one who called it GOLEM," she said quietly as they both stared at the computer. "Grant had a fondness for myths and fairy tales. And he told me more than once, before the end, that he wanted to make all my dreams come true. Do you think that's what he was trying to do, Jase?"

He hated that she sounded so sad. "I don't know. Maybe. I've been on a few cases where someone who passed away had left unfinished business behind. Sometimes people linger long after they should've gone on. How long have you been using this program?"

Chelle hesitated. "Honestly, he gave it to me before he left for Arizona, but it was hidden. I didn't find it until about six months ago. How long ago did these odd things start happening?"

"Six months ago," Jase said.

Chelle looked stricken. "It *is* me. It has to be."

"Well, there's one way to find out." He tilted the laptop toward her. "Write something."

The room was filled with helium balloons.

Chelle sat back and looked around the room. Nothing had happened. They both looked at the screen.

"Do you do anything else?" Jase leaned forward to look at it.

"Well, I usually write more than that." She frowned, looking at the document. "But otherwise, no. Not really."

She laughed. Then a bit louder. She shook her head. Jase gave her a curious look.

"All of this is a little hard to take in, that's all." She nudged him with her knee. "Right? I'm sure you're used to it. But I'm not."

Jase grinned. "Trust me, every time I start a new case, there's something I'm not used to."

She couldn't stop herself from touching his face, tracing the line of his jaw and then letting her thumb run across his lower lip for a second before she leaned to brush a kiss against his mouth. "Just making sure this is all still real."

"Write a little more, maybe," he suggested when she pulled away.

She did, spinning a little tale about balloons and rainbows and pots of gold. Nothing happened. With a sigh, she saved the file into the Works in Progress folder.

The room filled with balloons. Hundreds of them, multicolored, bouncing and bobbing. Every time one popped, a rainbow shot out, covering them with glitter. Chelle laughed, hands out to catch it, watching as the colored and sparkling bits of light cascaded through her fingers.

"Boom," Jase said.

She looked at his face, cast in rainbow-shaded shadows. Glitter had settled in his fair hair. She brushed it off his shoulders.

"Now we know," she said. "The default setting to save files is the drafts folder. But if I put it in that one, it happens. I just don't know how."

He shook himself to let the glitter fall away. "We don't need to know. We just need to know how to stop it from happening anymore."

She thought about writing good things. Winning the lottery, finding a cure for cancer, world peace. A roomful of balloons had been fun and easy and hadn't hurt anyone. What if she used whatever this was, as crazy as it seemed, to make a better difference in the world?

"Jase…"

"Do you want that responsibility?" he asked quietly, though she hadn't said anything aloud. "Think about it, Chelle. You don't know the limits of this. Do you want to be in charge of the entire world?"

She definitely did not. More than that, she suspected she wouldn't have been allowed to be. Jase might've kissed her breathless no matter what she'd written, but he was here to do a job, and that job was to stop all this stuff that had been going on.

"I'm going to delete it," she said.

"The story?"

She shook her head. "No. The program. I know Grant wrote it for me because he wanted me to reach my dreams, but he couldn't have meant for it to hurt people. That's why he didn't give it to me outright—he was still working on it. He must've known it had issues. And he's gone and will never be able to fix it. I'm going to trash it."

Jase looked solemn. "I think that's a good idea. But all your work…"

"None of it was much good," she told him. "Besides, you do your best work in the revisions. I'll be okay."

"Trash it, then," he told her.

Her fingers nudged the trackpad to position the cursor, then dragged and dropped the program's icon into the trash. She waiting, expecting a warning or something to pop up, but nothing happened except that small crinkling sound that always occurred when she deleted something.

"Well," she said. "That's that, I guess."

"How do you feel?"

She'd expected a sense of loss. Months of work, tossed aside. Sorrow, certainly, at deleting something Grant had left her. Yet all she felt was unburdened. A weight, lifted. She twisted in her chair to look at him.

"I feel…inspired." She grinned and put her hands on the keyboard, fingers resting lightly on the keys but not typing anything yet. "I feel free, Jase. Is that weird?"

"What isn't weird in this world?" he replied with a laugh and sat back in his chair.

Chelle laughed, too. "Maybe you can tell me all about it sometime."

"So you can write a book?"

She pressed her lips together on another laugh. "You never know. Might be a huge bestseller. Romance sells, you know. Especially when it has a happy ending."

"Would you say this has a happy ending, then?"

She leaned forward in her chair to offer him her mouth, hoping he would kiss her. "You tell me."

He did. Sweet and slow and smooth, exactly what she'd been wishing for. His hand slipped beneath her hair, cupping the back of her neck.

"I think it's a good possibility," he said against her lips.

His phone buzzed, not a normal text tone but something harder. Jase pulled away, leaving Chelle confused, eyes half-closed, mouth half-open. He pulled his phone from his pocket with a muffled curse.

"What's wrong?" she asked.

"It's Reg. He says we should get our asses over to the beach. Now."

Chapter 15

"I was on the phone with Eggy, seeing if she'd had anything she could put together about this thing you said about the computer program," Reg said from his place on the condo's deck. "She hasn't, by the way, though there were a couple cases of computers being possessed by former owners and stuff like that. Nothing about a program that makes hallucinations with physical manifestations, though. And then… Shit. That."

He pointed. This time of year, there weren't many people on the beach, not like if it had been the height of summer, but you still had a few dog walkers and joggers and shell seekers strung out along the sand. All staring out at the way the ocean had retreated, not a normal low tide but much, much farther than that. Several sandbars had been exposed. Some flopping fish.

"Is it what I think it is?" Jase asked around the tightness in his throat. "Shit, Reg. It is, isn't it?"

Chelle, face drawn, touched his arm to turn him to face her. "What's going on?"

"It's what happens before a tsunami," Reg said. "The water pulls back, way back, because the wave is gathering."

"We don't get tsunamis in Delaware," Chelle said.

Jase took her gently by the upper arms and looked into her face. "Chelle. Did you write about a tsunami?"

She let out a choked gasp. "Oh my God, Jase, I never wrote about it, but I did make some notes about it in one of the plotting folders. I never researched it or anything. It was a ridiculous plot point I was thinking of using to beef up word count. It never went anywhere—"

"But you put it in the program." His stomach twisted, dropping.

She nodded and looked out again to the vast expanse of sand the retreating sea had left behind. "Yes. It was in there."

"What did you do with the program?" Reg asked.

"I deleted it," Chelle said.

Reg shook his head with a frown. "Right to the trash? You didn't run an uninstaller?"

"No. I didn't know I had to," Chelle said with a look at Jase.

"Yeah, he wouldn't, either," Reg said. "Shit. We have to do something about this. And fast."

"We'll take my car. C'mon." Jase grabbed his keys and headed for the steps, Chelle and Reg on his heels.

The gorilla stopped him at the bottom of the stairs with a single punch to the gut that sent Jase to his knees. With a roar, the ape then grabbed him by the back of the shirt and shook him until his teeth rattled. When his head connected with the wooden railing, everything went dark for a moment, though he could hear Reg and Chelle both shouting.

When he came to, it was under a stinking, sweating pile of fur. He couldn't move. His head hurt like a sonofabitch. He blinked, catching sight of Reg to one side and Chelle to the other. Together the two of them rolled the gorilla off Jase and got him to his feet.

"I think we're in some trouble," Reg said. "Girl, you'd better start remembering every story you ever wrote."

Watching Reg take down the gorilla with a single shot to the head had been awful. And it was all her fault, Chelle thought as she helped Jase take a seat on the bottom step. She'd done this.

"We have to get to my laptop," she said. "Before anything else starts."

"It's already started," Reg said with a jerk of his chin toward the shadows coalescing at the end of the street. "More zombies. Shit."

Chelle recoiled. "What? Oh. No. God."

"At least they're the slow kind," Jase said as he got to his feet with a wince.

"Of course they're the slow kind," Chelle said. "That's the only kind of true zombie. The kind that can run fast, they're not zombies."

Reg snorted and holstered his gun to grab up the car keys from the sandy grass where Jase had dropped them. "I'd love to debate this with you, but right now I think we'd better get our asses in gear."

She hadn't thought about the mess a pack of shambling undead would make when a car ran through them, and she'd certainly never written about it in any great detail, but it was a giant, disgusting mess. Chelle watched them scatter in a spray of guts and teeth and rotten flesh, then waved away the sudden rainfall of glittering light that lit up the inside of the car and faded as they drove away.

"It's the same thing," Jase said from the passenger seat. He'd argued with Reg about driving, but only for half a minute. He still looked as though he was hurting, and no wonder. An eight-hundred-pound gorilla had knocked him around like a rag doll. "If we shone the black light, we'd still see that glow. All the cases. Definitely from the program."

"We'll get there in time," Chelle said with more confidence than she felt.

She screamed, though, when the shrieking pterodactyl scraped its claws along the car roof, tearing open the moonroof to peer inside. Its long beak snapped, missing her by inches. Then it dropped a dog onto her lap.

The dog peed.

But at least it was alive.

Chelle was losing her mind. All of this, everything she'd ever written or researched or used in a possible plotline in the multitude of files and folders in that program—all of it was coming true. Right here and now as they drove through the streets of Bethany Beach.

Civil War soldiers fought robots in the town square. The totem in front of the police station had been toppled by a dead-eyed pack of dolls in lacy dresses that swarmed like a school of fish, devouring whatever lay in their path. A carousel horse galloped past, kicking up stones.

And the water, she thought. The water was coming.

"Drive over it!" she cried at the sight of an enormous snake stretched out along the street. It was consuming its own tail. She didn't remember ever writing about such a thing or even researching it, but there it was.

She was never going to write again.

By the time they got to the house, she'd broken out in a chill sweat. Hands shaking. Yet determined, she followed Jase and Reg out of the car and into her house, where she flipped open the laptop to find a black screen.

"Shit, shit, shit," she breathed, dragging a finger along the trackpad. "Battery's dead. The program must've been sucking up power while we were gone. The charger's there on the chair—"

Reg found it and brought it over, plugged it in. The computer beeped, slowly coming to life. Chelle moved over so Reg could get at the keyboard, pulling up her trash can to get a look at the file.

"Where was it saved originally?"

"I found it when I was deleting some old letters and emails," she said. "It was in my archives folder."

"Got it." His fingers flew over the keyboard.

At the front door, a dragon hissed, staring in at Jase, who let fly with a string of curses and jerked the curtains closed. He turned to them. "Guys, hurry it up."

"No uninstall file," Reg said. "But there's a bunch of junk left behind from when you deleted it. Do you have a cleaner program or something like that?"

"I don't think so!"

From far away came a rumble. The ground trembled. Chelle and Jase looked at each other.

"Hurry, Reg," Jase said, too calm considering they were listening to the sound of the impending wave. "Hurry the fuck up."

Reg slammed his fingers on the keyboard, then let out a triumphant shout. "Got it. Shit, yeah. Should've known from the start. It's a GOLEM, yeah? And how do you kill a golem?"

Chelle had no idea. She knew vaguely of the legendary monster but few details. Jase knew, though.

"Erase the first letter written on its forehead," he said. "*Emet* becomes *met*."

"Truth becomes death," Reg said. "And...done!"

The front glass door exploded into a myriad of splinters. The dragon roared. Flame flooded the room.

But only for a moment, and then all that was left was that glittering light that slowly settled and faded, leaving the three of them staring at each other.

Reg held out the flash drive. "I changed the file name, which basically rendered the program inoperable. Crashed it. Then I saved it to this drive and uninstalled all of it from your laptop. But I'd wipe the hard drive if I were you. Do a complete reinstall."

Chelle nodded. She still felt as though the world were tipping and sliding away beneath her feet, but at least they weren't being swept away by a wall of water.

"What are you going to do with the program?" she asked.

"Vadim will probably get Eggy to study it. And then destroy it," Reg said. "Either way, it's going to be safe and can't cause any trouble."

He caught sight of Jase's look and tucked the flash drive into his pocket. "Look, I'm going to go outside and grab a smoke while you two say your goodbyes."

"You don't smoke," Jase said.

Reg dropped a wink at Chelle. "Take your time."

When he'd gone through the front door, she stood. Her palms felt sweaty, so she wiped them on the butt of her jeans. She cleared her throat.

"So. You're done, heading out of town right away, then?"

"I'll have to get to Florida and make my report," Jase said.

Silence.

"And then?" Chelle asked, kind of hating herself for being the one to pose the question.

She was in his arms before she knew it. His big hands warm on the small of her back. His mouth, kissing her. Oh, how he kissed her.

"And then," Jase said into the kiss, "I thought maybe I'd swing back up this way."

Her fingers linked behind his neck as she tipped her face to his, smiling against his mouth. "Yeah? And then what?"

"I figured we could see about that happy-ever-after," he told her. "Isn't that how this story is supposed to end?"

It was the best way a story could end, she thought and kissed him again and again and again.

* * * * *

MILLS & BOON®

nocturne™

AN EXHILARATING UNDERWORLD OF DARK DESIRES

---

sneak peek at next month's titles...

In stores from 10th March 2016:

Her Werewolf Hero – Michele Hauf

Immortal Redeemed – Linda Thomas-Sundstrom

Available at WHSmith, Tesco, Asda, Eason, Amazon and Apple

Just can't wait?
Buy our books online a month before they hit the shops!
visit www.millsandboon.co.uk

These books are also available in eBook format!

MILLS & BOON®

Let us take you back in time with our Medieval Brides...

The Novice Bride – Carol Townend

The Dumont Bride – Terri Brisbin

The Lord's Forced Bride – Anne Herries

The Warrior's Princess Bride – Meriel Fuller

The Overlord's Bride – Margaret Moore

emplar Knight, Forbidden Bride – Lynna Banning

Order yours at
www.millsandboon.co.uk/medievalbrides

MILLS & BOON®

Why not subscribe?

Never miss a title and save money too!

Here's what's available to you if you join the exclusive **Mills & Boon® Book Club** today:

+ *Titles up to a month ahead of the shops*
+ *Amazing discounts*
+ *Free P&P*
+ *Earn Bonus Book points that can be redeemed against other titles and gifts*
+ *Choose from monthly or pre-paid plans*

Still want more?

Well, if you join today, we'll even give you
50% OFF your first parcel!

So visit **www.millsandboon.co.uk/subs**
to be a part of this exclusive Book Club!

MILLS & BOON®

Why shop at millsandboon.co.uk?

Each year, thousands of romance readers find their perfect read at millsandboon.co.uk. That's because we're passionate about bringing you the very best romantic fiction. Here are some of the advantages of shopping at www.millsandboon.co.uk:

Get new books first—you'll be able to buy your favourite books one month before they hit the shops

Get exclusive discounts—you'll also be able to buy our specially created monthly collections, with up to 50% off the RRP

Find your favourite authors—latest news, interviews and new releases for all your favourite authors and series on our website, plus ideas for what to try next

Join in—once you've bought your favourite books, don't forget to register with us to rate, review and join in the discussions

Visit **www.millsandboon.co.uk**
for all this and more today!